CINQUE SORTITE: FIVE ASSAULTS OR SALLIES ONTO THE BATTLEFIELD

DOMINIC M. MARTIN

CINQUE SORTITE: FIVE ASSAULTS OR SALLIES ONTO THE BATTLEFIELD

Copyright © 2021 Dominic M. Martin.

All rights reserved. No part of this book may be used or reproduced by any means, graphic, electronic, or mechanical, including photocopying, recording, taping or by any information storage retrieval system without the written permission of the author except in the case of brief quotations embodied in critical articles and reviews.

iUniverse books may be ordered through booksellers or by contacting:

iUniverse
1663 Liberty Drive
Bloomington, IN 47403
www.iuniverse.com
844-349-9409

Because of the dynamic nature of the Internet, any web addresses or links contained in this book may have changed since publication and may no longer be valid. The views expressed in this work are solely those of the author and do not necessarily reflect the views of the publisher, and the publisher hereby disclaims any responsibility for them.

Any people depicted in stock imagery provided by Getty Images are models, and such images are being used for illustrative purposes only. Certain stock imagery © Getty Images.

Scripture quotations marked KJV are from the Holy Bible, King James Version (Authorized Version). First published in 1611. Quoted from the KJV Classic Reference Bible, Copyright © 1983 by The Zondervan Corporation.

ISBN: 978-1-6632-2377-7 (sc)
ISBN: 978-1-6632-2378-4 (e)

Print information available on the last page.

iUniverse rev. date: 07/12/2021

---Sortita: Italian, noun, feminine: Military, sally; Colloquial Exit or Way out; Figuratively, Wisecrack, smart reply, sally.

---Sally: Noun. 1 A sudden rush forward; a leap. 2. An assault from a defensive position; a sortie. 3. A venturing forth; an excursion; a jaunt; a foray onto the field of conflict.

---When I believe in something, I fight like hell for it.

Steve McQueen

---The art of war is simple enough. Find out where your enemy is. Get at him as soon as you can. Strike him as hard as you can, and keep moving on.

General Ulysses S. Grant

---For you were once darkness, but now you are light in the Lord. Walk as children of light for the fruit of the spirit is in al goodness, righteousness, and truth, finding out what is acceptable to the Lord. And have no fellowship with the unfruitful works of darkness, but rather expose them. For it is shameful even to speak of those things which are done by them in secret. But all things that are exposed are made manifest by the light, for whatever makes manifest is light. Therefore, He says: 'Awake, you who sleep. Arise from the dead. And Christ will give you light'.

The Epistle of Saint Paul the Apostle to the Ephesians 5: 8-14

CONTENTS

A Note On The Montecassino Bombardment ix

Preface xiii

1   Fatherhood, O La Paternita 1

2   The Absence Of The Imperative Command 33

3   Leadership Or Il Primato: The Rise Of The Suck-Up And The Inconsequential 61

4   My Supposed Homophobia 137

5   Dugri: Integrity Or The Importance Of One's Word 251

6   Postcript: A Quick Tossing Aside Of The Heavy Duffle Bag 283

A NOTE ON THE MONTECASSINO BOMBARDMENT

Saint Benedict of Nursia helped to construct the first Christian church there, locating it upon an old pagan site once devoted to the pagan god of Apollo, that most handsome god who could prophesize the future. Benedict wrote his well-known Benedictine Rules within that first humble church, and lived there in prayerful silence until his death in 543, after which he was buried within its chambers. Later, unfortunately, the church was destroyed by the Lombards in 581, and then by the Saracens in 884, after which it was re-built to a much higher standards by Pope Alexander II in 1071, making it the wealthiest monastery in the world. However, that greater level of solid construction could not prevent or deter damages from both an earthquake in 1349, and also a partial sacking by Napoleon's unguarded, renegade troops in 1799. The monastery's relatively close location to the capitol, Roma, and its prominent location on the top of a massive ridgeline which dominates even today the entrances to the Liri and Rapido Valleys have made it over the year an easy, malleable target for marauding troops of many stripes. And it was so attractive to the German Axis powers during World War II that they early on seized the monastery and its higher ground in anticipation of an Allied attack coming from the South and Anzio. Montecassino would thus form in the ravaging months ahead the key linch-pin position in the defense of the Gustav Line. The coming battle would pit Germany's Albert Kesselring and Heinrich von Vietinghoff against the Allies' Harold Alexander, Oliver Leese, and

Mark Clark. And all of these generals well understood even before the battle commenced that whoever won this upcoming, difficult battle would most likely win the war.

Providently, two German officers, Captain Maximilian Becker and Lieutenant Colonel Julius Schlegel, in those confused Autumn months of 1943 prior to the eventual bombing of the Benedictine Monastery on the following February 15 had the simple intelligence to propose the evacuation to the Vatican of the thousands of priceless antique religious documents and religious tomes that had been stored there, most of them for centuries. That job was accomplished; however still the monastery was destroyed by 1150 tons of bombs dropped by 142 B-17 Flying fortress heavy bombers, 47 North American B-25 Mitchell and 40 Martin B-26 Marauder medium bombers. No German soldiers were inside the monastery at the start of the attack, only 6 elderly monks. The mistaken order for destruction had been issued by Great Britain's timid General Sir Harold Alexander under the continual prodding of Lieutenant-General Mark W. Clark of the United States' Fifth Army.

Within days Pope Pius XII's Cardinal Secretary of State, Luigi Maglione, described the bombing as a:

>---a colossal blunder, ...a piece of gross stupidity.

In the same way that the Allies, undoubtedly on the side for good, annihilated the monastery, today through dozens of self-inflicted cancers our world is slowly and steadily destroying itself, as if on some mad, deranged purpose. The purpose of this work is to examine and study precisely how these always morphing and insidious diseases have been brought to birth and how they have over the course of many decades expanded and grown. Too, there is the further question of how these mounting sicknesses might be stunted or curtailed, truncated. So, naturally, two questions emerge: Is any of this true? And what should next be done?

Some may think that this ugly mess stems from our not being ready for battle, our not being prepared for the assaults and sallies of the battlefield, and that is because, commonly, the final words of all failed leaders are:

---I do not think that we have any reason to worry.

PREFACE

The further decline and complete fall of our country is the issue, and the kind or unkind fate of our children is thus also in the balance. These few discussions detail the five weapons now poised to be fired against upon ce champ laid et sale de bataille, this grimy and ugly field of battle. To list them in order: Every day, more and more, simple fatherhood is disparaged and the family of which he is a central part is variously attacked. Next, children grow to adulthood having never heard an order and thus are routinely spoiled, thinking only of themselves and perennially wishing for a fleeting happiness, the new nirvana of youth. Thirdly, we have gotten into the fruitless habit of voting for "leaders" who are not leaders at all but feckless suck-ups and inconsequential nest-liners, always afraid to stick their necks out. The following tale covers the necessary moral component of human sexuality, a fact which would ground and guard behavior if it were put to use; instead, we see that that component has been tossed aside, like so much old, tired lettuce, resulting in manifest coarseness and depravity. And fifthly, and finally, about us, prevarications, connivings, and simple lies are now the unhappy norm. These five issues arise, necessitating the Cinque Sortite, The Five Assaults or Sallies Onto the Battlefield that make up this book.

But, who among us wishes to read another predictable paean for traditional morality?

On the other hand, what have we done in our world with all our power and wealth but squander them or be dominated by those worldly things about which Christ warned us? So, let the dissipation and dissolution that surrounds us not come as any surprise, for this whammy thunderbolt did not come out of the blue, but, rather, we created it ourselves in the beginning out of whole cloth.

At this pivotal juncture, many may say that nothing is worth getting riled up about, that the culture is not degraded nor disgraceful. Yea, such is our yawning apathy! Does anyone wish to fight moral relativism anymore, or have we pretty much packed it in or given up the fight? One thing is certain: As we are surrounded by Luciferian forces, it is well past time to seize a weapon, here words, and move out onto the battlefield.

It is not correct to say that the relativists conquest of our culture was hidden or clandestine. Instead, this broad and brash foray onto the campo or veldt was marked by how bald-faced and brash it was, with each of the invaders saying aloud for all to hear:

---We will conquer you.

Routinely they chasten and swiftly mock all interlockers or those who do deign to differ. Often, we are told we are stupid retrogrades. Cleverly, these "prideful gladiators" acted as if the battle had already been won. Their campaign to banish God started with small numbers, yet it now numbers in the millions. One of their first tactics was to enter the arena of education since they understood that there in the public classroom they might wield the grandest ascending power. Starting in 1962 these inveiglers sought to banish religion from that classroom and in that quest they have been largely successful. All along they were smart and clever; however, as we were napping and somnolent, we let them in; we created conditions wherein they might flourish, and when they won a skirmish, our counterpunches were weak and most frail. So now, today, we are encircled by many battles unjoined, those that are ready and meant to be contested, should we muster the necessary vigor. Always it has been their intent and will be too in the future to lie to achieve their aims and also to demonize and mock the opposition, and to try to make us feel weak and inconsequential. Still, all of this will only take place if we let them, if we remain paralyzed and impotent.

It is not for a lack of a nemesis or antagonist that we suffer since deep-seated problems abound. Rather, it is our present lack of focus and an absence of will which encumber and enervate us and which the "prideful gladiators" then in turn so smartly exploit. This lack of focus and absence of will daily rob us of a greater speed and make us mightily less likely to engage in and complete any task. Thus, a strengthening paralysis reigns over us now, a constant, spreading, and debilitating paralysis.

For, what good does it do to say that we are not in a war, one contested simultaneously on so many fronts? Socially, physically, economically, morally, psychically---everywhere a contest rages, though sometimes it is little discussed. What good does it do to deny that such a battle exists and will continue to be fought as far as any occluded eye might see? Always on my mind is the other looming question on the horizon of the future: Who will be victorious in this new battle? Only the childish or somnolent among us will maintain that our world today is not in the gravest danger.

Yes, we are in some pickle or jam! We have become far

too passive, and too materialistic. And, perhaps due to an over-reliance upon technology and all that it entails, we now lack the sequential key perspective of analysis needed to solve our problems, to find out precisely how things went wrong and exactly how to fix them. Since universities no longer instruct us in the four steps to solving a problem: To discover, to diagnose, to treat, and to re-assess, we loll and dither in expanding confusion and myopia. As the great German philosopher, Martin Heidegger, writes:

> ---Everywhere we remain unfree and chained to technology, whether we passively affirm or deny it. I know that only God can save us now.

Martin Heidegger: The Question Concerning Technology, Der Spiegel, September 23, 1966.

It is astonishing to think that he possessed such far-reaching, keen perspicacity over 50 years ago.

So, soldiers, new warriors, what bodes well? I say to those of you in the back squabbling, kibitzing, Connors, Ainsworth, Becker:

> ---Don't talk back! Concentrate on the job at hand! Finish what you start! Do you follow me?

Where will these moral divisions and embittered rancours lead us? Shattered? Shutttered? Moribund? But, a greater silence comes now, I do pray! Attention! That man who proudly says he craves a nemesis, that fairytale of vengeance earned, may he move or is he just all talk? A long battle, no, five of them do await us and must soon be joined. Soon therefore, we shall sally forth into the meanest thicket, onto the unforgiving battlefield, making a determined costly lieutenant's sortie into the woods, and such a man does not know in advance where such an assault from a purely defensive position may take him.

What is that caustic dismayed world that I hear outside? Carlo? Santo? It is fierce! Expect a tangled yarn, some vagrant quips hazarded and some lean legion wisecracks and howlers since all good soldiers have much time to kill before the fight commences. Why not? Perche no? So, let us move forthrightly now and with dispatch to the breach, fellow legionnaires and partisans, since it is well past the time to join the fight. I expect that it shall be fun and larky to be a fly in the ointment, to lance the relativists' boil with a sharp spear, and to broadcast to all who may listen that:

---There's the rub.

That last is for Will whose words do guide. And in the meantime, do not be shocked if Lorelei or others try to enthrall or divert our capacity for mettle and steel. Thus, we must remain most alert and tenacious, and not just close to it. Close is not good enough. We must be fast on our pins, use all stealth, and be gimlet-eyed, clever, keen, both by our sight and questioning all that we see with boldness and audacity in our minds.

Otherwise, if there is no long battle and eventual victory, only a giving up with the hands in the air, then it shall all be over and we shall see each other on the other side of the divide.

By the common, how important is this to you anyway? How badly do you yearn for victory? For, without desire and complete energy, all is lost.

Che e con me ora? Who is with me now? We need another breakthrough, like the one at Saint Lo, that is, a spiritual re-birth. There are some delivered herein, with words delivered by God. But who has the reins of progress? Who among us has the open ears to hear the old lessons, now abandoned? And who among us wishes to change course?

Yet...yet...if we keep going the way we are going... confronted against the sizeable arsenal now gathered against us...

FATHERHOOD, O LA PATERNITA

---Paternity: the word is from the Latin, paternitatem, meaning fatherhood, and pater, meaning father:

1. The quality of condition of being a father; fatherhood.
2. The quality or personality of an ecclesiastical father; used as a title.
3. The paternal relation viewed from the standpoint of a child; paternal origin or descent.
4. Figuratively, authorship, source, or origin (of a work).

---Listen, warriors: Go back to your posts and, each of you, think about what you are going to do. Take responsibility and act. We must banish all chaos. Form a line and hold it. This battle is what you signed up for.

---Children, listen to me, your father; act accordingly, that you may be safe. For the Lord sets a father in honor over his children and confirms a mother's authority over her sons. Those who honor their father atone for sins; they store up riches who respect their mother. Those who honor their father will have joy in their own children, and when they pray they are heard. Those who respect their father will live a long life; those who obey the Lord honor their mother. Those who fear the Lord honor their

> father and serve their parents as masters. In word and deed honor your father, that all blessings may come to you.
>
> The Book of Sirach from the Old Testament 3: 1-8

This late and tardy story begins in the early 70s. For some years now, the moral relativists, raising themselves above us commoners as if by unspoken fiat, these phony gendarmes have been making their own rules up as the days have tripped by, telling us how to live and, alternatively, what to abhor and what to embrace. And for far too long they have consistently denigrated, diminished, and dismissed as part of their ever-widening agenda or canon or dicta the very idea of paternity, the simple idea that fathers are important in the raising of a child. The old phrase, "hook, line, and sinker" springs to mind, since they will truck neither dissent nor argument, saying to themselves and us:

---It is my way or the highway, you got it, man?

As a result, more and more, piu e piu, men and women both are told by these false dream-tenders that fathers are not needed in the least, and instead, that it would be inestimably better if they were to completely go away, their manhood forever truncated and curtailed. Fatherhood and manhood, we were instructed by these self-appointed thought-police, are joined to become one unholy and unnecessary union. All of this is stated subliminally subsumed, and consumed as if it were an uncontested proven fact, though of course that be not true. We are told by various proud, clarion voices that most men are "Tits on a boar", il cinghiale, ungentile and useless, the crudest boars, that men are rank and worthless wastrels, inutile o vano. Therefore, bypassing all men and their rightful place in society, it follows that today one may make a baby with purchased sperm, an unfrozen egg, and a glass Petri dish; however, where does that artificial means of production leave men? Out in the cold? Impotent? Not invited to the dance? This persistent and pervasive hatred of both fatherhood and paternity is one of the key, doctrinaire mantras of the left; the sneaky, snide left has a great many rules as we shall discover. The left likes rules, especially those made to gain and secure their power; and too, the more hidden and various there are, the better. If a song, this chorus is one endlessly sung. Yet, it is a caustic and unproven dictum, something merely asserted as if unquestioningly true, and therefore wholly unsupported, all of which brings to mind the apt phrase in Latin:

    ---Ipse dixit

or

    ---He himself said

with no analytical justification or firm foundation in learning

For the sake of argument, as we make an analysis of the commencement of this battle, let us further assume that these moral relativists' deprecation of men and fatherhood began 40 years ago, and further that that defamation and castigation of one half of the human race shows today no sign of shrinkage. Much of this false and corrosive talk was started in the schools and most of it was taken in whole by young and unsuspecting ears without their asking any of the large questions, e.g., what will happen if a son has no father, or who might protect the daughter from incipient danger? Once the atmosphere in the class can be dictated, the gradual turning of minds to mush shall soon follow.

Down through all these lost years, real men regret lost fatherhood; and too, children miss their fathers, that abiding guidance and care. Yet, when did we go so soft in the head as to allow for this vilification of men and their natural role as fathers? Why would we, men and women both, accept this false bill of goods, this fraudulent diminishment of manhood? How did this mean slander arise? If one cares enough to tender the question, one is forced to take the time to ferret out and marvel at the answer and its simplicity. And to do so we must ply the caravel further backwards into unrepentant time, onto unforgiving waves and stoutly so, since we are journeying bare-hulled into the roughest waters.

And, so many years ago now and just as my own adulthood attempted to emerge, like a pupa trying to become a butterfly, with myself full of tardy half-steps, then just a fresh plebe at the academy of life, a fierce and unyielding feminism arrived upon the receptive cultural scene. And with it, generally, a broad and pervasive enmity against men emerged, as an unquestioned force of the broadest momentum. It became acceptable for many (and not just women) to engender a calculated hatred of men, to broadcast that mean message endlessly to all arenas, and to so say broadly all about the society's marketplace of ideas. That same hostility also leads symbiotically towards an antipathy towards the regular biology of fatherhood. Yea, how sudden it all was, and how unfriendly! It was shouted from the rooftops that all men were bad, very bad! How unfriendly was the climate between the sexes then, and still today! From many female quarters an almost frenzied hatred of men then came to birth. Some women were so self-absorbed in themselves that we males might as well have not existed. Such general unfriendliness was calmly blessed by the much of the Gargantuan media and then it only further gathered more strength to itself and grew. Women's studies, Queer Studies, American Studies, White Privilege courses and similar seductive pablum were soon taught in many universities and the subversive ideas within those courses began to subvert soft minds. Without a questioning or skeptical attitude, many professors pushed, prodded, and goaded the students to accept blindly these new and corrosive thoughts, ones entirely new to the world.

And yet, how could I help being a man, or nearly so? Was not that factor of my incipient, near-manhood one of God's gifts to me, one of undeserved many, like my nascent ability to sometimes slash wicked, rope-like line drives over the head of a leaping third baseman? As I stumbled towards adulthood, all of these factors gradually gathered together to make a fabulous and chaotic cultural stew. It was what the Italians term, presciently, a casino! It was a mess, yet one disordered and hurtful and complicated. Some brow-beaten men gathered together to drink, to commiserate, to wish for an earlier time. So, just as I began to sense within me that sharpest of primordial urges, to find a mate, a pleasant, beautiful, and obliging female with whom to couple, and to produce children, such cultural stridencies, always rising and usually shrill beyond all words, arose around me. Such meanness, what mocking derision and disrespect, I saw, felt, and witnessed. Because of my sex, inevitable catcalls and snide looks came my way, and not just from the distaff side. So, ironically, with the worst of timing, and as Mister Murphy hovered in his helicopter, it was in the middle of this atmosphere of ridicule and scorn, one announcing:

> ---Don't try anything with me, you jerk! Bastard! Don't even try, I tell you!

that I did set out like all young male voyagers and hunters might have done to find my pleasant Diana, my smiling huntress with whom I might merge and produce a family.

As I look back upon those days from today's somewhat refined vantage, I wonder about this idea of starting a family: Where did that notion come from? Is it simple biology or our culture that is the main catalyst? I maintain that that urge is as primeval and primordial as the deepest green of a forest or the darkest blue of the sea. And producing some progeny suggests leaving behind a vestigial tail, one which says aloud:

> ---Kilroy was here, or, I existed, and here plain to see is my fledgling son or my eager daughter.

A father may see in the face of his child both his own and his wife's. And in their successes and failures any proper father yearns for more of the former and little of the latter. Yet, where is the secure place in our increasingly selfish world for children? Hasn't their status also been truncated, curtailed? Many higher income, fast-track couples have eschewed childbirth in favor of making more money which may lead to greater so-called freedom or convenience. Still, in the midst of these unquestioned societal shifts, weren't children largely forgotten about or dismissed?

Cinque Sortite: Five Assaults Or Sallies Onto The Battlefield

All in all, weren't my tentative attempts at bridging the biological gap to produce heirs as basic as anyone else's clamor for bread, water, salt? Still, all along, like a repetitive incessant rapping knock upon an outside oaken door, we were told that men are useless, fathers are not needed, and children do not matter and may be just another extremely expensive pain in the rear.

Since they were insignificant, laughably slight and thin, I do not wish to describe my first fumbling attempts at love; but rather, I want to chart or sketch the chaotic, acerbic, and disconnected milieu in which this young man, I, first began haltingly to pursue that precious holy grail of ardent, lasting amour; moreover, as it happened and most unsurprisingly, all of my weak romantic rendezvous ended only in classic farce, as if played put by Chaplin or Tati. If well dramatized, my attempts at love would have been an excellent comedy of slapstick manners! Indeed, such an outcome might have been predicted. Mine were abject, ridiculous, laughable forays onto love's campo, lean, scant efforts only to be pitied, if not mocked. Such tentativeness I exuded! I made only the weakest nods to Naiad! Soon, as if in a dream some lowly disappointments emerged, predictively. As I now look back upon those most feeble efforts at life-long tryst, ones clearly destined for the most obvious renunciations, that fallow time of my nearly spent youth seems to me now as a period of singular lost circumstance that might have been better served simply skipped or postponed. Yet, to spy the silver lining in the midst of things, as one must, it was a good thing that those endeavored-upon clinches never took place since in those days I was not at all, of course, yet ready for love, nor even close to it.

At the same time as feminism, most injudicious in its

timing, the sexual revolution came unannounced onto the cultural scene, stoked by the invention of the birth control pill (Just a little more estrogen! Just a little more!), and, shortly thereafter, as too much beer does lead frequently to Nod, sharply slipping moral standards. The moral relativists, who then thought they were in charge and who made up all the rules as they went along, they told us, they announced it as a medieval magistrate might have done, that a man no longer had to be faithful, and also that a man need not worry about producing children (such a bother!) or, at least, so we unimportant docile minions were resolutely informed. These self-appointed elites appointed by nobody told the rest of us that that massive change in standards would carry with it only unrivalled gifts, and most distinctly, no down-side or detriments of any consequence would take place; instead, with the calm insouciance of the arrogant, they flatly guaranteed that the looser moral standards would bring only limitless gratuities, or what the Italians might call:

---Quali regali generosi

or:

---Only the most generous presents.

However, instead, over the intervening years, what has happened? Pray tell, where they correct, these pushy, non-skeptical moral arbitrators? As a cruel substitute for those gifts, one which of course never materialized, there arrived huge numbers of new and highly virulent sexually transmitted diseases, thousands of fractured homes, millions of children and teenagers with essentially no father, declining manhood throughout society, and finally, rampant, unending sexual confusions of all manner and spent trial. It must now be admitted that we had been warned from on high against all of these disasters, yet we did not well listen, afraid to resist the progressive's pervasive mantra. Also, abortion soon became the unwise and clumsy form of birth control, its legality assured by Associate Justice Harry Blackburn's illogical sweep of the privacy wand, at a rate of roughly one millions babies per year in our nation alone. In the name of convenience and faux sexual freedom and because we let it happen, abortion in many progressive circles overnight became an unsacred "right", a faux sacrament, one presumably as fundamental as bread or heat or clean water, and sanctioned and blessed, if that is the correct word, in a flash by society's inability or unwillingness to defend the unborn. Thus, as if overnight a new culture of spreading death was tightly embraced.

So, then, pre-AIDS and as might have been foretold, a period of unleashed couplings ensued. All types of unrestrained sexualities were praised, practiced, explored. Since the relativists had driven out the moral component, excised and truncated it, any sexual action was possible, probable, and necessarily good. Skepticism did not impinge in the least, so any possible drawback to these carnal wanderings, one saying from the rooftops to the ribald and licentious:

---Vagano! Vagano! They swirl! They swirl

were ignored, never mentioned or brought up. Millions, perhaps not knowing any better or, more likely, not recalling the simple lessons earlier they had been taught by their parents, teachers, mentors, therefore put into most vigorous practice all these dangerous bedtime strategies, and of course many later paid a very steep and high price for that prolifigacy, both physically and psychically. And in this corrosive process that new form of extreme experimental carnality automatically, ipso facto, meant that the role of the father in society had been degraded and shrunk to the miniscule, and for the first time millions of children were raised with no father in the home.

Too, over time this new hedonism approved and promoted by the higher-ups of society produced some other cruel manifold effects. For example, I just read the other day that 25% of adults in New York City (that once most charming burg) now carry the Herpes Simplex Virus 2. Many of those so afflicted suspect that nothing is wrong, making them much more likely to transmit the virus to others. All of this was not true in that magical year of 1961 when I was nearly ten years old and the fabled "M & M" boys were chasing the Babe's single season home run record. One wonders whether those living a life of promiscuity, instead of faithfulness, consider themselves to be children or adults? Do they think it their right or obligation to so tempt sexual diseases of so many forms, the incipiency of that fierce biologic onslaught? Moreover, once infected, do these experimenters presume that they are entitled to a perfect cure, and one paid for by the government?

Also, at that time an entirely new complex of sexual diseases arose, and many of them were particularly virulent and easily transmittable. Yet, is that not always the usual mechanism for any disease?: To morph, to mutate, and thus to spread to someone untouched. Given the demanding mechanisms for transmission and the strong overriding pathology for many of these diseases, what did those fresh populators, those with so much either curious wonder or wunderlust think was going to happen, that they would remain disease free? Unlikely is the clear answer.

One of my uncles, an astute doctor with a lancing and sardonic wit, once allowed to me that the toughest job in the country was not to be the President, nor Notre Dame's Head Football Coach, but rather the Chief Medical Officer at any large university. He asked me once, plaintively:

> ---How do you stop them, these fervid, unfervent, rabbits, from coupling with each other all over the place, once they have had a catnip's taste of it? For, they simply do not listen to that singular word, No.

Then, many fresh-faced apostles, gurus for this unrestrained hedonism as well the death of the traditional family, acting on the fly as if they were our self-appointed Praetorian guards, they came to the fore, advocating:

> ---Go with the flow. Stay in the moment. Love the one you're with...

and the like. At this time, they did not in the least regard themselves as self-indulgent sybarites or lazy sensualists or slayers of the family and fatherhood. On the contrary, they defended themselves by offering, but no, insisting upon this simple, fraudulent thesis: All sexual activity lacks any moral component, and, concomitantly, one should be willing and free to follow (traipse behind?) whatever instinct or desire or wish or want or dimply perceived need that does walk on its own two feet into the room. Why not? All of this and much more became the accepted norm quickly and quietly, 50 years ago, when I was barely 17 and just starting that chaotic dating combine that we term college. So many factors were not questioned! So many assumptions were made overnight! And I was so green and bumbling! Manifestly foolish as well! And, yes, I was plainly just a big geek, all of which could have been judged from afar. And in those first days of university so may years ago now, if I were to argue with many of my fresh, fellow students that society's new, tainted mores might be fraught with illusion or disease or loneliness, or that they might lead to fatherhood's decline and then, inexorably, to millions of unguided, father-less youth, well, that approach was to risk right away the most severe and compounding scorn and haughty belittlement from my new peers whom I then had hoped to befriend.

And soon enough, as might have been predicted if one knows anything about biology and the history of disease, AIDS impinged upon the world's population; however, with scant surprise, its moral ramifications were so little discussed. Because uncontrolled sexual activity and prowess had become magically an ersatz right, that rampaging and lethal disease, one initially untouched by conventional medical techniques, only slightly held back or restrained the new-found profligacy and licentiousness. And despite the efforts of medical doctors and nurses, the many other various sexual diseases reached even higher levels of contraction. In some cases, the newer forms of viral and bacterial complexes impaired permanently a woman's ability to ever carry a child to term; however, since bringing a child to birth was daily becoming less and less important, at least on the opaque surface of things, this salient fact was often ignored and skipped over.

Cinque Sortite: Five Assaults Or Sallies Onto The Battlefield

So too, the number of divorces skyrocketed and broken homes became as if overnight commonplace. Phrases like:

>---Semper fidelis

or

>---Real men stay for the fight. Only weak pansies leave

were forgotten, tossed aside. And from that last sad tale there arose the unexpected circumstance at the core of this dark story: More and more children were to be single-parented, especially lacking a father. This last salient even was not largely lamented, since so few realized at the time exactly what had just transpired. The new promiscuity, heralded by those blithering selfish Hefners who without grace masqueraded as our heroes, created this unintended circumstance. After all, we could have told them one simple word: No. Often we do not know what we do not know. These new faux preachers telling us to prance around like Priapus were, in reality, wolves in sheep's clothing, and they were in effect preaching a false religion, one that was not new, since there is nothing new under the sun, as Ecclesiastes tells us (I 90). So, due ex machina, their phony dicta, we as sheep avidly followed, and many millions of children today are raised without the benefit of a father, without his guidance, without his usually firmer hand, and without his often stricter discipline. Indeed, in this atmosphere wherein men were roundly castigated, defamed, thought of as useless or inconsequent or harmful or worse, some of us, both men and women alike, took the stance that a family without a father was a good thing, maybe even a better thing, and therefore, that perhaps it was a glad and happy occasion when that man had gone down the road. However, so much for God's plan!

Also, beyond the pale, deep beneath the surface of things another closeted ulterior motive maneuvered and lurked about gaining traction, since if the father is gone, the family is destroyed, and the state itself then may march into that intentional vacuum to fill a greater role, calling to mind that scary book title:

> --- It Takes A Village: And Other lessons Children Teach Us
>
> Hilary Rodham Clinton; Simon and Schuster; 1995

The truth is it does not take a village, but a mom and a dad, as Richard Santorum has written. But by then, since we let him do it, the devil thought he already had in his hand the keys to the kingdom! For many this gradual destruction of the nuclear family, something which had served mankind so well down through the ages, was intentional so that the state, which is all to some amongst us, may accede to an even greater power.

Am I too arch? Do I press this case for traditionalism too strenuously, too stridently, and in that course harm the very argument? I think not, recalling the demeaning slogan that swirled around my ears during those first ugly years of feminism:

> ---A woman needs a man like a fish needs a bicycle.
>
> A nasty phrase coined by Irina Dunn, and later popularized by Germaine Greer

Cinque Sortite: Five Assaults Or Sallies Onto The Battlefield

Or, please recall the snide title of Maureen Dowd's recent book:

>---Are Men Necessary? When Sexes Collide
>
>Maureen Dowd; G. P. Putnam's Sons New York City; 2005

Why should men, or the larger population including balanced women, have to put up with such trashy and disrespectful talk? What have we done to Dowd and others of similar ilk to deserves such foolish lances? Did she sometime in her past have an especially bad boyfriend? If so, she ought to have left him, recalling the wise words of Lear:

>---No, no, no, no! Come, friends, let us away...
>
>William Shakespeare; King Lear; Act V, Scene 3, Line 9

Often, within the privileged progressive bastions of New York and Los Angeles, all of those who have taken over the cultural media praised such hateful speech, or perhaps worse, fed it, allowed it, and encouraged it. In sum, the pernicious idea that men and fathers were at best incidental and unimportant was floated and then was fully taken in; further, some extremists held that a father might be harmful and detrimental to the rearing of a child, especially if she were a young girl.

For half a century I have witnessed the promulgation of these hari-kari ideas. I have seen them absorbed whole, willy-nilly, as if gospel true, as if they emanated from on high. And too, I have seen the considerable damages that they have then wrought upon our culture. And it has been in this unusual atmosphere, one of off-kilter hate, continuing renunciation, bad ideas, and an illogical forsaking of the past (It is obsolete! Obsolete, I tell you!) that I have tried to be both a decent father and a favorable composer of this small and cautionary tale.

***

May we step aside or perhaps charge outside for a breath of fresh air and there amongst fragrant zephyrs demur to another world whose warnings do apply? I recall these words from Fellini's Amarcord:

---What have you done? Are you crazy?

Amarcord; Film script by Federico Fellini and Tonino Guerra; 1974

I ask this question taken from one of my favorite movies since it begs the making of another: How could we ever have assumed that a destruction of the traditional family, based upon the relentless belittlement of the father's role in that nuclear group, would not necessarily carry with it unforeseen problems of a glacial and stupendous nature? Has society ever before tried raising such a large percentage of our youth without a father in the house, a loving authority figure there to guide and advise, to demand and console, to praise and nurture? Did we think that we would know in advance what would happen? But really, scouts, guides, were we not just guessing? Did we like apes hazard that there would be no downside? With these false assumptions we set in place the notion that it should be just the culture, one largely debased and demeaned, then, which was to raise a child, and not two loving parents who at one point in time had conjoined with God's kind grace to produce him or her? This is what has happened, and clearly, in a majority of cases that is the unwise path that has been chosen to the full detriment of the child.

Example? On December 14, 2012, a young man who had clearly been deeply troubled for some time, "went off" and killed 28 students and teachers at Sandy Hook Elementary School in Connecticut. What devilish, deranged thoughts must have swirled in his tangled mind! This teenager was the product of a broken home and lived with his mother whom he had also shot dead. I read that the young man had wanted to join the Marine Corps but that his mother had refused to give him her permission. By his frail looks it would seem that his weak stature would have led the corps to declare him perhaps unfit for service. However, one wonders if he had been raised both by his mother but also by a loving, but sometimes gruff, father whether things might have turned out differently. His father, if he had been there, could have schooled him in exercising and lifting weights, on conditioning and proper nutrition, thereby strengthening and building up his body. Too, his father, if he had been present in the home, could have showed him how to change the oil on the family's truck, how to fire a .22 caliber Henry Lever Action Rifle, how to pitch a two-pole pup tent, how to build a proper hardwood fire that would last an entire evening and night, and which then could be re-stoked for a breakfast of Sourdough toast, Back bacon, and black coffee in the morning. Perhaps under his father's active prodding, pushing, compelling, and coaching the son might have gained the strength, maturity, and sinewy tenacity that would have been needed for the Marine Corps to accept him into their elite unit. Instead, absent a guiding, protective, and loving father, he wallowed into his weak-sister mode, a puerile and lasting sissyhood. More and more teenage boys are like that today, never really growing up, never becoming men.

Lately in my job as a teacher, I have been exposed to hundreds of young adults, and usually, especially with the males, I see still-children marked more than anything by unmistakable drift, endless dreaminess, and an inability to focus for ten seconds on anything. Far too many lack a work ethic, drive, grit, vigor, and concentration. They operate as lemmings might, constantly closely considering what their peers might think or will do. This passive tactic leads them to shortly become slow-moving blockheads, cube-of-butter numbskulls.

How things have changed from not too long ago! My father and other men from The Greatest Generation, since it was nurtured by adversity, that ilk possessed determination and simple courage by the bucket. They always led by the example of swift action, followed then by only a few words. They were taciturn, gruff, hearty. My father would sometimes say to me:

> ---If there is an enemy, find it, surround it, and then it must be vanquished! If you do not see the enemy, it is because you are not paying enough attention. Are you paying attention, listening? Awake, my man in brown, awake!

By contrast, many of today's youths, since they have not been schooled by a demonstrative, demanding father, they often seem intent on looking for an "out", some sort of lame excuse. Surely, there is a correlation between the lassitude of so many young men and the disappearance

Cinque Sortite: Five Assaults Or Sallies Onto The Battlefield

of their fathers, some of whom back in the day used to be pretty darn somber and pushy, always saying things like:

> ---What shall you accomplish today? How many things will you get done?

Many young men have never been groomed to chase and achieve their dreams, to find that man that they were meant to be. Recall General George Patton's speech from the movie of the same name:

> ---In about fifteen minutes we're going to start turning these boys into fanatics---razors. They'll love their fear of the Germans. I only hope to God they never lose their fear of me.
>
> Patton: December 4, 1969; Screenplay by Edmund H. North and Francis Ford Coppola

Of course, with little doubt, promiscuous sex is at the heart of it, the nexus, of the fathers' decline and diminution: Too much, too early, with the wrong people, or perhaps, the wrong sex. Surely, one must hazard, a rabbit-like, jumping-jack life is not a good preparation to become a faithful husband and cautionary father. This is quite simple really, and much simpler than we today understand or grasp. So, how did it start? Well, for easy starters and most carelessly, we tossed out the Ten Commandments, saying blithely that they no longer applied to us, and not in the least. Those dicta which had stood for thousands of years were tossed into the trash bin like yesterday's newspaper. Instead, and perilously, the culture began in those early years to tell all of us that a person can do whatever he or she wants to do; said another way, my individual desires are paramount, above all else, something sacrosanct and almost divine, ironically enough. To sum up: The idea that sex is not the center of life, that it is a tiramisu (Pick me up!) or dessert at the end of the meal, that it ought to be reserved for the private marriage bed, so that the couple might joyfully express a reverence for each other even as, with age, their bodies grow slack, flabby, or protuberant---well, that concept, one rooted in both biology and religion, one for ages as omens of the augurs, that notion is now laughed and scoffed at, mocked, incessantly derided and defamed, since sex has been deemed by the false preachers as some sort of inconsequential, and harmless sport underneath the covers.

So, dusters, cowboys, horse traders and all the legions' foot soldiers who walk through the same brown and grey dusty polvere, the thought that an 18-year-old of either sex might wait is termed as impossibly old-fashioned and anachronistic, something foolhardy, inane, laughable. To many, abstinence is simply not considered, since sex is "my right", just like for some women today in our death-bent society, abortion is "my right". Society has pushed for these new alternative strictures, ones that are, as we shall see, paradoxically at least as confining as the traditional.

So, among our ardent ranks, let us consider that most important word, one said aloud:

---Instead

Instead, in today's so-called evolved society (Read: Bent or twisted) men in general are mocked and emasculated. Instead, male promiscuity is encouraged and praised by that same society since, in so doing, that future father whose strength only derives from fidelity and constancy, he will be automatically weakened, since as promiscuity rises, real manhood declines. Instead, we men have become endless constant fodder for jokes by female (and male!) comediennes who draw raucous cheer for that sort of humor that says that all men are stupid, silly, smelly, worthless, oafish, uncultured, clumsy, clodhopping, dumb, half witted, boorish, negligible, unnecessary, scornful, useless, despicable, contemptible, valueless, simply foolish, ad infinitum. By the way, after having listened to these shrill and strident attacks for decades, many males are fed up with such gutter talk. Instead, young girls may be told to anticipate courtship by a young man who is a miraculous combination of Zorro and Saint Francis, and when he falls short of that impossible standard, he must be dismissed. Instead, those same young women are told to experiment, to perhaps become a dedicated, man-hating lesbian or menage-a-trois aficionada. Instead, too, in a further demented embrace of the arcane and the occult, transitioning to the other sex will be roundly considered, if that unwise choice is allowed. Instead, mothers in television commercials routinely speak of "My daughter", instead of "Our daughter", thus minimizing, perhaps unconsciously, the place and station of her husband. Instead, in this hookup culture supported by the false prophets, abortion has become a murderous form of birth control; we have therefore embraced a culture of death, to the tune of 1 million dead innocents of the womb per year or roughly fifty million dead innocents since Roe v Wade became law back in 1973. And instead of fighting against abortion fifty years ago, religious groups mostly acquiesced, thinking it could not be defeated and doing what can only be termed as a piss-poor job of fighting against this national disgrace.

Instead, and further, single women (and men) may adopt orphaned or abandoned children, and by the way, this massive change in mores and familial norms was done with scant discussion. Instead, we began to hear too much talk that women must be empowered; however, with their amazing biology and will, were they not powerful all along; and too, what shall they do with that new power? Shall it be more chin-ups? Pull-ups? Sit-ups? Should women so vigorously chase a gaining power? And why was that singular word, power, chosen amongst all the others? Why don't those women ask for more kindness and or tenacity or patience or grace, instead of more power? We have been told by the false preachers, the "prideful gladiators", that more power is important; however, what folly that gains! Instead, men rarely are granted child custody in the event of cruel divorce, even of young sons. Instead, a father is rarely consulted by the mother when an abortion is pondered. Instead, increasingly for employment women are often chosen over a better qualified man, solely on the basis of sex. And instead, finally, when all of these sad trends are gathered together, they form a new, rolling ball of momentum, one mounding and mounting, and one determining that men's crucial paternity, the important right of fatherhood, is forever diminished, as if on cruel purpose.

This sneaky, accepted hypothesis-in-tandem that

1. Biological fathers do not count for much, and
2. It takes a village and, distinctly, not a father and mother to well raise a child

needs to be re-assessed and challenged anew. Surely, after all this exculpatory evidence is considered, most right thinkers, those not yet tainted or warped by today's flimsy and false values, will reach the unassailable conclusion that this social experiment, essentially banishing or getting rid of fatherhood, did not turn out so well. Surely as well, we can grasp that a turnback of the clock to some earlier values would hold favorable results. However, will we? Will we return to the old, better ways of living? And surely, we will discover that to do otherwise---to let an awry, crooked, twisted, and obsessed culture raise a child instead of his two parents---will only harm those children more deeply, though they in the midst of the ensuing chaos may not regard it so.

Again, sailors and soldiers both, think, though you may be by now a little tired and growing listless, rise and do not slacken! Oliver, are you made of strong stone yet? Again, ancora una volta, let us turn backwards to look around ourselves, as any keen-eyed, yet sleepy, dog does a proper giro or spin before his laydown onto his soft brown feathered cushion. Three score years ago, why would any culture wish to take on and promote such crazy ideas, e.g., that a father is not necessary in the least, that a kin-group would be better at raising a child than a set of parents, and that cultural affiliations were more crucial than blood? The answer is clear: Social forces were loosed sixty years ago that announced these new doctrines as fact, even though they were only craven and unproven propaganda; this sponsorship and endorsement accomplished by self-appointed big shots was done on purpose to destroy the family, to make it simply go away, so that society and the state might better raise our children. All of this was done right under our noses! It was a frontal attack like any other, and our necessary counterattack, long overdue, must be firm and resolute, long-lasting and made of steel. In an atmosphere of diminishing religion, the media and the culture, such as it was, simply proclaimed that fathers were unnecessary so that society might take a much larger role in child-rearing. Familial independence declined, with the state filling the new intentionally created vacuum. All of this was done on purpose, as part of a planned stratagem. Why else would the media, which more and more tells us how and what to think, so quickly and so unquestioningly give its false imprimatur, its faux benediction, its phony blessing, to such mammet pap, and to so many other dangerous and destructive ideas?

All of this suggests that by now paternity itself should have completely disappeared, yet such is not the case. Therefore, one must ask: Is there not a vestigial pull backwards toward a calmer, better place and time? What would the Evangelists think of Eve? Still, we can no longer dither nor dally, since a larger battle awaits, and one which must be brought to the recognized enemy. This contest shall require all our tenacity, full requisite speed, and unyielding, intrepid resolve. This new shift to join in battle in the long culture war cannot wait. It must be brought to the enemy. Speed is key, as always. For, our society will continue to implode and destroy itself unless we move and confront fiercely all those who deprecate the importance of fathers in a child's life or mockingly scoff at traditional ideas of manhood. And if we continue to dawdle, to dither and loll, our children will continue spiritually and psychically to be undernourished and only partly fed.

In the meantime, and to garner and muster to ourselves a building strength, something needed for all battles

Cinque Sortite: Five Assaults Or Sallies Onto The Battlefield

and forays, all assaults and sorties, as we gird ourselves for another, endless fight, one more sally or charge into Dante's deepest thicket of the darkest wood, we may wish to recall two more snippets from the Italian lexicon which well demonstrate the simple rudiments of this story, all the better to embellish its telling. Example Number One: Once more in the film, The Godfather (In Italy, they call it Il Padrino), Don Vito Corleone has a frank conversation with weak Johnny Fontaine, saying, directing him to:

    ---Act like a man!

A little later, more to the point of the present discussion, Vito slowly and convincingly gives Johnny a stern lesson: To not be a good father, to jump from bed to bed since one may, since it is possible to do so, to encourage the incipient Priapus in all men, to not be constant and faithful is to implicitly undercut one's important role as a father and husband. Vito implies that any man who does not act as if his family is his first priority after God, well, that man is less than a man, perhaps a half child, half man assemblage, a confused and desire drenched perpetual adolescent, another childish and giggly phony like High Hefner, whose whole life was a play or tableau upon the world's stage demonstrating how not to behave. Here is the scene in the movie, with Vito asking Johnny:

    ---You spend time with your family?

Johnny answers:

    ---Sure, I do.

And Vito responds:

> ---Good. Cause a man who doesn't spend time with his family can never be a real man.

The Godfather script written by Francis Ford Coppola from the novel by Mario Puzo; 1972; Page 17.

Here is the brilliant art in Coppola's telling of the tale: Just as the don speaks these words to Johnny, over his shoulder the viewer see's Vito's first son, Santino (ironically, the name means "little saint" in English), who has, just minutes before, committed adultery with another woman, all of this done during his sister, Connie's, wedding. Implicitly by this sharp juxtaposition between faithfulness and unfaithfulness, Coppola derides and mock Santino's behavior, gauging it as a stain against his manhood and as blasphemy upon a sacrament, as one stronger generation, Vito's, gives up its leadership mantle, its sceptre of manhood, to the immeasurably weaker next one, Santino's. This is how generations decline, enervate, and wipe themselves out. Why did Santino not listen to his father and lead a more righteous life? Answer: Because he did not wish to, since all the time the crafty, never-pausing-to-relax devil was whispering bad, nasty thoughts into his ear, thus convincing the weaker man to do otherwise.

Example Number Two: Finally, as a linch-pin, or a way to clinch the argument in God's favor, should He with grace may grant it, another example from the Italian world comes to mind. The case, one built slowly brick by brick, is made that fealty to family ought to be re-found, re-embraced, re-strengthened. So, let us for a moment regard a father's simple love for his son. Such a thing must not be savaged

Cinque Sortite: Five Assaults Or Sallies Onto The Battlefield

or truncated. Such a love re-enforces paternity, the very idea of a proper manhood. Nothing is more pure than that love, or too, a mother's love for one of her progeny. When a father or a mother share a son or daughter, each of the parents perennially worry about everything, his Achilles' heel, his shoes, his health, his mind, his mind, and his soul. Will he fall from a tree? Will he develop rickets? Will he learn to master a favorite language? Will he have and keep good teeth? Will he be close to God? Will he become a productive citizen, a loving spouse? Will he know that God is important and, if a man, that all woman need to be respected? In this way, by caring for them, our children as part of God's perfect and complicated plan, that love necessarily takes all parents out of ourselves so that we may see the face of God in them, in our children, and too, so that our own desires and advancements, since we have had our time, may then be viewed as paltry and secondary next to theirs.

So then, after this rambling but necessary preamble to the telling of the tale, please consider the writer, James Joyce, who with his wife, Nora Barnacle, lived in Trieste, Italy from 1904 to 1920. In Trieste, the Joyce's produced two children, Giorgio and Lucia, a name incidentally stemming from the Latin word, luxe, meaning light. One day, the great writer, il grande scrittore, took his only son, Giorgio, down to the lonely sea and sky to a sheltered bathing spot upon the shore called "Fontana", une bella posta right on the sea where his son might cavort in the shivering Adriatico. The Great War was about to commence since a few weeks earlier and not too far away, in Sarajevo, Archduke Franz Ferdinand of Austria and his morganatic wife Sophie had already been assassinated by a Bosnian activist. Giorgio was only a skinny nine years of age that July of 1914. As he would later write in his poem "On the Beach at Fontana", Joyce see his:

>---trembling fineboned shoulder and boyish arm.

The caring father saw his son's slim body, its inherent fragility and weakness, and how defenseless and in danger his son might be without a father to protect him from all the mean, unseen dangers that do lively lurk about in this world. Prophylactically, protectively, tenderly, the father wanted to guard his son against all dangers and tragedies as fathers have done down through the ages.

This parent's love is a purer one than any other, since it is one untouched by erotic love's carnal cravings and vaulted tremblings; too, it is one unstained by promises of financial gain, and one unblemished by a consideration of a possible advantage that might accrue, or, as is implied by those most common words:

>---What is in it for me?

We should be wise to study this inherent benign strength of a father's love, and at the same time how much is lost to the child and to society at large if it were to go away or be diminished. We should all be more prudent now to embrace that love. And we would be sensible to no longer castigate interminably those fathers from whom it naturally flows. With that in mind, here is James Joyce's full poem, "On the Beach at Fontana", taken from his poetry collection entitled, Pomes Penyeach, written in Trieste, Italy in 1914 as a kind of spontaneous paternal hymn from father, James, to his young son, Giorgio:

Cinque Sortite: Five Assaults Or Sallies Onto The Battlefield

> ---Wine whines and whines the shingle.
> The crazy pierstakes groan;
> A senile sea numbers each shingle
> Slimsilvered stone.
>
> From whining wind and colder
> Grey sea I wrap him warm
> And touch his trembling fineboned shoulder
> And boyish arm.
>
> Around us fear, descending
> Darkness of fear above
> And in my heart how deep unending
> Ache of love!
>
> Shakespeare and Company Publisher; 1927

So, in conclusion and right in front of our sleepy eyes, we have seen a disastrous experiment, this intentional diminishment of the father's place in child rearing. How quickly social standards change, alter, morph, and with scarcely a cogent discussion or full debate! We must understand that all around us today we see complete pandemonium, something we alone have created from scratch. And therefore, we must ask ourselves:

> ---Who is in charge of this disintegrating, disassembling, chaotic jamboree?

Life is a somber trial, one full of choices that bear a lasting imprint upon our lives, and our souls. Bad choices then lead to evil and endless anxiety. So, today, let us fully reject this false and dangerous trial, since it has not worked and is directly counter to God's will. Let us regard it for what it has been: A asinine and foolish attempt to belittle both fathers and men generally, and at the same time, willy-nilly, in one fell swoop, at the same time to destroy that traditional family. As well, let us recognize the failure of all replacements for the family, since they have been wholly inadequate and faulty and, moreover, not part of God's plan. Finally, let us return again quickly to the earlier model of the family which worked quite well when both the man and the woman put their full minds, energies, and bodies to it.

It, this titanic turnaround, this gigantic effort, this long combat against all of these compounding and now-entrenched treacherous ideas shall not be easy. No, sailors, foot-sloggers, militia men and women, all my partisans from the hillside, do steel yourselves well for the long foray onto the campo. We shall need surpassing intelligence, dedicated resolve, and a sinewy tenacity on all fronts. Expect adversity and then mightily vanquish it! It is high times, today, at this late date, to put our ship around, to speedily turn her about, spin her perpendicularly into the sea's onrushing rollers, seas that hasten to swamp this ship lest we move most speedily. Mates, abruptly now! Bosuns all, gather your finest mettle and prepare for battle! Man the oars! Steel the lanyards! For henceforth, all mustered diligence and dispatch shall be demanded since there is both a nation and the world at stake. Who among you shall be the first, il primo, to step forward into the fractious fray and volunteer for action? There is nothing better than the heart of a volunteer. It is important immediately to strive to make things better. Each of us share that stiff assignment and large obligation. And before you launch into combat, have some large quantities of both soup and wine since you will need all strength and fortitude for this long battle that lies ahead.

And in the meantime, as you gird for this sortie, think about these short, simple lines from Proverbs, prudent words that have lately been fully discarded and mislaid, words that tell us the simple truth that being a father is a most important and necessary job:

> ---Train up a child in the way he should go. And when he is old, he will not depart from it.
>
> Proverbs 22:6

THE ABSENCE OF THE IMPERATIVE COMMAND

---Be resolute and make rapid preparations to store food and water in your position so that your supplies will last through intense barrages.

> Preparations for Battle by General Tadamichi Kuribayashi (1891-1945), a set of instructions prior to the Battle of Iwo Jima meant for the soldiers of the "Courage Division", 1944.

---You want to know why this outfit got the hell kicked out of it? A blind man could spot it. They don't act like soldiers; they don't look like soldiers; why should they be expected to fight like soldiers?

> Patton, film script written by Francis Ford Coppola and Edmund Hall North, 1970.

---You will laugh at violence and famine. And you will not be afraid of wild beasts.

> The Book of Job 5:22

Those that do not know how to work, who have not yet learned or been taught how to do it, when first confronted with it, they will invariably talk about how hard and difficult it is. And that is what we see all around us now.

First, we all need to remember that six decades ago, long before we tacitly agreed that technology rather than strong hands and legs and backs ought to carry out our work, most Americans, yes, most, lived on ranches and farms and dairies and orchards and forests, performing there those necessary tasks which today are labelled menial, lowly, or simply beneath one. Before farming had become a corporate tax write-off and an endeavor that other people should carry out for us, there in those fields and forests and on those ranches those laborers then worked long, hard hours under the glinting implacable sun or scudding clouds that raced across the impervious sky. Both cold and heat beat down upon those long-gone workers, enveloping them, yet, since they were rugged and formidable, sinewy, those forces did not in the least enervate them or made them weaker, since, over time a pervasive implacability or stoicism had been gained, earned, stored, and trusted within their bodies and souls. To never be upset or deterred, to grasp the now rarely uttered word "long-suffering", and to be inured against anything undesirable or painful by prolonged subjugation to it, all of these were character traits adopted generally, regardless whether the difficulty was crop losses, bodily injury, inclement or ill-timed weather, disastrous market conditions, or anything else that might be termed a setback or bad break or humbling reversal of fortune. During these long and arduous efforts, and more to the crux of this small tale, Americans were constantly being told what to do. Then, not now, we were subject to the constant onslaughts of the imperative command, our friend (Yes, it is a friend indeed!) "Il imperativo" as the Italian might term it. And, I hold as the main theme of this short story, we were that much better off for it.

So, let us then, shipmate or private, pivot some and

jettison ourselves far backwards in time. When I was young most farmers for whom I worked had been in the war, which would be World War II. Some had seen brutal combat, and likely had participated in the calamities of Dunkerique, the deprivations of Operation Shingle at Anzio on the way northward to Roma. Perhaps they had witnessed the FUBAR of Pearl Harbor, or the crazy luck of Midway Island. They later had survived, the ones I knew of at least, D-Day in Normandy and latter, the long siege of the Battle of the Bulge at Bastogne in the shrouded freezing Ardennes Forest of late '44. In ways that we today may not be able to fully comprehend, these soldiers and sailors and airmen had been completely and fully toughened by war, by all of it: The training, the mayhem of bloodshed, the lousy food or the lack of it, the worn-out or improper boots, the drenching cold and wet conditions, the wrenching wounds, and by the long ache of the deaths of their surrounding comrades. From this training and by what they saw firsthand, they understood right away, as Kuribayashi above intimates, that solid preparation is the simple key to victory, to vanquishing and squashing the enemy, and so they believed implicitly in the importance of drills and conditioning, so that the odds of survival might improve a slim tick, no matter how strenuous or grueling, before any contest should be joined or might be won. These combatants knew that such training would surely make the outcome more favorable for their side, that it would, in their military parlance, "pay off". Of course, in the cruel course of this preparation for and engagement in war, something none of them had asked for, some of these warriors became too aggressive, too vicious, by what they had seen and what they had done. At the same time, all knew that to claim victory one always had to be ready and prepared to fight, and also to work well together with fellow warriors, even if you did not much like the other guy; too, all grasped that exercising rare speed was key to victory, since, as Frederick the Great once said:

---L'audace! Toujours l'audace!

After the war, after victory both in Europe and in Asia had been accomplished, automatically most of these warriors in the trenches, on the sea, and in the sky, they brought these ideas and principles and automatic, reflexive modes of conduct home with them as they gratefully returned to the farm, forest, or ranch.

Not all of them became farmers to be sure, since farming was quickly becoming much more automated and industrialized. Some returning became factory works, truck drivers, managers, you name it, since they did what had to be done to feed their growing families. However, many of them, fifteen years after the war's conclusion, became bosses, this metamorphosis happening because from the war they knew deep in their bones precisely how to lead. They ran the show. They naturally became the guys in charge of whatever needed to be done. And, jeepers creepers, it was men like this, hardened beyond normal measure by war's long compounding adversities, who happened to become my various bosses as I, then but a weak tad or scamp or skinny slip of a thing, then barely thirteen, first set out to work in the fields and orchards. And at first, what a fearful and daunting lot of men they were for I, a small, teenaged, pimple-faced freshman kid to run up against!

The first thing I noticed about these guys is that they

were universally skinny! Even though middle aged, since they were used to strenuous exercise, interminable tramps across the fields and up steep mountains, usually carrying heavy, bulging packs upon their shoulders, they were most lean and sinewy, holding absolutely no extra weight, even around the belly. Secondly, I noticed right away about these guys that they were really happy not to be sniper bait, not to in the enemy's mean crosshairs; so, they smiled and cackled and teased each other most of the time. Third, I observed, and most happily so, that these former combatants were hugely racy, ribald, and profane, for such exotic, almost perverse language I then did hear! It was quite something for an impressionable whelp who had just become a teenager. Such words, such phrases, such arcane and howling expressions! From that first day in the fields, I loved every minute of it, and why not? Every expletive, every dirty, misunderstood nuance, every surplus and excessive, for-the-hell-of-it phrase---all of it was terrific, fantastic, and otherworldly to my young ears, making me laugh and feel young and giddy. They never used words like:

---Would, could, should, maybe, perhaps.

Instead, they always spoke with a simple, direct diction, using real tangible words, and never, ever used the subjunctive or conditional cases since they imply doubt. Given my sedate home life, where bad language or anything close to it was simply not tolerated, this new work situation, where spicy and naughty talk was a daily potion, up-to-date and de rigueur, it was a delight, a treasure, and a verbal glory to listen to those lusty words and phrases and to which every happy day I did cling. Right away I looked forward to going to work with these gruff, curt guys since each day I would likely learn some new naughty word! Why not? To a growing and aspiring teenage mind this peace-of-cake joy could not have been keener! Of course, much of their profanity and verbal boasting was derived from their years in the military, where they had used gallows humor to dodge the ominous threat of death. In that warfare they learned to loudly pronounce to all about them only the most lively words and risqué phrases, unique diction picked up maybe from ramrod stateside staff sergeant who relished his roles as provoker and derider, and who only wished to turn his young recruits into tougher men intent upon a greater victory.

I worked for a lot of characters like the ones I have described in those days, but two of the main ones were two Army guys named Mike Flynn and Vincenzo D'Onofrio, one of Irish extraction and the other, of course, of Italian. During the long Fall of 1944 they had met in the 28th Infantry Division at the Battle of Hurtgen Forest just south of Aachen under Major General Norman Cota; and later, they fought at the Battle of the Bulge after a transfer to the First Army under General Courtney Hodges, and somehow, both young men had survived both battles. For the long six months of those two battles neither one of them got hit, shot, or injured in any way despite the fierce and endless fighting, so both with no true logic assumed that each guy was somehow mysteriously lucky for the other, some kind of instant rabbit's foot in battle. Quickly then, they became a team, like a shortstop and a shortstop are when they turn a quick-as-anything double play. After the war both returned to the wives back in the states and saw there their first-born children for the first time, since when the war had heated up back in '42 each of those yet-to-born ragazzini had still been camped out in their mother's watery womb.

Over the course of time, both Mike and Vincent (by then quite proud to be an American, right after the war, Vincenzo decided to ditch the Italian version, Vincenzo, and to call himself Vincent) gravitated to the orchards of Ventura County, since the pay was good and regular and both liked to be outside away from the preening bigshots that even back in those distant roamed offices like preening, self-important warlords. I still recall that first day when I showed up for work at this big citrus ranch off of the long and straight Gridley Road, with Vincent saying to me, after he first laid his eyes on me:

> ----What's the deal, kid? We got to pay you $1.25 per hour? What the heck! You're weak and stupid and don't know jack diddly. Heck, you're just a wimpy little piker and no stud muffin, that's for sure. By the way, dingleberry, star-gazer, our new pup, you got a heck of a nasty complexion there, squirt. Fix your face, will ya? You can't lift much, you can't drive truck, you can't drive tractor. What the blazes! And I can tell in a flat second just by looking at you that you know less than zip about construction, plumbing, and all the rest of it. And we got to pay you $1.25 per hour? It sure as hell sounds to me like we are getting royally screwed!

More than a little intimidated, I answered:

> ---You are going to pay me the money, aren't you, mister?

Vincent responded:

> ---Yeah, sure, you little whelp, whippersnapper. But, I want to no dilly-dallying, no sauntering, no dithering or lolling, and no lollygagging; you got that? The word for the day is hustle, always! And two more things, dirt ball: Concentrate on the job at hand, and finish something once you've started it. Got that, dingus? So, you must never be a cripple. Stand on your own two feet and learn how to move, sprint, pivot! As they used to say about boxers, to rest is to rust. You got to keep moving. You follow me, Jasper?

Right from the get-go, I just loved working for those guys, Vincent and Mike. They were fearless and obstinate, and almost seemed to relish all difficulties and problems, so that they could fix them and right away! Too, for both of them, their word was as good as gold, and even though the ranch's owner was miles away, neither of them would have shaved hours or pinched supplies. Mike was always talking about how Ireland was HIS island, how he owned the whole darn country, lock, stock, and barrel, and then he would get this faraway, dreamy look in his eye. They were always making jokes about anything under the sun, and I could tell right away that they were just glad and happy and content that no joker Kraut German was shooting a Muser-Werke Karabiner 98k at them. The years of the war had steeled them, just having to get through it all had automatically made them more resilient and determined about everything. During the war there was a whole lot of seeing death first-hand and they had to learn how to survive everything that came at them. So, they always enjoyed going back to the salt mines in the orchard since nobody was trying to shoot them. Out in the field both liked to have fun, and because of all their joking around, the gesticulations and teasing and guffaws, the days out in the field, while we were working hard, digging ditches, laying pipe, planting trees, fixing plumbing manifolds, whatever else that had to be done, those days passed us all by quicker than lightning. Somehow the days actually became shorter, as if by accident or miracle. Too, both of them were always coming out with some odd or obscure turn of a phrase, something like:

---Chop chop!
---Turn tail!
---Lions led by donkeys!
--- Pass the buck, why don't you?
---Go off all half-cocked!
---Full tilt.
---Make a pass at.
---Make it snappy, will ya?
---Go to work on…
----Half the battle is…..
---You are as useful as a bump on a log, tits on a boar
---You got that done by the skin of your teeth
---He'll have to face the music, that's for darn sure!
---Another rube rookie.
---Dummy run
---Holy Moses!
---Make do.

Sometimes they would say stuff I didn't get, so I began to carry a little grimy notebook in my jean pocket, thinking it might be something a little racy. Tantalizing to me were these words and phrases, and they were endless. Some of the stranger ones were:

> ---Shack up with a blister.
> --- Fiat money.
> ---Grease ape.
> ---Shit on a shingle
> ---Tickety-boo
> ---Gravel crusher.
> ---Shavetail in the box
> ---Grunt and growler
> --- Irish promotion
> ---Check out

There were jillions of them, so I'd write some of them down in my grubby notebook and then, later at night, I'd ask my dad what the heck Mike and Vinny were talking about and he'd usually say:

> ---Heck if I know. Those guys were in the Army and I was an old shell, a full looey in the Navy, a ninety-day wonder navigator working on tramp transports steaming out of Pearl. So, it beats me, son, it sure as hell beats me!

So, sometimes I never did decipher their wordy gibberish since it came straight out of the Army argot from across the ocean wide and never got into any proper dictionaries where I might learn about them. Too, since both of them spent a lot of time in good old Deutschland, they would use words like:

> ---Bitter

Cinque Sortite: Five Assaults Or Sallies Onto The Battlefield

---Snell
--- Feine Bruste
---Schones Madchen
---Mit schlag
---Kirschlager
--- Essen ein Schlafchem
---Unverschamtheit, that lovely weiblich or feminine word which many years later I learned means always present impudence, and
---Strafe.

all of which, and many dozens more, gave to me the clear impression that these former soldiers had a private and special access to another, larger world beyond me about which I knew nothing. Many years later I found out that that last word, strafe, means to punish, and therefore that it is an appropriate word to describe what happens to a jeep when it is shot at repeatedly by machine guns from low-lying aircraft, exactly like what happened to Generalfeldmarschall Erwin Rommel July 17, 1944 near Sainte-Foy-de-Montgommery deep in the infinitely variegated Calvados country.

Sometimes too, I would hear little snippets from Vinny, undecipherable Italian phrases that he had picked up from somewhere, maybe that prisoner of war camp that he called Fontanellato (but I am just guessing on the spelling of the jail since he never spelled out the word for me ever) where he had spent some time in the middle of the war's chaos and that was close to Parma of the hard cheese fame. Or perhaps it was more likely that these hardened field ruffians or fun-loving desperados had picked up these exotic phrases and strange words in a seedy bar or cheap osteria, words like:

>   ---Ma donna buona
>   ---Porca miseria
>   ---Ascolti! Vedi! Il petto. No due!
>   ---Una bella ragazza!
>   ---Una buona figura!

And how the heck was I as a dim witted, naive teenager supposed to make any sense of that nonsense? Mike and Vinny sometimes talked in foreign languages, mostly Italian but sometimes in Deutsch, which to me sounded exactly like a toilet flushing itself, so that I would not be able to follow any of it, like parents do all the time to their kids. My two bosses in the orchards never seemed to forget the foreign words and the army lingo since all of that had been learned in the war and under the most desperate pressures, so that those strange and exotic words must have permanently stayed there, firmly and forever etched into their brains.

Yet, more than that, this surprising and sometimes rough language was like seasoning for the day, like lots of coarse black pepper sprinkled over a nicely grilled Flatiron steak. It reflected the teller's odd and tenacious habit of mind and showed, demonstrated, that once he had been compelled to pass a very long period of time at some tedious chore. I could imagine both Mike and Vinny sitting around a Quonset hut or bivouac or seized lodge or impromptu tent camp telling nothing but the tallest of tales, that is, in the intermittent, unplanned lull between the fighting and skirmishes. Always, soldiers have lots of time to kill, then periods of intense activity where everything had to be right on the tick, or else caustic death might loom. Mike and Vinny, and all the other orchard bosses that I had back in those days delighted in stupid stories, obscure tales, rankest jokes, and letting strange buzzwords words fly. Crazy Irishman Mike made a silly game of numbering his most well-known jokes, so sometimes he'd just leer at Vinny and me, wink some, and then say to us:

    ---Number 8!

and the two goofy jaybirds would start laughing like a couple of off-the-beam kids. The ceaseless and speedy banter among these guys was rapid fire, as short and fast as the time between mortar rounds. On some days when we were out in the boonies working our rears off, the jokes flew so thick that the day passed as if were mere minutes. Heck, I knew right away that Mike and Vinny were just happy that no cloak and dagger Kraut was trying to take a pot shot at them. Those two guys, they sure did their bit. Simply put, foot sloggers and boys in blue, here was their drill about working on the ranch: All the work had to get done, and so they thought: We might as well have some tiddly fun doing it. The work simply had to get done. Had to. Pumps wanted to get fixed, trees needed to be braced, their trunks painted white to reflect the sun, weeds had to be sprayed, drag-line irrigation lines had to be pulled, and Nitrogen fertilizer had to be spread properly just before a soft rainfall. There was no sense in ever saying that the job could be finished tomorrow. No, sir! These guys were not used to talking about tomorrow, no way. So, all of this work had to be (Had to be!) carried out perfectly, precisely, dead nuts on, and to the flippin' letter. With them nothing was ever lackadaisical. I then understood early on that all of these bosses, but especially Mike and Vinny, had been made tough, sinewy, and tenacious by a hard and relentless determination that they had earned day by day in war, and too, that they sure as hell were not going to put up with anything dumb or half-ass or hard case from me, else sure as anything, there would be major hell to pay, and as a sure thing they would know how to dish it out.

All of this means that out there in those vast fields and bucolic orchards, whenever they ran into a SNAFU or problem, they never gave into it or capitulated to anything. If a screw-up of any sort arose, right away in their toughened bones they knew instantly that all efforts to conquer it had to be mustered, marshalled, and re-doubled, and not down the damn road, but exactly then. They knew how to make duck soup out of everything. Made stalwart by war, when they saw a difficulty, that was their signal to step it up a notch, but, no, more than a notch. Right away it seemed to me that Mike and Vinny did not shirk from these contests and difficulties; instead, they luxuriated in them, almost smiling with relish, grinning like a gleeful teenager about to drive a fast care to pick up his good-looking squeeze on a Saturday night. Conditioned earlier by so many adversities, they then expected them at every turn, around all corners, under each door. And I knew early on that they would no more turn away from or retreat from a nasty-ass problem than they would drink ethyl gasoline or curse their mothers.

So, over time and through character-building incidents, I grew up to near-manhood under their strict tutelage; it was an almost military atmosphere that enveloped me, one saying that all work was some sort of mythic battle to be fought proudly and quickly, and won, vanquished. Soon,

I understood with them that to give up was the only way you would ever lose. Mike and Vinny had immense, fearless tendencies, feisty and reliable instincts that told them to never give in to any damn thing, that said that only we are the masters of our own fate, that we are never subject to some mysterious outside force that compels us what to do. They taught me to never quit at anything, but rather, to always give a 100% effort in all things. From them, as well, I learned to, as they both said to me dozens of times:

---Do it right and do it once

and correspondingly, that any slap-dash, ronchie, or careless job was only done by some stupid gink or rube idiot who was simply less than a man. Most of the time they were smiling and laughing, and the only time they cussed was when either one of them nastily skinned a knuckle somehow, making it bleed like a stuck pig, and then the blue language would really start to flow out of their mouths, like a fast river coursing out of the mountains. Too, from these rugged men I learned that it was never right to waste time, or be in any way a shirker or lazy man, since to do so was automatically to steal from the boss, whether he was a jerk or not, and even if he weren't around. Finally, as they had instructed me from the get-go, I came close to mastering the idea of concentrating completely on the job at hand, and also to finish the darn thing fully once it had been started. Focus was key! How many times did they yell at me, and harangue, hector, bellow, pontificate about my idleness or slowness afoot, all done so that those keen and sharp messages about work would enter my pubescent brain and there reside and settle to better task? Truth be told, very rarely did they bark at me, and when they did do so I surely deserved it anyhow. And finally, these ways of working, getting many things done at once, these instinctual attitudes, over months, through lecture, and by example were absorbed by me seamlessly, without me knowing that such a transformative thing inside me was taking place.

Then, as a way to better survive the difficult conditions, as any other soldier might have done, I did not object to their commands, their strictures, their occasional bellicose demands, slights, and reprimands. For one thing, I did not wish to get skinned; no, that would not have been helpful. To protest anything to them would not have done any good. They were in charge, not I. Without my realizing it, I was fast on the track of becoming a worker's pragmatist. Anyway, they, these men 10 or 20 or 30 years older than I and who had fought in an ugly, long, and distant war that I had only read about, they were inestimably stronger than I. They, not I, had been hardened by war's depravity. They, not I, had been shot at, though never wounded. They had tramped with heavy backpacks through sloughs and swamps, up ravines and escarpments, not I. They had gone days and weeks without hot food and dry socks, not I. And they had seen many of their friends' faces turn in silence to stone when killed, not I. Sometimes in their faces I could see all of these things, all the past deprivations and ugliness. Sometimes then, as we might gather at an orchard's edge to discuss quickly what next must be done, to craft an agricultural strategy, I could see and read in their sad eyes a retreat back to some mean, long, lean burrow of the war, and I could sense that behind them in their sequestered souls there resided pain of a deeper sort, a large and unspeakable sorrow inside each of them that would never go away.

However, we usually we did not sit around gabbing. Instead of discussions of strategy amongst us, they gave out orders, clear unmistakable orders and scores of them, often yelled or shouted or roared above the repetitive din of the Ford tractor. Sometimes their tone was rough, gruff, brusque, but after only a few days of that, I no longer cared in the least what kind of tone they used to convey the darn order. What difference did tone make? None. These men, my first real bosses really, outside of my parents and teachers, they meant no harm to me, none at all; too, they were always watching out that I did not hurt myself doing something lame ass stupid or clucky. Soon, after a few weeks, I began to expect them, these endless razor-edged imperative demands. Why, in short time, I would not have been able to live well or function decently without them! For, I had begun to expect them coming towards me as assuredly as I expected a good night's sleep to give me a greater strength in the morning.

Even today I can still hear their commands and orders which were always made with sterling precision:

> ---Move the Ford tractor to the north side of Block #2. Do you hear me now?

> ---Transfer the 18 50 pounds sacks of Urea fertilizer from the pallet in the barn to the bed of the green pick-up, you know, the '49 Stude.

> --- Deliver exactly 6 hours of water via dragline sprinklers to the 2-year-old grapefruit trees in

> Block #4, and at the same time, patrol it for leakers and also look for any other sort of foul up.

And on and on. Since they had been trained 20 years before with absolutely no sloppy or ambiguous commands, whether in boot camp or in transit or in the bloody war itself, it was no surprise that their belligerent and barking orders to me showed the same degree of exactness and precision and specificity.

Over the next few months hearing this habit of speech trained my mind to always look for greater clarity in all things. Too, occasionally I was not paying full attention when the commands flew my way. So, sometimes but not very often, I would ask for greater clarification, saying to them:

> ---How many hours of water did you say to apply to Block #9?

> --- Which block needs the 2 pounds per tree of Ammonium Nitrate, #3 or #5?

This was only fitting for me to ask those questions since I was just a kid, a rookie, one whose small brain had already been trained and exercised by all these demanding bosses, but especially by Mike and Vinny, those true men grown much stronger than I in much tougher times, those who knew deep in their bellies that sloppy thinking could easily end up in somebody croaking, or maybe many of them all at once.

The key is that all the time there in the fields and ranches, I was never, never asked what I thought of felt or believed, and quite rightly so. They did not have requisite time for that, nor did they care. I was but a functionary, and an infinitesimally small part of a much larger team. I was meant to do a job. It needed to be done, that job. I never said to myself:

>   ---It is not my job.

If they told me to do something, I did it, and pronto.

Mike and Vinny would ask me:

>   ---Listen, kid. Can you move? You're slowing down some, chump. Can you get the job done now?

I was told simply what to do, and what the gang of us (since I was usually working alongside a gaggle of similar dweeb, weak idiots) was expected to accomplish if the day were meant to be a good and blessed one, one uncommonly led and productive. Once on the job, I was never asked my opinion about any darn thing, only about how the job or travail might best be done and with all available speed.

And in all of this I was neither special nor splendid in any regard. I was just one of the guys humping it out in the boondocks. All the time I was being molded, groomed, formed, yet I did not know any of that at the time. My bosses' dynamics of precision and bellicosity were normal and constant all through those now long-distant days. My desires were unimportant and never discussed, and all the work had to get done and properly so, and that's it. How about that? And all the bosses at the various ranches were pretty much the same: Barking looeys, and always pissed off and eager privates from the war with no moaners or complaining Dilberts among them.

Dominic M. Martin

Is it possible or likely now to make a small, slow, flanking maneuver within this discourse, to tack the boat some, directly back into the waves? That is, may we presently look at how things in the workplace have changed, how orders are no longer given as they once were, so that tasks are left undone, sloppiness reigns, and a new foolish emphasis on feelings has arisen like a naughty Poseidon from the depths of the ocean to the surface of the sea. Such a study of that stark juxtaposition of then versus now will prove illustrative to all those who believe we have a problem in surrendering, abandoning the earlier norms. All of those who did not think we have a problem have already departed for Zanzibar or Marrakech or perhaps to the couch, or maybe to the honkytonks of Alsatia, intent upon pleasure or unkind oblivion.

To put it plainly, one's own desires have been made (by society?) that much more important. So, it is no longer:

> ---How many hours of water is needed for Block #9 this morning?

but, rather:

> ---Do you wish to irrigate Block #9 today?

So, as the imperative command has withered away, many (or, is it all?) younger workers now need to be coaxed, cajoled, and talked into doing things; however, this sad event happens not just once, but continually. One command or order will no longer suffice; further, simple obedience has disappeared like smoke out of a chimney drifts up into the sky. Upon prompt command most now do not labor instinctively; indeed, that gruff brusque, rough manner of speaking has pretty much gone away, having disappeared entirely from the working landscape. In many fields of work, the feelings and thoughts and inclination and biases of the employee have become predominate, seemingly more important than the job itself. Something termed a "micro aggression" has emerged in the workplace, where slights are engendered, sensitivities have grown, and now diversity is now all. This is where we stand today, and explains why less real work gets done. And, in that course, what else has been lost? What has been left behind when an employer must constantly have to beg, to convince his charges into carrying out a job?

In the first place, via my high school French lessons, we have lost the stern concept of time, or what the French call, la Vitesse. There, then, back in the days when I first had demanding and remonstrative bosses like Mike and Vinny, I discovered that the French named their most fleet trains, those which would steamroll blastingly, alla Strelnikov whose real name is Pasha Antipov, across the mostly flat Gallic countryside, "TGV", for Tres Grand Vitesse, that moniker signifying a very great speed. During those days, toiling on various farms and ranches across the county, usually laboring under a very hot and searing sun, with neither hat nor lotion, hearing dozens of clear, shouted, specific directions, and commands always in my open ears, we all got much done and speedily so. For I was not alone, but surrounded by other cubs and bruins around the mother bear. Yet, today, with the rights and tender feelings of the worker much more to the fore, speed or la Vitesse has been irredeemably lost, cast aside. Therefore, we can no longer get things done quickly. For example, it took only a meagre 13 months to fully and completely construct the

Empire State Building (20 West 29th Street, Manhattan), yet today that same job completion would more likely take 13 years! Since speed is no longer deemed important to the job, it takes too much time to get things done, and all of that is simply because the good-time Charlies-in-charge have never been to war. The result is that the ability to move quickly has vanished. Presto. Subito. Basta.

Secondly, foolishly, with the near disappearance of the imperative command from the workplace, we have lent to employees the captivating, yet corrosive, idea that their own individual desires are paramount. And the wide ramifications of this notion cannot be over-stated. With no surprise, a self-absorbed and unrestrained selfishness has taken hold at work. It follows that gracious loyalty to a firm or boss has shrunk drastically, if not disappeared. A company's goal, usually to provide a service or good while making a profit and paying its bills, has been supplanted by the constantly altering desires of the employees who have been led by our wayward culture to presume that what they want matters.

And on the distinct, other hand is the thought of "What Must Be Done", echoing the sage words of Saint Luke in chapter 3, verse 10. Due to the creeping massive transformations that we have discussed, much labor (most?) is not carried out properly, carefully, assiduously; rather, it is done sloppily, piecemeal and slapdash. Precision has vaporized, disappeared, evanesced. Consider the cost over-runs on the Callaghan Tunnel under Boston Harbor on the way to Logan. Consider how anti-trust regulations are not enforced. Consider how teachers' unions always demand more money, yet the test scores of their students only decline. Consider thousands of other examples of sloppiness and the haphazard...

   Back in the day I was lucky since I used to work with the Mexicans, some legal and some distinctly illegal, in those orchards and ranches, and then, later I led dozens of crews of them, growing grapes and making wine. Why Mexicans? The native locals by that time in the sharp devolution of our culture were disinclined to do such long and dirty work. Somehow over the years menial farm work had become declasse, out of fashion, looked down upon. Of course, the work itself had not altered, only our perception of it. As Herman Melville writes, they, these lazy, white natives:

   ---Would prefer not to...

engage is such menial and tedious labor. Why, it was beneath them! However, here is the question central to the tale: Why would the Mexicans so quickly and happily follow my direction and command, while the pasty white locals, who were born here, would not show up for a job, or, if they had, engage in arguments about how things really ought to be done. What is the answer, Margaret, Marvin? The Mexicans have not yet become exposed (read, corrupted) by this country's new and expanding culture of entitlement and entertainment. Consider how debased and degrading our culture has become, and in such a short time! In truth, the Mexicans on the other hand, were and remain good family people, asking little of life, carrying about themselves an easy and natural stoicism; also, they are indefatigable, never tired or stanco, consado, since they know from their church that this coarse and chaotic life is but a brief and temporary one. Routinely, just like my earlier bosses, Mike and Vinny, they wear a constant smile and look of contentment upon their faces. Their strong and faithful beliefs lead them to always see the glimmer of the light at the end of the tunnel. Uniformly, they tend to be true to their mothers and wives, much more than gringos, who often grow some lousy vice to Gargantuan proportions since our fully dissolute culture encourages them to do so. Indeed, many of the bachelor solteros that I knew back then gratefully sent much of their earnings back to their mothers in Mexico since they figured correctly that mom needed the extra cash more than they did.

Some readers may here posit that I am too burdened by a burgeoning nostalgia, for a tilted windmill's past which is irredeemably departed, and further, that today's laborers have secured considerable workplace rights that did not exist before, ones which the courts have expanded, confirmed, and exonerated. Ah yes, 'tis true: I suppose that I do yearn for an earlier, simpler time!

All of that is true, yet still I fret, since near everywhere I see lassitude, slovenliness, even paralysis. When I ran wineries, by many yards the hardest part of my job was finding and then keeping decent employees. Many would wander off the job after only a few days of sloppy labor. Many potential workers simply did not want to work, so I had to talk them into it. Many were listless and forgetful, lolling and passive. Many were incapable of or disinclined to do what they were told. And many young people today lack any sort of work ethic, having been schooled by technology that engaging in social media or playing a video game, anything along those lines, they conjure, is akin to using a time clock; unbelievably, they think using those techno elements is a job!

Too, I see the stark inability to move quickly, with a smile on my face, like Mike and Vinny used to do, to attack a problem not with a frown, begrudgingly, but with glee, a most forceful glee. As young people jump from job to job like fervent, jumping rabbits, I see a growing lack of loyalty to anything outside of the self. I see that the ethics of the worker, something that would dictate a full day's work for a full day's pay, have diminished. I see a nation gone obese and rotund, rather than sinewy and lean. I see the absence of the imperative command since today employers have to gingerly suggest or cajole that a job might be done. Might? I see everywhere the simple inability of many to plainly obey. And I understand that this absence of the imperative command has made many workers weaker rather than stronger, and weaker by miles and miles.

To sum, somewhere along the line, we told people or made the assumption that a worker's wants, needs, and desires were more important than the job itself; however, if we are to save ourselves, that idea needs to be reversed or truncated, subsumed back into the realization that getting the job done is the thing upon which one must focus.

A keen and watchful reader may anticipate the next words, that we ought to return to the earlier standards, that we would be wise and thrifty to emulate the hard-working Mexicans who in the vast main do not shirk work; rather, they are indeed most grateful for it. Also, it would be prudent to grasp that all life is hard and then you die, that a painstaking endurance and tenacity at work ought to return to the workplace; further, that following through on a received imperative command is not that difficult; and finally, that we would be wise once again to value the clear satisfaction of getting copious amounts of work done. This current course of self-absorption we have lately adopted is a baneful curse upon our disintegrating culture! So swiftly, we have become, instead of razors, couch potatoes. We have become lazy, lardy, cubes of butter! So, now, today, it is not so easy to get off the sofa!

Please know, please understand, please grasp (to use at the last in this writing, yes, that tool called an imperative command to better emphasize a now-lost message), please recognize that in all battles, all difficulties, all efforts, and all work that speed is key. I forecast that all life…if we do not change our ways…well, it is going to get harder, yet again, harder still. Yet, it is time now to fall in line, to regroup, to toe the line, to bear down, to focus and concentrate, and to give a 100% effort in all things. Here is where this small tale shall end.

I guess that giving up the family farm fifty years, forsaking forever that idea of shared, rough, tedious, familial labor, was not such a grand idea after all.

Finally, in our retreat from the use of the imperative command, the very idea of obedience has been lost. For, ponder our infrequently that very simple infinitive, "to obey", is even said! It is almost as if someone in charge of things waved a wand, banishing the word from the dictionary, from our daily lexicon. So, assuredly, we ought to bring it back now, today, doing so with the understanding that obedience to a goal or fealty to a faith always makes one stronger. Therefore, we ought to recall to better ourselves these words of Saint Paul the Apostle to the Romans:

Cinque Sortite: Five Assaults Or Sallies Onto The Battlefield

---For as by one man's disobedience many were made sinners, so also by one Man's obedience many will be made righteous.

The Epistle of Saint Paul to the Romans 5:19

LEADERSHIP OR IL PRIMATO: THE RISE OF THE SUCK-UP AND THE INCONSEQUENTIAL

> ---I don't have to tell you the story. You all know it. Only two kinds of people are going to stay on this beach: Those that are already dead and those that are going to die. Now, get off your butts.

The words of Colonel George Arthur Taylor of the 1st Infantry division, 16th Infantry Regiment, uttered on Omaha Beach on June 6, 1944. For his actions that day Colonel Taylor was later promoted to Brigadier General and received the Distinguished Service Cross.

> ---To exhort: The verb is a 15th century coinage, deriving from the Latin verb, hortari, meaning "to incite" and it often implies the urgent urging or admonishing of an orator or preacher. To incite by argument or advice, to give warnings or advice, to admonish earnestly; to encourage.

> ---If you want a decision, go to the point of danger.
> ---Show me a man who will jump out of an airplane and I'll show you a man who will fight.
> ---You think the world owes you something, and it just doesn't work that way.

Three quotes from General James Maurice Gavin (1907-1990), also known as "The Jumping General"

Today self-centered puerile hucksters, con men and grifters, leaders in name yet not in deed, dominate the political and even the military landscapes, a sorry condition which once was not the case. So, naturally now, we find ourselves in an ugly, confining cul-de-sac, one devoid of real leaders. By slowing tracing the parabola of that broad arc resulting in what we have today: The lax and puerile as the norm, perhaps we can discover once again how to be great, how to be resilient. This small tale is meant to answer the question: How did we blunder into this absurdity where evil is dressed up as good and weak leaders are portrayed as strong ones? Why do we constantly promote and elect ass-kissing shills, cagey carnival barkers, phony stooges engaged in covert and false advertising, who know nothing of what it means to move, to accomplish, and to get things done pronto? If you are grifting and glib, you are good, or so goes today's terrible logic. For myself as a very small potato, so small it can hardly be seen, I am quite tired of being lied to by those dilletantes in power. So, I say: Do look around and think back to when we used to have leaders who actually knew how to lead? Or, think back in time to the last instance when you heard someone these two simple words:

---Let's go,

those two most seductive words in any language?

And, speaking of opportunity and drive, whatever happened to that terrific, yet now lost, word: Gumption? Along with so many others, has it mysteriously been struck from our lexicon? If so, by what mischievous word warlord? Instead, in no longer nurturing and developing true leaders,

Cinque Sortite: Five Assaults Or Sallies Onto The Battlefield

we are buggering ourselves, it is as timple as sat, or should I just say that we are in a mell of a hess? For, we have set this strong and rusty booby trap for ourselves, and now with insouciance we walk right into it, putting our tender ankle into the robust, nasty vise. In essence, we are making our own new prison, and slowly building it ourselves brick by brick and mortar by mortar. Essentially, this sharp decline in the quality of our leaders amounts to a total failure of our will and commitment. And the whole issue can be boiled down to the asking of two key questions: Who is your hero? And, who is your enemy? Both of those questions need to be asked, else the battle shall be forever lost.

One thing is for sure: To be a real leader, it is not an easy or automatic thing to do. It is not enough to, as Lee Marvin as Major John Reisman growls in the 1967 film, The Dirty Dozen, to:

> ---Just act mean and grunt.

Screenplay by Nunnally Johnson and Lukas Heller from "The Dirty Dozen" by E. A. Nathanson

There is much more to true leadership than that; however, today new arcane depravities have marred our sublime aspects and coarsened our collective soul. Expecting glee, we who are fools have embraced the unknown darkness. We put our trust in fake leaders who lean into mediocrity and fatuousness, saying precious little and doing next to nothing. As my father used to say about the lazy:

> ---Those boys are simply all show and no go or the pits. There're nothing but grunts and growlers!

Too, using eyes that are no longer keen, we no longer know how to recognize a good man when we see one emerging amongst us. Therefore, as if following somebody's errant orders, routinely today we elect amoral losers who love to preen and prance, handsome mirror gazers who know absolutely nothing about real leadership. These fatuous phonies lack any spine, or, as used to be said in some rougher quarters:

> ----Those guys have no balls; perhaps they need to grow a pair.

By doing so, we are weakening our culture every day, first by inaction and secondly, by proposing these lousy and false models of leadership that shall only disappoint and circumvent the will of the people; moreover, by constantly picking fake leaders we only create new and expanding problems. Thus, our society does degrade itself to its newest nadir daily; and, of that, there may be no doubt. And here is just one of the ramifications of that intentional pervasive enervation: As a culture we no longer produce and elect proper quantities of real, rugged leaders that may come out of the woodwork like streams of happy fat termites! So, instead of creating the conditions for the genesis of true leaders, the suits are here, and some might say:

> ---They have bloody taken over!

'Tis true, the phony suits are here, those empty and spiritless suits, quisling whistle dicks, wormy jerks, the lackadaisical suck-ups and the slimy inconsequentials who are only in the game for their own ascendant power and what financially they may personally gain. They do not wish to serve the people, since it is the other way 'round. They tell us we are the land of milk and honey, content in God's sweet pocket; however, true connoisseurs of the truth, what do they really know? These phonies and bootlickers, these sloganeers and shyster keepers of the treasury, our treasury, they do not know how to lead; and, of course, they don't! These few ideas have only formed in my mind from witnessing for decades the clear, manifest corrosion and corruption of our leaders (sic) that now are everywhere. These jerks are in charge; they rule the roost! How did we get here, to this tight pickle? Is it not high time in these deep waters to push back and to study the catalyst we unwittingly have engineered for this obvious decline? For, to better chart our path forward often it is better to gaze backwards in time, since that vantage of the old, yet only if it is acute and keen-eyed enough, may chart for all of us a better, more lucid path for our future.

Still, after tall and stepping backwards a tittle, or to take a dekko, aren't all earth-bound supremacies temporary and fleeting? Is it not engraved or set in stone in our genes that all earthly empires shall one day fall, just as a man shall pitch forward when he is drunken? Therefore, we are in the long process of simply disgracing ourselves. Are we not dispersing ourselves chaotically into the caustic mists of history when later scholars will lament our obvious corruption and nepotism? As a once proud and proper nation are we not right on track in that inevitable sliding decline? All of these questions are crucial to this discussion.

For, I see again that only suits surround us now, empty suits, guys and gals who probably have never worked a true day in their soft and easy, perfectly networked lives; and they are what used to be called "weak sisters" or "pansies" before those entirely accurate phrases became problematic due to their possible inference that in any battle or contest the distaff quadrant is inherently less formidable. Quixotically, are we not now attracted to someone who always is in need of sumptuous aid, who does not stand out as superior, and who is not as strong as others in a group? Do we think implausibly, irrationally, that the weakest among us would make the better leader? What the heck ever happened to the phrases: Row your own boat! Stand on your own two feet! Do the right thing! Or, instead, have not our notions as to what constitutes a good and effective leader fully changed over the years? The obvious question arises for the purpose of this discussion: How did that sharp shift in ideas happen?

It makes the greatest sense (that is, it follows and not just happens) that most of the world's strongest leaders, and not just the military ones, were not born to that lofty stage; but rather, upon exam one studies that they themselves in the early days had once been wood choppers or plebs or lowly hod carriers or simple foot soldiers; that is, as they gained and advanced upon, and eventually secured manhood, that they themselves were sometimes cursed at, berated, maybe mocked, and often along the bilge were considered the lowest of the low, below the salt. By fortuitous design and perhaps some middling chance they worked their way up the tall totem pole to secure those positions of higher leadership; that is to say:

---They did it the old-fashioned way: They earned it.

The Paper Chase written by Mr. John Jay Osborn, Jr., Houghton Mifflin, 1971.

Cinque Sortite: Five Assaults Or Sallies Onto The Battlefield

And it was this long training (when given an order they simply obeyed it!) that made possible their later unsurprising rise to the pinnacle from which they later led with clarity and distinction.

For example, Omar N. Bradley, often dubbed "The Soldier's Soldier", perhaps would not have become such an accomplished general had he not earlier been the greenest private. Indeed, that transforming mechanism explains why or how whenever later in his career he gave an order, he delivered that command with a small smile. We may now muse: Was he just a tad ashamed or embarrassed to be a leader, to have assumed such a wide swath of power and authority over so many others beneath him in rank?

As we gaze backwards into time's interminable tunnel, we view in our future, true leaders, as if they were characters within the play, an uncommon toughness of mind, something subcutaneously groomed, fed, and nurtured by one adversity after another, and something which gave thankful rise to the thousands of leaders of World War II. Where would we have been without them? As we trace it, earlier through their youth, they, all of them, from the average bosun to the highest admiral, had confronted and then mastered all of these historic and unprecedented nemeses:

1. The Great War of 1914-1918,
2. The Spanish Flu epidemic of 1918-1920,
3. The "Black Monday" Stock Market Crash of October 28, 1929, followed by

4. The Economic Depression of the Thirties, only ended by
5. The Big One, World War II against the Nazis and the Japanese.

It is no surprise and little wonder then, after all of these compounding calamities, that they did not naturally think that the world would be an easy or comfortable place in which to reside. They knew that life would not be a bowl of cherries, a mountain of fresh and sweet oranges, or a tasty gravy train! Probably without knowing what was happening, they hatched within themselves and then grew to taunt fruition a hearty and healthy stoicism and skepticism. Early on, they would have known in their bones that it would necessarily be a good thing to be always extremely fit, tough, and rugged. Then, many of them must have said to themselves as they joined that last spontaneous armed conflict, one whose outcome no one in advance could have foretold:

> ---Ah, what the heck! This is just another battle, one more adversity in a long line of adversities, something difficult and mean and hard and long-lasting which, like all the other difficulties, must be surmounted, vanquished, brought fully to its knees; and in any case, since there are no other nearby viable options, one must carry on and trudge forward throughout this nasty sortie, if only to prevail upon the enemy who must be soundly defeated.

I think it today serves us well to study in some patient depth this sturdy and resilient mind-set, one they closely held to themselves as they entered any fractious fray, just as we ourselves now enter into the harrowing days of our own future, those days ahead of us that may now appear so bleak and surpassing; still, I bet it is true that the more that we do study them, the longer that study will give us needed strength and the more than we may learn about how to behave and how to select amongst ourselves the better man or woman to lead us out of all oncoming trouble.

Today, using that rare attribute called "common sense" (now that it is so uncommon!), we may grasp that though all of us may not achieve the highest rank or station or pinnacle in life, all of us can be strong, which is to say, all of us can be MADE strong. Please do recall how all of us are born most weak, yet over the years through trials many of us do become strong. This is how it should be. We must again have men and women who are no longer green or mincing or full of evasive lassitude or the lamest excuses about everything under the sun, but strong. To do so, of course, is no accident. If you would, think about how infrequently that simple word, "strong", is used nowadays. One wonders: Has that word too, along with the other word "gumption" also been fully struck from the dictionary? I pray: To what distant domain or hidden mountain bite-the-dust buco or bivouac has it fled? We can look back upon my parent's generation, that greatest generation that survived all those trying events listed above which culminated in the horrific World War II, and see that nearly the entire people, whether inside the war or outside of it, had become strong and then immeasurably stronger still, what General Patton often called:

---Fanatics! Razors!

Dominic M. Martin

Throughout the course of those compounding precipitous events, the people had become inured or protected against both pleasure and pain; and that state or condition is the very definition of stoicism, that philosophy of life first presaged by Seneca and then fully wrought by Christ. Conditioned by events that they neither invited nor disused, those that survived all these events, the deprivations, the setbacks, the shortages, were then not much bothered by some later unfortunate turn of events. At the same time, accordingly, they were not excessively buoyed by pleasure, titillated by temptation, or enslaved by outlandish desires. The great majority of this generation had not cultivated vice of any form, for, if any vice is to prosper, it must be fed and nurtured. (Isn't that not correct, Hugh?) In short, many of them had become perfect stoics, perhaps without knowing it at the time; and in so doing, they understood that true happiness, what the Greeks term Eudaimonia, itself should never be a goal, but rather that that beguiling state is a possible or likely or natural by-product of a disciplined and productive life. Ironically, the more happiness is NOT sought, the more it shall arrive, walk in the room. That leads us to what President Kennedy liked to say, paraphrasing those same Greeks, by his saying that happiness is:

>---The full use of your power along the lines of excellence.

In 1945, just as the long war was mercifully coming to an end, my mother learned some of these same hard lessons, not that she particularly wanted to know them. For in that year, she was diagnosed with Tuberculosis, a disease that she probably had contracted as a nurse-in-training working with Arikara and Mandan Indians in

Fargo, North Dakota burn wards many years earlier. The illness had festered within her body for close to a decade, and then, for some obscure reason, it then metastasized, exploding in runaway growth, as diseases are wont to do. And in that cruel, unforeseen, and unjust diagnosis, her life was changed utterly, in a flash, since thenceforth, she would always be short of breath and on fatigue's soft edge. In 1950 a pneumonectomy of many hours was performed on my mother, removing a lung and change. Once a superb athlete, a young woman who could jump her own 5'7" height, she now, most suddenly, could do so no longer. Still, through all of these mounting difficulties and trials, she never complained, moaned, groaned, lamented, keened, cried, sobbed, wailed, whimpered about or regretted her fate. So, as a child, whenever I was tempted to squawk about something silly or minor that had happened to me, seeing her constant example of cheerfulness and steadfastness, then I did quiet myself. For, who was I to complain next to her? Was I to be a wimp or simperer, but another hammy milquetoast, Mister Jitters? Instead, I would sometimes say to myself:

> ---Why not shavetail and go the max, fly by the seat of my pants, praise the Lord and pass the ammunition?

Indeed, by her constant example of fortitude, my mother had become my quiet leader; always she guided me with her continuing example of firm, smiling resolve. She never gave up hope and knew that all life, no matter how difficult or taxing it can be, is a gift from God. She, and my father too, were tough and pragmatic and resilient by any measure, especially when stacked up against today's slack, mincing standards of behavior; therefore, both of them without exception rebuffed any problem, whether physical or mental or financial, as if it were a flick, flea, or mere fly. The two of them together through it all, they had garnered to themselves or coalesced what is called character, though then, that sort of thing was not considerable remarkable, but rather, was just thought of as normal behavior. (How things have changed!) Their elevated character automatically made them excellent leaders. So, in their 35 years of marriage (before she died early at the age of only 61 due to the lingering vestiges of the awful disease), they withstood dozens of trials large and small, but none vanquished them or even came close to doing so. And in all of those years, it almost does not need to be said, my parents were not unique. Their tough attitude and mien of endurance, strength, and vigor were the way that most people were back then in time.

We must ask it: How have our values so forcefully shifted? In the context of this short history and with an eye fixed upon the idea of true leadership, let us examine the ethos of our nation. It cannot be disputed that by this time, today, we have as a people become imprecise and wanton and careless. As a people, it is true to state baldly that we have become impossibly soft, both the purported, ineffectual leaders and those passive ones, we commoners, mere Chaplin cogs in the wheel, who are led and generally do exactly what we are told to do. So many freedoms have been lost! In so many places today we may no longer speak freely! And, in such a short time this new lassitude has blossomed! We accept and vote for leaders, (faux ones, doubtless) who neither possess any capacity to lead, nor will they ever. They may well please and pander, but lead, they do not, for they know not how to do so! Was it the lure of easy money from Wall Street or circular lawyering or cheesy real estate deals that has made us go as a people so quickly soft? We have become a nation of consultants, not doers, arbitragers, brokers, and land swappers, rather than plumbers, fence builders, or car mechanics. Our bosses no longer say:

> ---Disperse. Go do the job. You know what to do. The old man says you really cut it today.

since we can no longer get the smallest thing done without our being a gink or dead battery, without screwing it up. Therefore, now, mundane multiple mistakes are tolerated everywhere; too, today, all sharp precision has left the stage. Many people today say that they will do something when they have no intention of doing so. Itinerant scam artists abound. Expediency and deception are now king.

    Example? I once did some grape processing work for a client with 5 phone numbers (yes, five!) and one Tuesday at 10 AM (the best time for a business call, or so at least I had been told) I called all five, left a polite message, and yet received no answer; then I did the same thing on Wednesday with the identical result; so, finally, on Thursday I rang all five for the third time and at that time left very stern, distinctly profane messages, after which his father called me and asked me plaintively why I had been so mean to his son. I told the protective father that his son needed a kick in the butt, so I gave it to him, and at this writing he is a very successful winery owner. Today, most folks do not call you back. People say they shall call; however, they do not. So, to be sure, to be a practiced time waster, a namby-pamby or inveterate complainer or practiced phony is now the new model.

    Contraverting the dicta of people like John Wooden, George Patton, Vincent Lombardi and thousands of other true leaders who promoted teamwork and resilience and endurance, today, since the model of a good worker or leader has changed utterly, it is normal and acceptable to moan and complain, and then to moan and complain some more. The focus is no longer upon the job to be done, accomplished, but rather, it has shifted to focus upon the employee's rights, prerogatives, and feelings. Today, it is our rights and entitlements, our fleetest wishes or basest desires, no matter how extreme or trivial or unusual, that are focused upon, rather than any productive work that should be accomplished. In this weakening process, in this studied and calculated enervation, we have morphed to become singular pansies, mommy's sissy pants, camp-fire girls, knocker jerks, smokescreen makers, eight ball goof offs, and that unkindest cut of all, victims. Encouraged by the childish likes of Oprah Winfrey who would like to make victims of us all, it now is acceptable for a young male to say, for example:

> ---I was made to eat too much tomato soup over the years; therefore, that was some bad abuse from which I suffered greatly and which still to this day weighs me down, for which I need steady and proper counseling, and which necessarily keeps me from reaching my full potential.

What a phony gas bag she is! She has made a fancy, lucrative career for herself by promoting victimhood for all. Thus, egged on by this moping, fault-finding, victim-obsessed culture, we create artificial ceilings for ourselves. Because of people like her, people who say we are ALL victims, it is no surprise that we are cranking out sissy men and soft women as fast as we can. Whatever happened to meeting a challenge and then besting it? Therefore, as perennial babies, it is not surprising that we worry about fluoride levels, vaccine safety, coffee risks, bone density decreases that may occur upon aging, body fat indexes, you name it. Did Wyatt Earp think about any of these unimportant things, or Harry Longbaugh, the Sundance Kid? Heck no!

To further demonstrate this point, once when my family was in a New York City coffee shop right after the September 11, 2001 terrorism attack (which ought to have never happened, had the president not been distracted by his carnal wanderings), another female patron, clearly traumatized and clearly a New Yorker by her strong accent, she asked me as the father pointedly how I could subject such a nice family to such a second threat. Her inference was that we ought to have stayed in our hotel room watching television, sipping chilled orange juice through a straw. Why, this woman, she was afraid of her own shadow! I told her that we must not be afraid of ghosts, the past, or unseen diseases, but instead, putting our faith in God, we have to go on freely living, without useless worrying, and accomplishing the task at hand. Our national model of how we ought to work and lead in such a short time has altered from focused and unifying goals saying:

> ---Get it done! Finish the job! Speed now! Hop to it, dingleberries! As Senator Kennedy of Louisiana

> says, I like breakfast food and straight answers! What's next?

to today's sad emphasis on the worker's feelings, desires, and entertainment.

To return to D-Day again for a moment, Colonel Benjamin H. "Vandy" Vandevoort there used to speak of:

> ---The necessity of unified effort"

to push ferociously towards a common purpose. How dismayed he would be, I do wager, if he saw how poorly and sloppily we work and lead today! And, once again, this is simply because these words:

> ---Let's go!

are now so rarely used.

Often, and no doubt part of my growing siege mentality, my son and I now watch dozens of war movies, mostly about World War II, but also delving into our many later far-flung fiascos, and usually after only ten minutes into the viewing, I will ask of him:

> ---Could we today muster up, coalesce, the same sort of intensity and strength and determination and vigor and simple speed that those tough soldiers daily demonstrated? Would we today volunteer for action and possible death in great numbers like those brave men did? Would we not dither?

Invariably, impatient and not letting him answer me, I would answer my own three questions with:

> ---No. No longer. And yes, we would dither and dally, saunter and loll, loiter and stroll.

Thus, right under our sleeping eyes, right under own noses, a stark metamorphosis of our ideas on leadership has taken place. So, nowadays most leaders (sic) no longer lead, but instead, simply cash their bloated paychecks. Decisiveness has retreated, replaced by cohesion-building and focus groups. Clear and striking independence of thought has fled the scene, supplanted by herd mentalities, George Orwell's good old groupthink analytics. Because universities no longer routinely teach the rudiments of cognition and thought, many graduates do not know how to question, to examine, to reach proper conclusions; instead, they are swayed by the mob and coached to only move upon deeper feeling, not thought. Too, often it seems that dereliction of duty is now the norm. Therefore, a great and growing vacuum at the top exists, caused by the Sheep Mentality that is all around us now, engendered too by the Peter Principle that works like a bad charm or nasty rabbit's foot every day, and finally confirmed every day by the needed Cover-Your-Ass Syndrome, a terrible disease which has, as if suddenly, become our new disgusting, non-golden standard.

Therefore, more and more we are ruled by those that govern, guided only by private gain, convenience, and expediency. They believe in (or say they do, always speaking for effect, to create that constant mist of misdirection and confusion) the ubiquitous task force and consensus building. And that is because first a flag needs to be raised to see which way the wind blows! Today, no voice frank, hectoring, or clear is heard. Sometimes I do trust that many of the faux men have actually been gelded, less a mustang. In this placid milieu no one ever exhorts, picks a fight, decries any action, or starts a substantive quarrel, since to do any of those things would be to risk one's career, that most hallowed and precious modern entity. However, that justification or excuse is not a sufficient one. If we may recall, was it not that readiness to challenge and to debate that led our valiant Founding Fathers to eventually revolt against penurious Great Britain? Why, to fight and argue, to castigate and blame, to rebel and charge, all of those actions used to be part and parcel of what used to be called in the now sadly distant days of yore the American Character.

In looking at all of this, the pitiful condition of our so-called leaders, most of us commoners (Yes, we must use that word since so separate and apart we are from the ruling elites whom we have allowed to assume their permanent ungracious ascendancy), we commoners know that the leadership at the top is broken and full of rampant corruption, that many of our leaders are mere grifters, and that we are now governed by faux leaders, "empty mere suits" as my father used to term them, adept only at pandering and phoniness, preening and empty gestures; that they are people of sizable sleaze and makeshift quicksand beliefs always accepting less than the best from themselves; more, they are afraid to rock any boat, and are ruled by convenience, money, expediency and, finally, a ruthless pragmatism that only regards their singular benefit as central or paramount. Since this type of fake leader has had plenty of practice time, he is adept at only two things: Trashing an opponent and feathering his own nest. Self-promotion is all; moreover, with practiced guile, persistence, and relentlessness he will emasculate any foe. The concept, crucial to this nation's founding, that the rulers only gain their power from the consent of the governed has been fully forsaken; it has become mere useless theory, detached from the true world. In that process our Constitution has been ignored and set aside; therefore, today just a meaningless piece of parchment that might as well line the bottom of a bird's cage. This is what happens when corruption takes over. And the first thing that these fake leaders do is to raise the flag high up the pole so that they may see with clarity and distinctiveness which way the wind is blowing, perhaps in the meantime asking around to their sycophantic attendants as an attempt at ingratiation:

>---Tell me, is that breeze a ventoso or maestro or tramontana?

If we have lost any concept of leadership, if we no longer know how to lead, perhaps we would be wise and prudent to gaze backwards into our collective past, to ponder some of the pertinent sayings of real past leaders, in particular, one General George S. Patton, with the idea that some of his quotes may shake us out of our present lethargy and point us as a people once again into the right direction. He writes:

>---Better to fight for something than to live for nothing.

---Don't tell people how to do things; tell them what to do, and let them surprise you with their results.

---The test of success is not what you do when you are on top. Success is how high you bounce when you hit the bottom.

---Pressure makes diamonds.

---Do you duty as you see it and damn the consequences!

--- When in doubt, attack!

---If a man does his best, what else is there?

---Achievers are resolute in their goals and driven by determination, discouragement is temporary, obstacles and overcome, and doubt is defeated, yielding to personal victory. You need to overcome the tug of people against you as your reach for high goals. Accept the challenges so that you may feel the exhilaration of victory.

---Anyone in any walk of life who is content with mediocracy is useless to himself and the American tradition.

His sage words seem as if they emanated from another century, a region and time far from our own.

So, in only a few short decades, we have gone from General Patton's dictum of decisiveness:

Cinque Sortite: Five Assaults Or Sallies Onto The Battlefield

---We herd sheep, we drive cattle, we lead people. Lead me, follow me, or get out of the way.

Pocket Patriot: Quotes from American Lives. Editor Kelly Nickel; Page 157, 2005

to this cryptic, yet accurate, line from the cynical mystery, Ross MacDonald's explanation or description of our society's venal elites:

---Only cream and bastards rise.

A line from the 1966 film Harper; screenplay by William Goldman, from Ross MacDonald's novel, The Moving Target, written in 1949, published by Knopf.

What a stark and stern juxtaposition we observe! How far the national general character has fallen, so precipitously, and in such a short time! And if this contrast of personality is true, we owe it to ourselves to immediately ask these vexing questions: How did the collapse happen? Why? And what can turn the ship around and back onto the correct course?

Today, many of our leaders are gelded, castrated, emasculated, whether man or woman. Usually we are "led" by the ineffectual and the inept, the get-along boys and girls who often and sooner or later become grifters, thieves, since it is so easy and placid to do so. Somehow in our country, it has become a job to be rich and well-connected. Therefore, doing the right and simple thing for the majority, the great unwashed and disconnected, has been replaced by endless accommodations and the fanciest maneuverings. Displays of righteous temper have been replaced by the phony mantra of consensus. Acceptance of all behavior has taken over. All precision in the workplace is lost, gone, departed out the back door in favor of sloppiness and expediency. Describing the goals of labor, Shakespeare writes in Macbeth:

---To leave no rub nor blotches in the work

William Shakespeare: Macbeth; Act III, Scene 1, Line 138

Yet, lingeringly, that sort of common exactness is gone. Where did it go? Did it evaporate into the thin air above us? Nobody knows what the hell he is doing anymore. Nobody knows how to wag it and shag it, make it and shake it. Simply put, sailors and flyboys, seabees and foot-sloggers, people do not do what they say they are going to do. Example? Back in 1946, one day in Kansas City, Missouri, 292 trains came and went in the gorgeous palatial train station, the Union Station downtown on Pershing Road; doubtless we could not muster that sort of exactness today, nor even come close to it! People say that they will do things with no intention of doing anything, and such a mode of speaking is the very definition of speaking for effect. And political correctness, that new clever malarkey from the left that obviates free speech, means that it is only acquiescent ones at the top of the ineffectual pile who get the nod. Today, if a man is decisive or forthright in our too-soft, feminized climate, he is characterized as mean, exclusive, threatening, or worse. Secular humanists who run the show promote the current moral relativism, a code saying that all actions are equal and sinless; and any statement made against a perceived evil can no longer be safely uttered, so unquestioned is this new commandment (sic) of diversity and acceptance.

What has happened is this: If I may risk a metaphor of liquids, a clear separation has taken place, a settling out

Cinque Sortite: Five Assaults Or Sallies Onto The Battlefield

of one liquid from another. As MacDonald (plus Goldman) writes once again in the film, Harper:

---The bottom is loaded with nice people.

We nice people at the bottom have watched too much and done too little to stem the obsequious, the bs merchants, and the nest-lining grifters who run this, our new tilted and unfit jamboree. Accepting too much, neither listened to nor with any real access to power, the bottom-dwelling nice people have been trumped, disregarded, forgotten. Those with a traditional predilection for old and true ideas of leadership, and those with normal moral values are now told simply to shut their gobs and to be forever quiet. They (or we since I include myself among the traditionalists) have been curtailed and truncated. Simply put, we have lost our voice in this new America of soft leadership, lousy standards, and endless diversity. And the Woke culture has won, at least temporarily. Therefore, many of us see our land and culture drifting away to polluted, nether regions. In a flash as if in a dream, we are losing our character and core, beset by declining standards of monstrous behavior. And all the while we are told by the self-appointed cultural guardians, those most intimate with the diversity and flexible standards crowd, to be silent and to keep our old-fashioned beliefs and attitudes to ourselves. In classrooms and city council meetings, free debate is neither taught nor tolerated. Universities no longer teach students how to manage a free and open, non-rancorous debate. And many of us have adopted that cage of silence since we feel in our sequestered hearts quite discouraged and dismayed, knowing that our country is already quite a long distance down this twisting road to perdition.

Clearly, to turn back from that treacherous course, new truer paths need to be embarked upon. But first, the quiescent nice people at the bottom need to re-find their lost voice. Secondly, the excessive power of the ruling elites needs to be sharply reined in, else our shrinking liberty shall perish to the full. If we do not soon join in these efforts, our country is lost, and the totalitarian state shall be all. In truth, we are nearly to that broken point already. Indeed, the situation is already so dire that a return to normalcy, to strong leaders who cleave to traditional morals, may no longer be possible, save some sort of mean catastrophe taking place which then may later act as a saving catalyst to change.

In the meantime, whilst we argue amongst ourselves whether a turning back to old value and standards may take place, let us return again to the original question, and perhaps with a set pair of more keen eyes. That is:

>---Would we able to muster it, that strength, now?

Clearly, for so many long days we have been out of shape. Surrounded by such compounding lassitude, and too, such huge gaps in logic and precision and execution, if any "big show" war were to suddenly open up again, if such chaos were suddenly thrust upon all of us by unexplained and unrecognized forces, how would we respond? Would we retreat or commit suicide. As Shakespeare writes:

>---Why should I play the Roman fool and die on my own sword?
>
>William Shakespeare: Macbeth; Act V, Scene 8, Line 1

On the other hand, having spent so long a time without real true leaders, should we choose action, and would we be able to move quickly enough? As confirmed, soft, compliant coach sitters, would we continue to be a nation of simpleton watchers; or quickly, blessed by God's grace, would we be able to stir towards a new vigor and vibrant action? Is this nation now too old a bunny to move, to plant a foot and then to pivot, to go?

And, in thinking about my own answers to these vexing and persistent questions, I shall say I do not trust our condition. Why? I doubt whether we any longer possess the right habit of mind to follow or engender strict leadership. And I muse again to myself that every other past empire has fallen, whether through poor values, corruption, the rise of the shirker to preeminence, excessive debt from too many distant wars, nepotism, or too many "entangling alliances". (Thank you, President George Washington). There is nothing new under the sun. So, perhaps it is now our turn for that demise, to slip under the roiling waters, to rest in this false, but now required, peace.

Too, all around, instead of true leaders, I see sleaze and corruption, cronyism, almost as if we embrace them. Most of these feckless leaders are as useless as a bump on a log, or tits on a boar. Quisling traitors, rank pullers, and all-American chumps now rule the roost, because we let them in the door! And this sad state is monitored obliquely by the oddest group of post turtles, all of whom as somnolent sheep we have foolishly elected to positions of power. One may ask in this discussion: What the heck is a post turtle? A turtle resting upon the top of a post. The answer explains why we are in such tall gras upon the resplendent veldt today. For, our current crop of leaders, faux and phony, are themselves mostly post turtles; and, just to clarify who these demons are, an individual post-turtle is one who:

1. Did not get there by himself,
2. Does not belong there,
3. Does not know in the least what to do once he is there on top of the post, and
4. Is elevated way beyond his ability or capacity to function or be productive.

Does not the image of the post-turtle aptly describe and delineate our current crop of lousy leaders? To the tee, I'd say, to the tee. Without wanting to sound uncharitable, we may describe them as a motley and mutinous collection of half-men and half-women who either cannot act or who prefer not to, but they all look pretty good in a suit, an empty suit. Their concept of leadership is to kick the proverbial can down the road, offending no one, and accomplishing nothing.

On the other hand, in stark and illustrative contrast, consider the dozens of on-the-beam leaders who arose from the heartland and the cities before World War II to help lead our country to hard-earned victory. Two common character traits of these men, generally, were self-effacing humility and the ability via simple steadfast determination to accomplish towering, momentous goals. I do not speak only of the famous, but those from all ranks who knew how to get things done. Please recall these officers:

>Lieutenant General Geoffrey Keyes,
>Lieutenant General James Maurice Gavin,

Cinque Sortite: Five Assaults Or Sallies Onto The Battlefield

>Brigadier General William Orlando Darby, the creator of the modern American Rangers,
>Major General Ernest Nason Harmon,
>General Oscar Woolverton Griswold,
>General James Harold Doolittle,
>Lieutenant Colonel Mark James Alexander
>Major General Terry de la Mesa Allen, Senior
>Major General Ernest Joseph "Mike" Dawley
>General Henry Harley "Hap" Arnold,
>General Lucian King Truscott, Jr.
>Marine Corps Gunnery Sergeant John Basilone
>Marine Corps Lieutenant General Lewis Burwell "Chesty" Puller

There are dozens more men beyond these stalwarts. What would have happened to our world if these men had not appeared and been there to lead our hapless world away from demon tyranny??

For a clarifying moment let us study more fully the demonstrative case of General Gavin. Born March 22, 1907, the product of Katherine Ryan, an unmarried Irish woman, and possibly a James Nally, the child was put up for adoption at the Convent of Mercy Orphanage in Brooklyn, New York two years later. (By the way, it just closed in 2008.) The very young boy was then adopted by Mary and Martin Gavin of Mount Carmel, Pennsylvania, and given the new name of James Maurice Gavin. On his 17th birthday, seeing little economic opportunity in the hardscrabble coal town and without telling his parents, he took the train to New York City, only later telling his adoptive parents where he was. A few weeks later, after contacting the US Army recruiting office, he talked a local attorney into becoming his guardian, and even though he was not yet 18, he enlisted in the army. He assiduously became self-taught, and used long hours to study all subjects, and eventually made it into West Point. There, a chance consideration of Stonewall Jackson encouraged Gavin to join the new paratroopers group. Training at Fort Benning, Georgia, he formed the 505th Parachute Infantry Division, as part of the 82nd Airborne Division. In total during the war, he made four jumps:

1. The attack on Gela, Sicily as part of Operation Husky and the vicious fight upon Biazza Ridge on July 10, 1943,
2. The drop on Italy's mainland at Salerno as part of Operation Avalanche on September 9, 1943,
3. The drop on Normandy, France on D-Day as part of Mission Boston on June 6, 1944,
4. The drop on Nijmegen, Holland as part Operation Market Garden on September 17, 1944, when General Gavin fractured two discs in his back, as he landed on hard pavement rather than upon an open, soft field.

All of these jumps quickly earned him apt moniker: "Jumpin Jim". Then, after fighting for months at the north flank of the Battle of the Bulge in late 1944, he helped to secure the Ruhr, and then crossed over the Elbe, capturing 150,000 German soldiers under General Kurt von Tipelskirch 21st Army. His soldiers loved him since he never told them to do anything he would not have done himself. He carried the infantryman's trusty M-1 Garland to be more like them. Usually, he fought at the very front of the fighting. He did not act like a big shot, like some officers did. At the age of only 37, he was the youngest major general to command an Army Division in World War II. Further, after the war, he helped to fully integrate the armed forces, and also, after being asked to do so by President John Kennedy, he served as Ambassador to France in 1961 and 1962, successfully soothing the sour relationship between Kennedy and President De Gaulle.

Here is a man who clearly came from precious little, yet through self-determination, grit, and perseverance he made himself into someone bigger and better, yet not that he ever was boastful or arrogant. Indeed, among those whom he led, he was most revered and respected, since he was selfless and humble. When he drove them hard, they knew that he was only trying to make them stronger, tougher, the better to enhance their slim chances of simply surviving the war. Therefore, General James Gavin was precisely the type of leader those soldiers needed. He came along, as did all the others, at precisely the right time. One may ask: Was he intentionally placed there by a benevolent God? General Gavin taught them that true teamwork was needed, else they might not survive. By the way, given our present society's malaise and funk, our endless self-absorptions and deepening depravities, most if not all of these military leaders from that earlier war are in the speedy process of being completely ignored and forgotten. Nevertheless, we may be confident that we shall never see their kind again.

Here too are two additional quotes from General Gavin which demonstrate his keen propensity to lead and too, his complete and overriding sympathy for his fellow soldiers:

>---The place for a general in battle is where he can see the battle and get the odor of it in his nostrils.

>---I have always believed that it is important for a general to be with the infantry and to look like the infantry.

Another general from that same war, General Lucian King Truscott, Junior, also understood the importance of grit and resolve, and once said to his son:

>---Let me tell you something, and don't forget it. You play games to win, not lose. And you fight wars to win. That's spelled WIN! And every good player in a game and every good commander in a war...has to have some son of a bitch in him. If he doesn't, he isn't a good commander....It's as simple as that. No son of a bitch, no commander.

And back in those now-distant days of the war, it was not just the higher ups that instinctively knew how to lead. The keen habit of mind and the resilience of body that marked these officers was also demonstrated by those lower in rank, and it was generally assumed that one private would by example or action always aid another. Yet, in any case, I today marvel at how far we have fallen from these prior models of proper leadership!

To learn more about true leadership and too, as a grateful nod to my father who served in the South Pacific with the Navy, we ought to look at a few quotes from his superiors from that time, first from Admiral William Frederick "Bull" Halsey, Junior, next from Admiral Chester William Nimitz. Admiral Halsey writes:

Cinque Sortite: Five Assaults Or Sallies Onto The Battlefield

> ---There are no great men. There are just great challenges that ordinary men like you and me are forced by circumstance to meet.
>
> ---All problems personal, national, or combat, become smaller if you don't dodge them, but confront them. Touch a thistle a thistle timidly, and it pricks you; grasp it boldly, and its spines crumble.

And Admiral Nimitz tells us:

> ---Leadership consists of picking good men and helping them do their best.
>
> ---Some of the best advice I've had comes from junior officers and enlisted men.

With leaders like these two men, and so many others, it is little wonder that a sound victory in the Pacific was achieved.

Ahoy, mates, swabbies, bosuns! If we turn to the Navy for advice, equally to find out the score we ought to again turn our eagle eyes to the Army. Let us consider for a moment the life of Audie Murphy. Born in the small town of Kingston, Texas in 1925, he grew up in a large family of 12 children in deep sharecropper poverty. His father, Emmett Berry Murphy, soon deserted the family after the birth of his last child, and therefore in fifth grade Audie stopped school altogether to pick cotton to help supplement his mother's small income. He also hunted for small game and worked in a radio shop to make some money for his family. When he was 16, his mother, Josie Bell Killian, died from pneumonia, and at that point many of his siblings were put into foster homes. Refusing passivity and mirroring General Gavin, though also only 17 at the time, Audie was intent upon entering the war, so with the help of one of his sisters, he falsified birth documents to say that he was born in 1924, finagling his way into the Army. (Earlier, both the Marine Corps and the Navy had rejected him due to his small size, 5 foot 5 inches and only 110 pounds, and also due to his baby face.) During the war Murphy invaded Licata, Sicily, fought at Salerno, Anzio, and Cisterna over the Volturno Line, and helped to liberate Roma; in two years of solid combat he was wounded many times and at one point after a hip wound had become gangrenous, doctors in Aix-en-Provence removed a nine inch swath of the infected tissue from his left hip; always he returned to the front as soon as possible; later he fought valiantly at the Colmar Pocket in the Vosges of central Alsace, and at Holtzwhir where he was wounded in both legs. Usually, he was the front of the battle, where the fighting was heaviest. At one point in the vicious fighting at the Colmar Pocket he mounted a burning tank and for an hour using a .50 caliber machine gun killed or wounded 50 German soldiers. For that heroic action he received the Congressional Medal of Honor. Always he insisted on staying with his men while his wounds were treated. Throughout these many contests Lieutenant Murphy was self-effacing and humble, fearless and steadfast. He was Mister Can Do! He would never ask his men to do anything that he would not do himself. Later in life Murphy was plagued by gambling debts, nightmares, and depression, what we would call today Post-Traumatic Stress Disorder (PTSD). Plagued by reoccurring nightmares and fears stemming from his years of fighting, most nights he slept with a loaded pistol under his pillow. Tragically, he died in the crash of a private plane in Virginia in 1971, having only attained the age of 45. First Lieutenant Audie Leon Murphy (1925-1971) was the most decorated soldier in our history. Here are some of his words which may guide us towards this new goal of stronger leadership:

> ---I'll tell you what bravery is. Bravery is just determination to do a job that you know needs to be done.
>
> ---I never liked being called the 'most decorated' soldier. There we so many guys who should have gotten medals and never did---guys who were killed.
>
> ---Lead from the front.
>
> ---Let each man hear his own music and live by it. The drums roll one way for one man, and another way for another. You have to listen for your own.

It is always inspiring to read and re-read the story of First Lieutenant Murphy, a man who from his earliest days as a skinny teenager in Kingston, Texas knew how to lead and how to get things done, and too, who instinctively never drew attention to himself or his bravery.

Of course, the fundamental questions that arise from a study of these courageous warriors are these simple ones: What sort of men or woman are we meant to be? (For, whatever we harken for, that dream shall arrive.) Whom do we revere? Whom do we wish to emulate? To whom do we look up or wish to pay homage to and respect? Who is my hero? If one chooses the wrong goal, it may be catastrophic, for, as the American Indians tell us, not all danger comes with a warning. Here is the common linch-pin: We are what we think. We become what our thoughts and dreams have made of us. So, therefore, it stands to reason that we must guard most carefully all our thoughts and all our dreams.

Yet, the leaders of today...alas! In shelving the proper model of true leadership, look at what we have done to ourselves! A specific case in point is needed here, so let us now briefly stop the train, for, if one makes a claim, immediately that assertion ought to be proven. (Now extinct, that kind of thinking has also gone the way of the dodo bird or the passenger pigeon, so poorly have our universities, intent only upon the dissemination of their cant of approved propaganda, schooled their students.) Recently, two of our top generals (who here shall remain charitably nameless) became embroiled in distracting and immoral sexual imbroglios with women other than their wives, and only one of them resigned. Our top generals were compromised utterly by this common vice, and in that pleasurable process clearly opened themselves up to obvious blackmail and easy extortion. However, should they not have known in advance where that sort of lousy behavior would inevitably lead?

Afterwards, one has apologized (big deal!) and the other skated away from any military judgment or tribunal. Therefore, we must ask ourselves: Everywhere, have not our nation's standards slipped? How did they rise through the ranks? What did they learn during that grand ascension? Why were their penalties so slim and paltry? Simply put, exactly what sort of men and women do we wish to be? Why do we not demand and flatly insist upon more honesty, steadfastness, and verve from our leaders and ourselves? We are the people from whom these fake

Cinque Sortite: Five Assaults Or Sallies Onto The Battlefield

leaders derive their power; however, we as the generators of power have simply lost the plot; so, therefore, in that lacuna that we, the people, have constructed, have not the suck-ups and the inconsequential, these so-called leaders of ours not won it all?

So, over acquiescent time, since we longer know how to choose true and diligent leaders, huge breakdowns of order and chicanery of all sorts have emerged on the public scene, wherein problems do not get fixed, but instead, they become systemic, the better to linger and fester; prodded by our own lassitude they metastasize and grow to new and always greater size. To give just a couple of examples:

1. The Veteran's Administration had been plagued by massive and continuing foul-ups that could not seem to get fixed until a true leader, President Donald Trump, came along to it the job done.
2. The Social Security Trust Fund has been raided since 1966 when President Lyndon Johnson accomplished that job of pilfering and nobody seems to care one fig or tender whit about it.
3. Medicare is rife with fraud which only climbs with every passing year.
4. In its establishment as a "quasi-government" enterprise, whatever the heck that means, Fannie Mae and Freddie Mac, dispersing away all responsibility, went looking for trouble, and, yes, they got it, helping to cause the Economic Crash of 2008 which affected nearly all of us.

Therefore, dispersed and triangulated responsibility over the years has become the rule over our land, part of the national mindset, and something leading to plausible deniability, saying:

> ---I did not know

and poor performance, reciting:

> ---But that was not my job. Someone else was meant to do it.

Notice how the following forthright confessional language:

> ---I own up to it. That mistake was my mistake. It shall not happen again.

is so rarely heard nowadays. One does not blame others, even if that excuse is valid. By the wave, sailors, bosuns, that list of four intractables could have plausibly been expanded to forty, but the reader shall mark the simple idea: Since we no longer produce true leaders willing to take some heat, we no longer have the ability or starch, determination or insight to solve problems, to get the proper things done and in the right sequence. And that can only be since we have become weak in the body and soft in the head, and also, unwilling to recognize and to promote within our ranks real leaders should they happen by God's luck to come along.

So, instead of finding and promoting real leaders, gauge this: Continually, as if by Kafka's rote or unseen doctrine, we promote and elect the glib, the ineffectual, the inconsequential, the kind of guy who goes with the flow and is afraid to ruffle any feathers. Back in the 1980s, we voted twice for a man (sic) as president who went on the Arsenio Hall television talk show wearing dark shades and playing the tenor sax. That pandering appearance made him appear to be cool, obviously a goal for some voters. However, this was his lame attempt at ingratiation, that is, to be seen as hip or cool by what Sir Edward Bulwer-Lytton in 1830 termed "the great unwashed", or what he haughtily might have termed the "hoi polloi". As a swelled head this half-man sax player had no competition. Still, the real question rests with us: Why did we think it right to vote for him just because he looked so cool? There is this most simple idea: Just because somehow looks cool does not mean that that person will make a great leader. Sixteen years later, we did the same thing: Twice we voted for a man despite his scant and paltry resume; instead, he secured the presidency since he possessed soothingly serpentine phrases and empty innocuous words and, more crucially, blood within him that was half-black. However, that action of ours begs the obvious question: Is that a good enough reason to vote for a man, simply because of his race? Why the heck do we not listen to Martin Luther King, Jr. when he tells us:

> ---I look to the day when people will not be judged by the color of their skin, but by the content of their character.

Doctor King's "I Have a Dream" speech in front of the Washington's Lincoln Memorial August 28, 1963

Therefore, this expanding paucity of leadership, real and true, is partially our own fault, since demonstrably we no longer hold the clear perspective, keen perspicacity, or simple insight to vote for the best man, the strongest candidate; instead, as somnolent sheep being led to slaughter, we vote for the most handsome, for the person with the most glib or calming voice, for the celebrity who may hobnob with other celebrities with little nervousness, for the one patrician most deft at manipulating the media through the use of money, algorithms, innuendo, and skyrocketing over-reaching propaganda. If we cannot recognize true leadership, we deserve instead the phony and slipshod louses that we receive. Too, when we promote and elect faux leaders, as we for decades now have been wont to do, real freedom and true democracy slowly die. That is exactly what we are seeing today. Fake leaders once in power often seize even more power, and then they exert rising control over the people. The result is that we are losing our republic. Why have we done this mean feat to ourselves? By electing these phony leaders, we have helped to make certain our own nation's early demise, that is, unless we come to our better senses and promptly so.

Too, too much of an emphasis is placed upon appearances. Therefore, if a senator is too good-looking, I argue just for the sake of sharper debate, he will not get much done. Put another way, did Abraham Lincoln's ungainliness paradoxically led him to be a better leader? For in his Illinois youth, he was relatively isolated, which led in turn to greater independent study, which again in turn led to his later, fully flowered literary genius. Perhaps if he not been homely, he would have joined more in the barroom rabble of his day, and not become the tremendous president that he became.

Also, many today seek the limelight, not to get things

done, but only for their own greater fame and fortune. They wish to be well liked and to be seen as hip or cool. Instead, it would be better to set this as a goal, with a true leader saying:

> --- I want to accomplish a great many things well and thoroughly, and to better aid the people whom I serve, those folks, equal to me in every aspect and from whom I derive my power.

What is the path out of this deepening quicksand, this compounding and spreading morass, one that doubtless we have made for ourselves? To step back a little, true leadership begins with an individual's self-reliance, that force that compels him to chart his own way, a force likely grounded in a healthy birth and successful adolescence, spurned and encouraged by nurturing parents who are both loving and demanding at the exact same time. Good parents must force and insist upon proper character; they know that it must be engendered and then arise within the child's soul; too, they must demand and compel in that child the complete acquisition of all available knowledge, since it is only after that life-long acquisition that proper decisions may be made. We must no longer raise simpletons, morons, namby-pamby Jasper milquetoasts, or spineless tools who do not know how to think. Thus, attentive parents will warn a child early on that frequent disappointments naturally are part of life, indeed, a necessary part of life, and therefore, that one would be smart to expect them to arrive at one's doorstep from time to time. With President John Kennedy, they will advise their children that occasionally:

> ---Life is not fair.

Accordingly, proper parents will want their child's Little League baseball game to go to a final score at its conclusion, they will want to attend a real, not fake, awards night, and they will expect a college to give out real grades, not pass and fail "gift" grades. In high school I once had a basketball coach who was well named Ferrari, for his speeches of high exhortation and vitriolic harangue were as fast and loud as the motor car. He demanded, and I surely do mean demanded, a full and complete effort all the time. If we gave him, say, only a 98 % effort our tightly wound coach whom we all universally revered and respected, he would instantly discern that flawed and half-hearted effort and then explode in a paroxysm of anger, a mountain of invective. Often, he used some pretty salty language, but they were all words that we had heard many times before. During preseason he would schedule basketball games at inner city black schools so that we could quickly see how fast the game ought to be played; and yes, we would lose those games by gigantic margins; but, in doing so he was only trying to make us better, much better. It is a sign of our sad times, that, though Coach Ferrari gave 100% of his energy and vigor to the school all the time, he was canned after I had graduated from the school for using "bad language". How overly sensitive and sissified our ears have become!

Today, however, so many of our over-funded, politically correct schools are only coddling, not driving, youth. Do they compel or insist upon determination, verve, and a full and unrelenting effort? No; of course, they do not. I have seen first-hand that public schools are now, more than anything, about the pension and health care benefits for the staff, period; hence, their primary focus is not upon the education of the student, no matter what mish-mash or bogwallow is alleged. And so many homes are broken that the prior model, the one which generated so many of the long list of military leaders listed above, it has been shattered, as if it were meant to be intentionally destroyed; instead, we have created or engendered, through that near-murder of the nuclear family, a new and all-governing society, one based only on constant power, which is meant to provide all services to all peoples, as it shall deem appropriate, thus circumventing the authority of the biological parents, and notwithstanding the salient fact that that sort of overriding governance is both unaffordable and unconstitutional.

Thus, it ought to come as no surprise to us then that the dynamic and fortuitous flow of leaders out of our population from both the farm and the cities (A miracle arising out of the woodwork it was, a true miracle, and one meant by God to save the world!) has slackened. And since government is now asked to do what families used to do, before the family essentially collapsed in upon itself, as a roof will fall if the supporting studs, purlins, and joists are not installed rightly, how can any new child, any individual become a true leader? Exactly how can such a genesis be engendered, since government itself shall surely not be up to that not-easy task? From what fountain, quale fontanta, quale sorrgente, shall the next needed Patton or Gavin or Truscott spring? I am talking about leaders who are wound tighter than nuts on a new bridge, since that is the kind of true leadership we now require. Where is it, this source of the fertile and demanding mind? Dalmatia? Up state? The further, Eastern, and most isolated reaches of Bavaria? And who shall be proximate to guide and lead that fledgling youngster, to challenge him to be a better version, to perhaps dub him an ersatz king, to groom him or her, to transform that young person to becoming a once and future king, a wise ruler, a benign despot? Who among us will be the clever Merlin or some other primitive guardian source meant to yield and produce these sterner ruling juices? For, how is any proper leader brought to birth and then caustic matured to both steel and grace if not by the constant praise and pushy castigation of loving parents? Those biologically linked elders who alternatively coddle and then reprise are simply the best team to get the tough job done, to teach a child, then a young adult to soon become a better person and one who can lead masterfully in the future.

Therefore, when all of these factors gather together and coalesce, that flow of real leaders, slowed by the family's collapse, is now not just a weak stream, but a puny trickle. And so today, more than ever before, leadership is defined, foolishly and falsely, as the inability to offend. What baloney! I say once more that the fake leaders today often wish above all to be liked, which is clearly a mistake in judgment. Recall another of General Patton's famous quotations:

> ---I don't want them to love me....I want them to fight for me.

How distant we are now from those better times!

After all, leaders are supposed to solve problems, not entertain, to aid the people and not to take advantage of them. A good leader will regard a situation and say to himself:

Cinque Sortite: Five Assaults Or Sallies Onto The Battlefield

---What is our goal here? How can conditions be improved? What is the precise situation? I fear it is past time to move! How do we get from A to B? What is the plan?

Do today's faux leaders think that way? Of course, they do not! Do they know anything about problem solving, or do they only take the stage to pander and connive, always catering to and fawning over the interest groups that got them elected in the first place? Many years ago, back when I was just starting high school, one of my many excellent teachers with a fierce quickness of mind foisted upon my new and slowly awakening brain this apt scheme or map for all problem solving:

1. To discover the salient issue,
2. To properly diagnose the problem,
3. To treat the condition, and then later,
4. To re-assess that treatment for possible success.

Given that our schools at any level have largely morphed into runaway propaganda spewing machines, is that simple formula for advancement even taught today? I was brought up and taught that these four steps would lead to success, and also, to assume that this common format was one used by all leaders when they needed to fix a problem. Imagine my consternation as I grew to adulthood when I grasped that this forma is now rare, if not fully abandoned! Looking around at our problem-filled world, where all these various problems sit and rest and grow and only fester, while being patently neglected, I conclude that those four simple steps for problem solving have disappeared, not even mentioned at all in today's over-funded, declining, and Pravda-like classrooms.

Further, as I then navigated this long and winding trail upon the front side of the mountain (though I am now distinctly on that mountain's formidable backside!), I was instructed that to be a good leader my own happiness or well-being was distinctly secondary. Accordingly, by my teachers and my parents and my coaches, I was rarely asked how I felt. They did not care, since getting the job or task done was more important, the key to the puzzle of accomplishment. One exception was when as a 5-year-old kid I gingerly stepped into one of the 10,000 lakes of Minnesota and there with my naked ankle found a broken glass beer bottle (It was probably a brown one from Hamm's Brewery of Saint Paul not too far away), lacerating it mightily; after that minor incident many asked how I was feeling. But generally, in not asking how I felt every five seconds, my mentors subliminally and subcutaneously were inculcating me with flashes of blessed stoicism that would become over time a deep-seated prerogative of my personality, that stoicism stating that it was best for one to be inured equally to both pain and pleasure, and too, there was the subtle supposition that life does not always bend itself to our individual will. By this way of reckoning and child rearing, my wishes were simply not regarded as paramount; instead, a full effort upon the work to be done was necessary, and then perhaps later on, some gingerly satisfaction would arrive. Goethe words come to mind in this regard:

> ---It is not doing the things we like to do but liking the things we have to do that makes life blessed.

Anon, I fear, that sort of tough lesson comprised of both resilience and grit is not much taught today.

Real leaders think first about those whom they lead. They value their opinion since those leaders understand that it is from those common folk that all their transitory power and authority emanate. If we look back in time and study the character reveals of proper leaders, we grasp that a real leader works for others, rather than for himself; moreover, a true leader does not think first of himself, but of the governed. Recall what the great Hunkpapa Lakota leader Sitting Bull (1831-1890) says:

> ---The real warrior, for us, is one who sacrifices himself for the good of others. His task is to take care of the elderly, the defenseless, those who cannot provide for themselves, and above all, the children, the future of humanity.

If we are to understand how our current leaders (faux, phony, fake; nest feathering skulkers, buck passers, and monkey shiners all) have let us down, how they probably will never possess the intrinsic capacity to lead (Where would that skill come from?), we need to study what led to the good leaders of the past, and also what led to the poor ones. Then we must return again to World War II, since a study of it holds many lessons for us if we wish to learn them, to incorporate them permanently into our souls. Accordingly, it would well serve us to concentrate specifically upon the German High Command as D-Day approached, since on those pivotal days it either did not correctly foresee or foolishly downplayed the possibility of an Allied attack. Thus, there was a failure of leadership.

Some of the Hitler's officers may have been fearful of his erratic and stormy wrath and chose to protect their careers (The word rhymes with rears) rather than to tell him what they knew in their guts to be the truth: That an Allied assault was imminent. Too, when they saw the blue-grey sea roiled by monstrous waves and the skies full of nothing but rain-filled clouds, they further discounted the possibility of an onslaught. They made many false assumptions. Among those German generals there was a paucity of skepticism, that most important character trait, one that always asks this key, yet quite simple, question:

---How do we know that something is true?

In those days those German generals could have used more intellectual rigor. They were not on their toes or keen, and they were not as alert and questioning as they ought to have been, thus inadvertently helping to pave the way for the eventual Allied victory.

Still, a few of the more alert and skeptical officers amongst the German upper echelon spoke out on those long ticking days just before D-Day, and one in particular we must turn to was Colonel Josef "Pips" Priller, a hot-headed pilot who during those pre-D-Day weeks many times warned his superiors about a dangerous shortage of German aircraft. On the morning of the battle, on June 6, 1944, and even though frightfully hung over from some unrestrained boozing from the previous night (Was it draughts or Calvados that they then imbibed, or perhaps some flagons of Pommeau de Normandie?), he and a few others, heads fairly throbbing from too much Acetaldehyde in the blood, no doubt, managed to get some Focke-Wulf

FW-190 or Messerschmitt fighter planes in the air and to strafe the swarming attacked beachhead. Prior to the attack he had urged a re-mounting of the air arsenal, something which he felt strongly in his Teutonic bones, but by the rear-protecting higher-ups he was not listened to. So, one may ponder the plain lesson: One may lead a horse to water, yet still that gelded or ungelded steed of four legs, he may not drink of it. Today we can muse that if wing commander Priiller's prescient and cautionary words had been more listened to, perhaps the war's outcome may have been much different. It is one such small points that battles are won or lost. Still, today, we need more leaders like Priller, i.e., those far seers that warn and caution of all possible dangers, some of them quite hidden and sequestered, and of damaging factors that lurk in corners and under beds and in closets, in disused trunks and garage boxes, and then to say one clear phrase aloud so that all may hear it:

> ---I warn you now: There may be still greater confusion or chaos, un fiasco.

Naturally enough, some among us are gifted by God to see a far greater distance than others, and it is they that ought to be the more listened, to whom we would be wise to adhere, since is that not what all good leaders are meant to do, amongst other things: To warn of possible danger, of unseen problems, of undetected complexities? All real leaders, therefore, must scour the countryside for any sort of errant trap, any booby traps, confusing diversions, fields of unexpected quicksand, false fronts, flimsy scaffolds, and any weak bridge about to fail. In short, before the deluge, they must exhort as they see fit; they must give out to us loud and prudent warnings and clear advice. And my advice today is this: Vast changes, improvements, in the quality and style of our leadership must take place directly, quickly, now, or as the German say:

    -Schnell!

since the needed reforms can no longer wait to be implemented.

Otherwise, to all the scouting Fremonts, Carsons, and Bridgers among us, what shall happen? What will take place in the morrow? It may not be doubted that all good leaders are scouts like John C. Fremont, Christopher "Kit" Carson, and Jim Bridger, all mostly mean men who knew singularly what would happen before it took place. This is a habit of mind of all good leaders, one grounded in self-reliance and independence of thought, and it is probably learned and absorbed way back in a distant childhood, taught by presupposing, demanding, and alert parents. It is a habit of thinking that must be learned and earned over time, and then later and once again, re-learned and re-earned. And so, charges, what? What is the gimlet-eyed gauge of it? If we stay on the same awful course of electing weak time biders, appeasing the sycophants, or encouraging the post turtles to even further inaction, what else may follow? Unless we break apart and destroy the old models, unless we bring to birth new and effective ones (Yea, but more truly said, "the old and effective ones") only more of the same calamities will transpire: We shall see only more reclining lassitude, full laziness, and a complete dearth of precision. We shall see only more corruption and nest-lining, more ineffectual and dilly-dally leadership, more phony and fake leaders who only seek to please, to pander to the well-positioned, so that they themselves become the more wealthy. We shall see only more self-aggrandizers who are afraid to step on any toes, and who are more interested in forming mutually beneficial alliances with those who will benefit them monetarily than in coming to grips with and solving a real problem from which all of us do suffer.

Otherwise as well, we shall see the continued expanse of the public sector, the ascendancy of a bloated amoeba-like government, a state so large it thinks of itself as a religion, though nothing could be further from the truth, as the old saying tells us. This always expanding state, it is an entity for which we all pay, yet which cannot and shall not solve any of the problems that now encircle us. Our nation is slowly dying from this burgeoning bureaucracy which mostly perpetuates itself and costs too much money. Thomas Jefferson once wrote:

---That government is best which governs least.

One must ask: What the heck happened to that idea? Many people join work in the public sector because of the security of a pension, yet our mounding and compounding debt to support those exorbitant pensions is killing us. Well aware of the miracle of compounding interest, Albert Einstein himself would not be able to calculate how much money would be needed to properly fund those pension plans; nonetheless, few among us seem to care, or to give a rat's ass, as we once, as teenagers, used to say. Surely our government must be trimmed; however, now that so many are happily feeding at the wide and ever-widening trough, how may that sensible cost-cutting be accomplished?

Where are the real leaders who would help get that done? Have they disappeared or evaporated into the cerulean sky? If we look at history, it tells us that most, if not all, empires do fail; further, why would ours be any different? Perhaps, we are already well past the economic and psychological tipping point; many believe that is the case today; maybe there are so many government employees that feasibly their numbers cannot be trimmed. We are well past the mathematical breakpoint. We must not discount the strong force of blind inertia. Don't all nations become overweight and porcine, and then do they not topple and crash to the floor like Humpty Dumpty, a clown or buffoon unable to support his own prodigious weight?

Here is a clarion example of this point. As he ran for office in 1980, soon-to-be-elected President Ronald Reagan sagely argued for the shutting down of the federal Department of Education, correctly maintaining that educational decisions ought to be made at the local, not federal, level. However, once he took office, for some dang reason he changed his mind and the wasteful department remained, employing many thousands, generating even more pensions that needed to be paid out, and tallying throughout the many elapsing years only many more millions of dollars we do not have, and that therefore need to be borrowed. However, wasn't his original idea absolutely prescient? Might not most educational programs be better administered on the state, rather than the federal, level? Of course, they should be, yet President Reagan by that time had lost his keener vision and critical momentum as a proponent of limited government; and though he did his level best, under his increasingly somnolent watch, government spending, during his second term in particular,

Cinque Sortite: Five Assaults Or Sallies Onto The Battlefield

only escalated beyond any safe level. And since that point in time spending has only increased exponentially since it is today clearly run amuck.

In the short course, what may be done now to obvert these impending disasters that surround us? What, specifically, can the "little man" or "little woman" do? The answer may be surprising to some. We ought to pray that we are tested, and then further tested since all difficulties automatically make us stronger; and further, as we have seen in the study of warriors, to be strong, not weak, is a good thing. In this regard, let us recall to mind President Kennedy's words:

> ---Do not pray for easy lives. Pray to be stronger men.

since to be tested automatically will make us more formidable, not less. Therefore, we ought to pray to God that He place more obstacles, not fewer of them, are put in our path.

Well in advance of taking the helm, most real leaders would have mightily suffered. Schooled by both strict parents and a demanding world, they in their youth would have been taught to run your own boat, sail your own schooner, to expect difficulties and problems, and too, that is not easy to achieve greatness. For example, Kennedy was sick throughout much of his youth, something from which he learned and profited, especially through his acute study of history, where he learned what other great men of the past had done to vanquish difficulties. George Washington lost his first wife and also most of skirmishes (Some allege all of them!) that he led in the French and

Indian War; nonetheless, those disappointments steeled him all the better, more surely, for the dangerous crossing of the Delaware River on that frigid night of December 26, 1776, and then the taking of Trenton from the Hessians then fighting as mercenaries for England. As General Washington and his troops made that perilous traverse of the river, our young nation's fate hung in the balance. And let us consider Abraham Lincoln: Losing his first election, a son, and watching the mental and emotional decline of his wife, Mary, he nonetheless through God's grace became the stronger for all of those heavy losses. Any man who is untested may then lack resolve, grit, steeliness; so, that means that we ought to pray for strife since it, just as surely as dawn follows night, shall make us stronger.

Therefore, one may now wonder this: Did our parents make a mistake in trying out of simple, normal love to makes our lives so much easier? Might it not, quixotically, have been better if they had made our lives harder? Without knowing it, ironically, did they help to engender a crop of lazy, meek, entitled people and lousy-as-hell leaders, those that have not been sufficiently tested and thereby steeled, made more tensile? Perhaps it would have been better, for our maturation as leaders, during our youth and eventual adulthood, if, to build that greater resolve one day at a time, we had been more thoroughly tested and daily challenged.

As I look backwards in time, I now understand that my father, of course, had the right idea on all of this! One day, as a brand-new teenager of only 13 years, I was, as all teenagers are inclined to do, loudly complaining, plaintively moaning and groaning, about something completely trivial and petty; and quickly, my dad stopped me in this predictable and self-centered harangue, and exhorted:

> ---Listen up, buttercup! Don't complain, don't wince, don't grumble. We are from Duluth, you follow? We hail from the cold country up North! Son, anticipate every problem, fix the damn thing, and then move on to the next difficulty. Am I going too fast for you, sissy pants? Life is a series of endless problems, one following right after the other, and distinctly not a bowl of cherries or fresh sweet peaches. So, expect adversity and then surmount it. Do you follow me?

On the other hand, we are taught by a weak-limbed society that everyone nowadays is a victim of one sort or another. As earlier mentioned, feeling-sorry-for-oneself excuse making has taken over the land. However, if you think of yourself as a victim, right away, in that very second, you have lost all power and in less than a flash you have become impotent and weak. To be "conditioned by the war" has been replaced by "excuses for failure". We no longer confront ourselves with the question: Am I a grown man, a grown woman? Consequently, we are raising a generation of pansies, wimps, cowards, pantywaists, effeminate limp wristers, crybabies, wusses, chinless wonders, weaklings, snowflakes, momma's boys, and nebbish milquetoasts, and, what is more, a dime to a dollar tells me that, when confronted with any real difficulty, and since most of us no longer know HOW to fight, most of us now will happily and quickly cave, bowing and capitulating to all adversities, whether they are Gargantuan or miniscule, real or imaginary.

Let us now grade the result of this experiment to make our lives easier. So often today, people (assiduously, we shall no longer call them leaders since they are not) will simply give up when confronted with a daunting opponent or a situation which is difficult and taxing. To again use that glorious Latin word, we capitulate:

> ---In part from Medieval Latin capitulates "to draw up in heads and chapters", from capitulum "chapter", in classical Latin "heading", literally "a little head".

Exactly at that time when we ought to re-double our efforts, to better focus upon and vanquish a tough problem or opponent, so often today we renounce all further effort as unnecessary and turn away from problems with disdain and weakness. We then may wobble a tad and mutter to ourselves:

> ---Yes, these are difficult problems, but...

One may wonder if, due to this important leakage of simple character, grit, and resolve, whether we might have permanently lost the ability to grapple, to struggle and wrestle, to contest, or find from somewhere inside ourselves the fierce determination and simple will needed to seize upon any complex difficulty, to take it apart bit by bit, and then to surmount it.

Of course, all of this points to a certain habit of mind, and how it is trained and conditioned. In a way, the mind is but a muscle like any other. Here is an example of excuse making from which we suffer: Not long ago I was building a garage deep in the woods of northern New York, a remote bel posto surrounded by the thickest forest of larch and hemlock and spruce, il mio refugio from our harping and

Cinque Sortite: Five Assaults Or Sallies Onto The Battlefield

impossible world. It turned out to be a splendid building except for one salient fact: Field mice would enter the shop easily, as if attending another mouse's coronation or baptism. I complained to the builder himself (a man meant to be a real leader) that the situation was not good, that the mice should not be allowed to saunter into the building with such rodential ease, and that other new ways must be found to fully exclude the mice from the building, and that he at that very moment must use his considerable wits to come up with better techniques to forever exclude any more mice from the building. However, instead of saying:

> ---You are right! I will work towards and accomplished that simple and proper goal,

the builder replied that the mice entering the shop so easily, so blithely, was something I ought to have expected, and further, that if we had wanted a mouse-free shop, we had made a serious mistake in locating the building is such a heavily forested location. At that strained point, I asked of the builder:

> ---Who is smarter? So, let me task of you: Who has gathered together in the mind the greater intelligence: You, or these sneaky and clever mice? Are they really that superior to us?

Not surprisingly, upon my asking that too-pointed question, our friendship began to melt away, as a pyramid of sand upon the desert's flat floor does dissolve against the wrath of a whipping sirocco. By the way, to this day, happy hordes of mice still do enter the shop with conversational ease, and in my mind's eye, I can even hear the older ones among them asking the younger mice, their proper valets or manservants, for a pipe and the evening's newspaper, or perhaps for a glass of cream sherry and slippers. I must make clear that this small story of easy excuse making is not insignificant but truly at the heart of this darker discussion.

Fellow soldiers and warriors, let us now regard it: Let us make all the more clear and lucid this assault or sally, this trek or foray of ours onto the surrounding battlefield into the deeper high reaches of the Hultgren Forest of dispersed responsibility and finger-pointing which now surrounds us. If we hope to do some good, we must study this map of the forest in front of us, since it shows to us notions of how we ought to lead, and with a thorough study it reveals how those ideas have fully altered from the old days; and too, that all those changes have been done to our collective belittlement, enervation, diminishment. Why, by this late date, we have all become suits now! Empty suits! Of course, we have done so! Let us examine the three lifting characteristics of proper leadership that we have nonchalantly tossed away, foolishly, like we might do with yesterday's refuse:

1. A strict precision, one saying to itself: "I shall do this thing right and do it once".
2. All possible speed, celerity, or dispatch.
3. The occasional audacity or aggressiveness, recalling to ourselves that once many years ago, a keen boldness was praised.

Note that the Latin base for audacity stems from the word, audax: To dare or to be eager. Who among us is eager or daring now?

And, contrasting most acutely, turning to traits that mark or delineate today's phony leadership, ponder the sloppy characteristics we have put in their place:

1. Lassitude and paralysis.
2. A paucity of concentration and requisite focus.
3. Endless finger-pointing, or the quick inclination to blame something on the guy "not in the room", a tendency to avoid all responsibility by forming what my father called 'the triangle".

I now see that his early cautionary words presaged the fall of real leadership. With the end of the World War II, right away some people were getting fat and sassy, and with the easy embrace of the flawed ethos of Woodstock of August 15-18, 1969 and the rise of the state above the family, that sage and good man, my father, well, he knew well in advance exactly what real trouble was then brewing.

These many years of lassitude and chicanery have led to the formation of a nearly permanent ruling class of faux leaders that threaten to take down our country. All of a sudden, then, we are surrounded by conniving baloney artists who have taken over the key positions of leadership, forming what many term the Deep State, one seemingly intractable and permanent. How did this SNAFU happen? These feckless leaders (not), intent upon only their self-aggrandizement and control, rule us serfs who, sleepy-eyed, let the gigantic Trojan Horse enter our gates to descend into the city. We have, all of us, been most remiss, to have let our culture be so truncated and transformed to but a shadow of its former form. So, given this sad state, what shall we do next, besides moan and groan, complain and whimper? A new and clear plan of action is needed, but upon this late date do we have the wherewithal or gumption to make one, and then the needed determination and resolve to carry it out?

When one surveys so many of today's leaders, skirting around the world (since this problem of lousy leadership is endemic and systemic, not localized or tribal), one may observe within all nations a shirking of responsibility, a going-through-the-motion's laziness, a uncountable malaise that only grows, everywhere the formation of study groups and task forces that do nothing, and only the softest feints of consensus building---all those factors that only lead to paycheck cashing and covering one's spreading rear. So, just consider for a moment the calamity at Benghazi of September 11, 2012! Afterwards, such finger pointing! Four good men died, and who was to blame? Those who engendered this irresponsibility were not punished, chastised, or prosecuted, not in the least! Let us blame it on the guy not in the room one more time! The bigshots skated by the tough questions again! However, where is our old and true friend, called precision? The net effect of this new ethos of irresponsibility is that many jobs are not done properly and that we often continue to make a completely bad hash of things. Yet, do we not more and more say now:

> ---That is just the way it goes

and leave it at that, shrugging our shoulders in abandonment? Or do we fight for a resurrection of the older ethos of doing the right thing and bearing the burden of accomplishment?

Cinque Sortite: Five Assaults Or Sallies Onto The Battlefield

Some observers may claim that is am too jaundiced and severe, too bitter; and correspondingly that our affairs are not as disastrous or dismal as I paint them. But, to pursue it the more: Why do I think this way? For over twenty years I have lived in New York State, the so-called Empire State. Yet, as before stated, do not all empires eventually collapse upon themselves and thereby fail? For those twenty years, living in the state that once housed the greatest number of citizens (now it is only # 4 and still dropping like a rock tossed off a tall building) I have winced at seeing the following screw-ups:

1. The manifest and intended inefficiencies everywhere in our government.
2. The foot-dragging, procrastination, and excuse-making.
3. The simple and compounding corruption and graft which is everywhere.
4. The impossible property tax so that the middle class only gets more pinched.
5. The egregious waste of energy and dollars on programs that do not work.
6. The subsidization of promiscuity, thereby encouraging the family's destruction.
7. The dull refusal or inability to take proper charge or do the right thing.
8. The coercive power of overly strong unions.
9. The damning level of deficit spending due to the funding of excessive pensions.

But, why stop at the number nine? Simply put, the state runs by compounding scandal and competing greed. Daily, political correctness grows, thwarting an individual's achievement. Daily, the cancel woke culture tells me as a white man that I am necessarily flawed and guilty. And daily, I have seen played out upon the nation's stage my father's famous triangle, blaming someone else for one's own mistake, all done to deflect or disperse blame and accountability, and also to distract attention from those really responsible for a given foul-up. After a while, even a stubborn mule like myself becomes weary of the spreading epidemic of laziness, since it is in truth a sickness like any other. One begins to look for a way out, and hence arose in my slow mind's eye this small tale.

As a concluding counterpoint (I do just now hear some jeers and more than a few whelps of small joy from the back of the room), and as a call to action, let us define real and true decisiveness. May we? The word comes from the Latin word, decidere, meaning to be:

1. Conclusive,
2. Indisputable,
3. Resolute,
4. One who puts an end to a controversy,
5. One who is characterized by little or no hesitation.

In that list of strong traits, I see little that describes today's faltering models of leadership. Indeed, those words echo may across the ages as mythic hints or dreams, anachronistic ghosts from distant realms and times and empires, all now-departed, from a distant heroic waystation about which today one may only read.

Further, in that definition, one does see a scant or glimmer of consensus-building, and nary a mention of that dreaded phrase, a task force! Who might have thunk it! Today's phony and shrill namby-pamby leaders remind of the 7th Calvary and how falsely they spoke back in late June of 1876 to the Sioux and the Mandan, the Crow and the Atsina: With a forked tongue, to feather their own nests, to disperse all blame away from themselves, to constantly speak only for effect, not to tell the simple truth, since to create an impression is all, and to engender the fabled red herring, one after another, by saying these dreaded and dreadful words:

>---Let us form a task force and see where that new consensus may lead us.

To sum, instead of taking charge and pursuing a direction based on a stubborn choice, now we raise the flag of public opinion to see which way the wind blows. However, what if there is no wind? What the heck ever happened to moral standards? Usually there is a breeze of some sort and that it is when the weak-limbed minions tiptoe off in that direction. We now longer ask:

>---What is the right thing to do long-term?

Instead, mincingly, we tender this malaprop:

>---What is popular? Or what will be popular tomorrow and the next day down the road?

I shall select two brief examples from our military history to more surely illustrate the point. If still mildly enthralled, I ask the reader to please do oblige me on making this concluding circle or giro upon the contested plain. Firstly, President Abraham Lincoln's general in the Civil War, one of many, was General George Brinton McClellan; however, though looking like a proper general, instead he was always mustering his troops, getting the troops prepared, yet very rarely did he attack the enemy. Most disinclined to fight, he was dubbed by the press, derisively:

---Little Mac who let John Pope swing.

That act of disengagement came at the Second Battle of Bull Run near Manassas, Virginia in late August of 1862. Throughout the war, and though he was a skilled organizer, McClellan was most averse to action, favoring in its place studied readiness for battle only. Eventually, after he let General Robert E. Lee slip away from the Union Army at Antietam which took place near Sharpsburg, Maryland on September 17, 1862, President Lincoln was forced to abruptly fire him for being overly cautious. Today, without a doubt, that hammer of cool dismissal by a proper leader does not fall to the anvil so quickly.

Secondly, once again at D-Day in Normandie, France, the German Panzer Division due to the success of "Operation Fortitude South" as implemented by the Allied Command meant that the German high command was fully distracted by General Patton's successful intentional feint movements; therefore, since so well tricked, that division was held resolutely far to the north, close to Calais, anticipating the Allied invasion at the English channel's narrowest opening there of only 21 miles. Moreover, when the top German generals, Rommel (who continually pushed to have the tanks at the shoreline wherever the attack might take place), Model, Guderin, von Schweppenburg and others finally understood that the attack had commenced over 201 miles to the south, at Normandie, even then all of the German generals, quacking in their boots, dithered, since they were simply afraid to call Hitler on the telephone; they were too timid to raise him from his famously long, early morning sleep-ins, and to secure his order to move the top Panzer divisions on-the-quick to the south to join the battle. Who knows what might have happened if that early morning phone call to Hitler had been made? What is more, their finest Field Marshall, Johannes Erwin Eugen Rommel was at that most crucial moment in the war precisely 638 miles to the East from the fighting, celebrating the birthday of his wife, Lucie, at their Villa Lindenhof in Herrlingen ten miles from Ulm, Germany; and therefore, unbelievably, he did not leave for the front so many miles to the West until 10 pm at night! Such foot-dragging and complacent lolling surely favored the eventual Allied victory. That day the German generals, in trying to avoid another of Hitler's perverse personal attacks, were most irresolute and indecisive; moreover, they wanted to retain their jobs and their lives.

The simple fact is that this sort of wavering, me-first leadership that the German officers demonstrated is all around us now. Such fake leadership must result in failure, and too, it must lead to small fibs and big ones, comic disingenuousness and protecting one's own flank above all else. Here is what I know as fact: Half of what these fake leaders say is a lie, and the other half isn't true either. By this late date are we not all tired of being lied to and misled? If we accept mounding mediocrity from our leaders, we shall only get more of it! On the other hand, tangle foots, all good leaders resist and are skeptical of conventional wisdom and authority.

How did we get here? Lately we have been raised, more by society as a whole than by our parents, to think it right and proper and correct that our own happiness is paramount above all other things. We ask of ourselves:

> ---Am I happy today? Will I be even more happy tomorrow? I own that right; yes, I do, and surely so.

Yet, such a self-serving attitude is clear unnecessary folly! If we think that sour way, we shall longer gauge what must be done; instead, we must say to ourselves:

> ---How might I today and tomorrow be more fully entertained?

With that sort of self-centered prerogative, it is no surprise that we no longer know how to decide or when to act.

And, in turn, as one logic doth follow the other, by habit of slothful mind and spirit, we are encouraged to avoid all difficulties, even though, as Seneca (circa 1BC-65AD), prefiguring President Kennedy's words, writes:

> ---Difficulties strengthen the mind as labor does the body.

More and more, given our culture of largesse and unchecked reverie, we do not choose the hard road, even though it is a central irony of life that we only progress when there is real suffering, and with the uncommon yet common thought we recall that sage advice of Job and Saint Augustine, amongst many others.

Real leaders, those of whom there is now a studied dearth, speak their minds freely and more. They do not spend an inordinate amount of time building coalitions, planning for obscure eventualities, or rear end kissing. They are skeptical pragmatists, yet far-seeing ones. They never say:

---Let George or Tom do it

since that would create the useless, if not harmful, triangle. Conditioned and steeled by problems and trials, each real leader knows the importance of sequential thought: First, how to fix his mind, then to decide on a course of action, and finally to sharply rise to the task at hand and most completely so until the job is done to the limit. Their favorite word is this one:

---Focus!

Or this one:

---Concentrate!

I understand that this natural habit of mind, one of a true and grounded leader, is now one quite rare, and lately growing as faint and evanescent as grey smoke on a short winter's day that long ago left the chimney.

Too, real leaders, by example more than word, spark an ethos that proclaims clearly:

> ---Let us now take good care of each other. All shall sacrifice equally and fully. The general will take the smallest piece of bread, the coldest cup of coffee. Each will rely upon another. All will stand behind one another, protecting each other from seen and unseen danger. And if one of your colleagues is down and out, hurt or injured, you pick him back up again and take him to safety.

Thus, leadership is a gained and learned habit of mind taught by a combination of word, action, and example. Real leaders are reluctant ones (recall General George Washington who had to be convinced, cajoled or talked into accepting the presidency), not someone who clamors for the limelight or fortune; they aim to serve and not to be a bigshot. We used to have humble and self-effacing leaders who told the whole and unvarnished truth; whither did they depart? Have they fully disappeared from the scene? Too, real leaders will not take one dollar from a corporation, since once a leader takes that very first dollar, that unelected corporation then runs the show, and the leader is now a once-leader, a weak and fragile pawn only, and fully impotent; and at the same time, stealthily, corporations become preeminent and greater than the state itself. Corporations next will tell these phony, once-leaders precisely which legislation to pass. Today we have made a disregarded habit of electing pawns, craven tools of the special interest group that put them in office in the first place.

In that regard and to conclude these ruminations upon what truly constitutes leadership (Not a shirker! Not a complainer!), let us examine what Major Richard "Dick" Winters, leader of Easy Company, 2nd Battalion, 506th Parachute Infantry Regiment, 101st Airborne Division and recently deceased after a life of turmoil, combat, and stress, says to us about proper leadership:

> ---If you can, find the peace within yourself, that peace and quiet and confidence that you can pass on to others, so that they know you are honest and you are fair and will help them, no matter what when the chips are down.

> From American History Magazine. August 2004

Here are five more quotes from Major Dick Winters that precisely tell us how to be a good leader:

> ---Physical stamina is the root of mental toughness.

> ---By taking full accountability for my life, I have been able to meet the standards that I set out for myself.

> ---We also looked for the men who accepted discipline. I already knew discipline is what makes a good soldier. On the runs and hikes it was discipline that kept the men going.

> ---Each man must conquer fear in himself.

>---Lives of great men all remind us we can make our lives sublime. And, departing, leave behind us footprints on the sands of time.
>
>---Once a man loses a sense of fear, a spiritual transformation has taken place, and instantly he becomes free.

With these words and many others, Winters lays out for all of us a clear blueprint about how excellent leaders spring to birth and then grow to a fuller maturity. I am not sure that we make them like that anymore. And that is precisely why we wrest with such a big problem today. How exactly does one begin the long road of transformation and metamorphosis from weakness to strength, from finger pointing to accepting full responsibility, from grift to honesty? That is the question that confronts all of us today.

Too, all of this means that today decisions are not made when they should have been made, and that if they are made, they are routinely made improperly, sloppily, and slowly, way too slowly. So, today, phonies and carrion-feeding vultures, blowhards and fake grifters rule both the day and the night. And, as all real leaders most assuredly know, in nearly all battles the key to any victory is speed, surpassing speed.

Here we would be wise to conclude this study with two quotes from President Theodore Roosevelt, he born asthmatic and sickly on Long Island's Sagamore Hill. Prodded by his demonstrative father, he strengthened himself by doing chin-ups on a low-hanging bough near his home; plus, he took up boxing to deter bullies, and also, he skinny dipped in the frigid waters of the Long Island Sound.

As a New York legislator he fought against the immense Tammany Hall corruption in the 1880s. Calamitously, on February 14, 1884 both his mother and wife died; so, undeterred, immediately he broke for his Elkhorn Ranch near Medora, North Dakota where he sought to assuage his profound grief; he found much solace in nature, camping out, grilling on an open campfire, spending long hours on horseback tending to his cattle, and hunting for all manner of game. Here are his words from a speech given a few years later in Chicago on April 10, 1899, one which has come to be known as "The Strenuous Life" speech:

> ---I wish to preach, not the doctrine of ignoble ease, but the doctrine of the strenuous life, the life of toil and effort, of labor and strife; to preach that highest form of success which comes, not to the man who desires more easy peace, but to the man who does not shirk from danger, from hardship, or from bitter toil, and who out of these wines the splendid ultimate triumph.

Assuredly that type of diction would not emanate from the mouths of today's leaders, where, instead, we hear the corrupt, conniving dictum:

> ---You scratch my back and I'll scratch yours

Such rank talk rules the fetid roost. Many of our present phony leaders do not carry out real work; rather they are simply professional rich people; they wish for an easy, not strenuous life; often they are economic analysts and marketing consultants who have no skin in the game; perhaps taught by fawning parents and going to the best (sic) schools, they prosper through post-university networking, not real work; they have made a study of "how "to be rich", yet they do not do anything since from birth they have been groomed by society and their parents to be fully incapable of any real action.

And ponder please, these additional words of Roosevelt from his justly famous "Man in the Arena" speech given April 23, 1910 at the Sorbonne in Paris, France:

> ---It is not the critics that count, not the man who points how the strong man stumbles, or where the doer of deeds could have done them better. The credit belongs to the man who is actually in the arena, whose face is marred by dust and sweat and blood; who strives valiantly; who errs, who comes short again and again, because there is no effort without error and shortcoming; but who does actually strive to do the deeds; who knows great enthusiasms, the great devotions; who spends himself in a worthy cause; who at the best knows in the end the triumph of high achievement, and who at the worst, if he fails, at least fails while daring greatly, so that his place shall never be with those cold and timid souls who neither know victory nor defeat.

Oh, how his words, however distant, do today ring true! We have moved miles away from his proper and forthright way of thinking. Throughout his writings, President Roosevelt asks us to ask of ourselves this key simple question:

> ---Who is your hero?

How I wish we had countless more leaders like Theodore Roosevelt around us today. If he were alive (and if we possessed at the same time the simple ken to elect him!), what a difference he would make in our corrupt, feckless, and leaderless world.

So, in that process of methodically moving away from straightforward honest leadership to embrace these false models of tainted leadership, are we not blind, cieci, aveugle, or seeming so? Are we not by this strained juncture tired of the lies which are everywhere? These lies are now unbiquitous; they surround us like vultures circling their carrion. Recall the words of Jonathan Swift:

> ---Falsehood flies, and truth comes limping after it, so that when a man comes to be undeceived, it is too late.

What is it going to take for us to see with lucid, keen eyes the compounding mess that we have created brick by brick, a chaos of lying fake governance that grows and enlarges all around us, to finally at the last wake ourselves up out of our deep stupor, to forge a new (actually, older!) model for leadership, and to ditch these new phony models for failure? The fake leaders of today twist the truth to help themselves and are only interested in the untoward accumulation of power, not serving the people. This is precisely how a civilization, once strong and forthright, collapses upon itself; and unless we wake up to learn to both groom and support true leaders, we are right on the sad track to its oblivion and dissolution.

When we lazily accept and acquiesce to mediocre and corrupt leaders, instantly we become part of the problem;

indeed, we become culpable ourselves. In this regard ponder the example of the brilliant German diplomat, Albrecht Georg Haushofer (January 7, 1903 – April 23, 1945): He was a German diplomat and in the beginning a Hitler supporter, and it was only after a measured time that he came late to the cause of Nazi resistance, creating actions and words which led him to be detained awaiting execution in the Moabit Prison in inner city Berlin. Consider his words from the Moabit Sonnets, one of which is entitled Schuld or Guilt:

> ---I am guilty
> But not in the way you think.
> I should have earlier recognized my duty;
> I should have more sharply called evil.
> I reserved my judgment too long.
> I did warn,
> But not enough, and not clearly enough,
> And today I know what I was guilty of.

His sonnets were found on his body after he was assassinated by the Schutzstaffel (Protective Echelon) in the chaotic Spring of 1945.

Some people nonchalantly and without full commitment say that they want change, want to make a better difference; but then, they do not act, do not move, and do not risk a thing. How much longer shall we embrace all these expanding evils that I have described? As complacent fools we have embraced the forces of darkness that now enwrap us tightly with their strong and paralyzing fingers. It is well past the time to unwrap those fingers, if we may with God's grace garner the strength to do so. Perhaps, though it may be difficult to conjure, things need to get even worse, perhaps much worse, before we shall see the need to make things better. There is that old expression of Thomas Fuller which comes to mind:

 ---It is always darkest before the dawn.

Yes, more and more, I am convinced that things shall have to get worse, much worse (One may ask the question: How is that possible?) before we are coerced and compelled to shake ourselves from our common slumber and lethargy. Now we are slow and timid, and perhaps we shall need to be forced by cruel circumstance to reject this embrace of fake leadership which seeks to destroy us. Maybe if things get bad enough, we shall at last see the light, a clearing of thought, and begin to change our ways back to the old model of leadership. As George Washington writes:

 ---All life is force.

There is much more than needs to be done to turn the ship around, to slowly and calculatedly gather to ourselves the vast quantities mental toughness and brave courage that have been lost. To begin to do so we could do worse than turn to the words of two sage prophets, advisors, seers, saints: Prophet Isaiah and Saint Paul, whose words tell us to pray with resolution, to step by step pray our way out of these Sargossa Sea doldrums; surely, should we finally follow their warnings, they shall lead us to a path out of this expanding malaise. Perhaps to both of them, we now ought to closely listen. Both tell us that if we do so, we shall re-gain the strength that we need to fight the many difficult battles ahead. The only question is this one: Shall we listen to their words, or would we prefer not to? Nonetheless, across all time the Prophet Isaiah writes:

> ---Do you not know? Have you not heard? The Lord is the everlasting God, the Creator of the ends of the earth. He will not grow tired or weary, and his understanding no one can fathom. He gives strength to the weary and increases the power of the weak. Even youths grow tired and weary, and young men stumble and fall; but those who hope in the Lord will renew their strength. They ;.will soar on wings like eagles; they will run and not grow weary, they will walk and not be faint.
>
> The Book of Isaiah 40: 28-31

And, should we listen to him, Saint Paul tells us:

> ---Finally, draw your strength from the Lord and His mighty power. Put on the armor of God so that you may be able to stand firm against the tactics of the devil. Our battle is not against human forces but against the principalities and powers, the rulers of this world of darkness, the evil spirits in regions above. You must put on the armor of God if you are to resist on the evil day; do all that your duty requires, and hold your ground. Stand fast, with the truth as the belt around your waist, justice as your breastplate, and zeal to propagate the gospel of peace as your footgear. In all circumstances hold faith up before you as your shield; it will help you extinguish the fiery darts of the evil one. Take the helmet of salvation and the word of the spirit, the word of God.

Cinque Sortite: Five Assaults Or Sallies Onto The Battlefield

The Epistle of Saint Paul to the Ephesians 6:10-18

So, in conclusion, we must task ourselves again with this key question: Why do we no longer produce productive razors like Hodges, Winters, Truscott, Allen, Keyes, Patton, Murphy and so many others? What sort of men and women do we wish to be? The answer? The values of our society have fundamentally altered to embrace other, fully false models. So, then we must ask: Are we not tired of the influence peddlers, the fawning suck-ups, and the thousand inconsequentials? It is now time for us to no longer embrace the mess-ups, the goof offs, the fawning ginks, the connivers, and the ubiquitous post turtles back-scratching each other for worldly gain. And, if we wish to generate, germinate, produce, trigger, foster, induce, engender, and crank out leaders of the early and true type, then it follows as surely as "B" comes after "A" that society itself shall have to return to its earlier and better standards. At the outset there must be brought to birth a fervent and constant desire for change, else all is for naught. If we don't do our best to change this sad, disquieting trend that I have delineated above, nothing will happen. Today, with Bernard `Malamud, everywhere we see before us:

---an absence of light.

Today we need new light. And now, if this key battle for our collective soul is to be joined, we shall need renewed confidence and concentration, fervent strength and direction, attributes which may only arrive within our souls by prayer, since at the end, all of those qualities, now so sorely needed, can only come in the first instance through the grace of God.

MY SUPPOSED HOMOPHOBIA

>---It is not true that the temptations to which I am subject are very great, but I trust in divine providence not to fall into the noose of the deceiver.

Words of Light: Inspiration from the Letters of Padre Pio; Compiled by Father Raniero Cantalamessa; Paraclete Press; Brewster, MA; 2008; Page 51.

>---Clouds arose from the slimy desires of the flesh and from youth's seething spring. They clouded over and darkened my soul, so that I could not distinguish the calm light of chaste love from the fog of lust.

The Confessions of Saint Augustine; Translated by John K. Ryan; Image Books; New York City; 1060; Page 65, Book 2, Chapter 2a.

>---Can I put in my two cents worth, or should I just cork it?

>---There is nothing new to see here. All of this compounding foolishness, these malarkies and shenanigans, have been tried many times before and, no sir, madam, they did not work then either. For, sooner or later, when someone makes bad decisions one after the other, it shall catch up with anyone. A stern price for sin is always to be paid,

exacted. At this time what an imposing phalanx of arms is assembled now against us! Shall it be victorious or shall we? Unaware or cajoled by tricksters, we have frittered away the right stuff, those qualities which once led to victory. I do not care what you say: Any man happy to take it up the ass cannot be called a hero. And, by the way and no matter what we may have been told, the kids raised by these cultish flunky minions are not all right, not by a yard or a woofin. Those in the ascendant opposition want us to surrender immediately; they act as if the battle had already been contested and further, that\ they had been the happy victors, that we had been soundly vanquished, and that we, the finally subjugated, ought to close our contrary mouths. In the midst of this marathon siege, it is no longer safe for traditionalists to speak one contrary word against the lavender circles. Through coerced disuse and truncation, the First Amendment continues to shrink and atrophy. We must ask of ourselves: Are we ready to join the sortie? Is our infantry too young, too green? Do we wish to achieve victory? Do we have the strong stomach for it? Are any of us proper soldiers who can actually get things done? Listen Oliver: Doesn't anyone around here believe in a comeback? Over long time, Knighttown's darkening rules have emerged and taken over many souls. Yours? Mine? Fresh action shall be required; so, one must ask: Are you up for it? Or, since our souls may be fully conquered by this late date upon the field of battle, should we instead demur, relent, surrender? I do warrant that more timid acquiescence shall only further harm the world. If we choose to take vigilant action against these moral marauders, we in the first instance should be wise to not soft-soap today's expanding quandary. However, throughout this discourse, I must pause and always tell myself to confine my caustic words only to the sin and not to the sinner. Still, I know one thing as sure as God makes those little green apples: This corrosive course, if the more followed and fully embraced, is precisely how any nation, blundering step by advancing, still-blundering, mis-step, shall surely destroy itself. And I know one other thing clear for darn sure: If I am not able to speak this truth in less than five minutes, I never in the first place should have begun to open my big gob, there to speak.

DMM

---Each, according to his like...

A brief phrase uttered by Sean Connery in the movie, The Man Who would Be King; screenplay by John Huston and Gladys Hill, 1975.

Harken, men-at arms! Gentle soldiers, adhere! We have a battle on our hands, another big battle, is that understood? For, all around us trendy modernists and agnostic secularists have seized the day. Sometimes I feel quite surrounded by that pressuring, errant ilk. Prayer is needed to fight the battle and we need to move most swiftly, soldiers, sailors; however, can you? Can anyone move to combat, or is the final battle already fully lost? There arises the futility of it all if we continue to do nothing, nada, zilch.

The debate begins with one very simple question: Who makes the rules, man or God? Man may say this or that; that is, he may allege, he can pronounce, he might maintain; however, does he have the authority, provenance, or power to make these rules, which here means new rules? For myself, I dispraise this course of accepted homosexuality as one of sedition, sorcery, and arrogance. Who designates the umpire if it is not to be God? Promoting their private false gen as if it were true, generally accepted standards of behavior that have been given to us as commandments and followed for ages have been haphazardly tossed out the window as if they were so many moldy, over-the-hill MacIntosh Red apple cores. And what has been put in their place, and by whom? Who in the Sam Hell is in charge here? Saint Michael the Archangel (Read: Someone who ought to know the ropes) tells us that this course is illicit and too dangerous; however, do we listen to him? And Saint Bridget of Sweden tells us that all the devils may be cast into confusion, but do we take her at her word or do what she suggests, implores? Those in charge, mooncalf fools all, have told us that "it" is all taken care of, or in the gravy, all of which, of course, is hogwash, baloney, and measly clap-trap, and exactly how all loathly deceivers commence any luring entrapment. While we slept, we have been lulled to gathering inaction and dulled passivity; and that is why, since it is quite late, as proper sailors we must make knots. For myself, I was once lax and laconic, a mere watcher of the tangle, but now I am asleep no longer; so, I have become someone resembling a mad, mangy, and insolent cur, a grizzled one to be sure, one tired of being kicked in the ribs, told to shut up and comply; therefore, I oppose it, a word now rarely said. Meanwhile, since this disastrous path has been embarked upon, we see that the mind of the lost suffers and too, the body of the perditious cries out in distress and anxiety, since the rules of God have become ignored, broken, trampled upon, traduced and mocked. Always, when a sin is committed, the sinner suffers, maybe not at that exact moment, but he certainly shall, perhaps in distant, graduated time. There is that idea that sin produces a perennial disquietude and distress, and concomitantly the observation that so few of them are really smiling, so deep is the natural depression that follows the sin.

I must assume, therefore, that religious freedom is not as important as it used to be. Many have adopted other priorities, or believe with no proof of any sort that there is no God. (Such a broad assumption to make, and a very costly one to boot.) Plus, the idea of simple obedience, that natural adherence to a greater authority, for many amongst us such a concept has in these last dark days left the stage, to be replaced by what the practitioners mistakenly term "freedom", saying this: I should be free to do as I please. So, fellow privates and brass hats all, let us go chop-chop and without undue delay straight to the front, to see there gathered against us upon the veldt, upon the campo, upon the battlefield, this formidable arsenal of weapons, minefields, and rusty beartraps meant for the tenderest ankle. By the tickety-boo, for those of you who yearned for some combat, like you Ernie, like you Inga, now you have your war. Here is your war, one which shall define the future for those of us on the backside of the mountain and too, for our children, those who do not yet understand clearly exactly what is transpiring right in front of their opening eyes, those that may finally see if God's grace is won.

Right now, I do warrant it as true, on this very day, we

are decamped, stuck at an isolated outpost just outside of Rawlins of Carbon County, Wyoming, perched there high upon the edge of the arid Great Divide Basin. We have been temporarily bivouacked there in a musty and dingy sheepherder's cabin making many pots of hot, strong, and black cowboy coffee, just as winsome Claudia made it, all the while hearing the whistling, wailing, and moaning from outside the window, from the high plains of big, black, and alpine sagebrush, common tarragon, and field sagewort, all swaying side-to-side in the constant zephyrs that never still, and too, growing well and stout in the very salty ground at 6834 feet in elevation; and we are once again hearing above the noise of the plants the constant bugle call of the devil's voice telling us what to do and what not to do; and so we are in a tight spot, whiling our time away, sitting on hot coals, cooling our jets, clipping coupons, impatiently wondering what to do next, asking ourselves exactly what ought to be done to combat this harmful scourge today and tomorrow. I say it is time to end the dither and move to action.

For, why would we as right thinkers assume that this corrosive path, the complete and common acceptance of homosexuality, would work, and that it would not automatically, incrementally scar men's souls? Why would we gauge that this road would be straight, and not crooked? Why would we anticipate that this house of cards would not collapse under its own prodigious mass? Why doesn't someone, speaking with Saint Michael, exhort:

> ---I shall not allow it. Those who play at this game will pay the steepest price. I know that it is wrong and that it is too dangerous. Well guard my words!

Why the heck did we think that this normalization is such a cracker-jack idea after all? Did any Army dick ever conjure that it could surely be a cockpit fog mistake or handmade boo-boo? False assumptions bite hard and long upon the ankle. There is not a melting snowball's chance in hell that any of this pablum shall work, or, to say it in another manner, that it shall grant true and long-lasting peace to its wayward perpetrators. Since, all of this pap and drivel has been countenanced and embraced before in time (it not working well then either), and that obvious thought reminds me of these familiar words from Ecclesiastes:

> ---What has been, that will be; what has been done, that will be done. Nothing is new under the sun.
>
> Ecclesiastes 1: 9

So, battlers, veterans, rube rookies, the next question in this difficult juggernaut or Mohawk gauntlet, one like any other, one which has been already uttered, but bears the more repeating, it must be this one: Who in the Sam Hell is in charge here? Some distaff play soldier, ribbon happy grunt, or carpet knight? Or, why do we have to trust any rube Tom, Dick, or Harry who saunters into camp, giving us as if we were stool pigeons or sour idiots our marching orders? So, I think to myself: Do you think that you are my mother or someone else who can tell me what to do? Whence derives such brazen authority? These proponents are illegitimate. Since, jayhawker: You have to be kidding me! Over these foolish years and by our silence we have opened up a huge can of parasitic worms and lice, for that is what this booby trap agenda is: Trouble, simple, expanding trouble. Point blank and unabashedly we are told by the lavender mob that we must comply, kow-tow to, and put up with these erroneous marching orders. The strayed mob demands our compliance, or else. In a commanding and cavalier manner we are being dictated to as if we were mere groundlings, less than serfs or slaves, as if we don't count for a mere whit or nickel; and finally, we are told that we, with neither question nor hesitation, must accept and acquiesce to this unlikely, ersatz notion that is now by meager rote broadcast over all the land, a false dictum saying: Homosexuality has no moral connotations. 'Tis a dangerous idea, that, and counter to God's will, if one may speak.

Do mark this, my comrades-in-arms: No doubt, this is going to be one, long, tough battle. Those who practice these forms of uncontrolled bedroom sport, they shall soon defend themselves (since that is what the guilty do), to justify false and pernicious actions, something which of course cannot be truly accomplished. This opaque and banal evil does exist all around us now, and it shall not soon depart. Still, they, these wagers of same-sex sport, will look for any hatchet or latch or trifle to try to find an excuse, to justify these faulty actions. For ourselves, those who think theirs is a fool's errand, finally we need to pull our heads up, to stop studying the ground, to watch and study the silhouette on the 11 miles away, dusky grey horizon across the Great Divide, perhaps looking northwards toward Riverton, towards the greyish waters of the Wind River about to become the Bighorn, to determine in advance what sort of day tomorrow shall bring. If we shall continue to do nothing, to acquiesce, to be tolerant, to look the other way, for all of us the pits or only more compounding disasters await. To do nothing, as we have done, is to lose the battle. The keen and eager Drill Sergeant asks:

>---Do you want to lose or to win?

For, today, we know that the world is turned completely upside down now, with two fools under one hood, both asking for a better wipeout. Some may murmur that I am sodden drunk, off my rocker or stool, and pissing against the wind, struggling against fierce forces larger than the incalculable; yet, halt and freeze, green hornets that surround, someone must protest this obscene, mean road that has been chosen.

Therefore, in the first instance, who among you wishes to join with me now to cross this Rubicon, this pond, no, this fetid swamp? Perhaps only some soldiery types already well-adapted to long, tedious, and contentious battles will agree to take up seasoned arms in such a lengthy siege. Rather than to rest in a lull in combat, certainly a battle needs to take place, with all appropriate armaments employed, with all mountain passes attacked and all rivers forded. Even then, perhaps, all will be lost, perduto or perdu, because so many past bad decisions have already been carried out and implemented. Certainly, mounting momentum is on the side of the clever proponents of normalization. Certainly too, due to the already committed defilements, the prognosis for our health is not favorable. However, as all true Irish soldiers inevitably shall say:

>---This situation on the battlefield is, yes, desperate; but yet, no, it is not serious.

These stoical Irish do so gladly witness, for this is but a temporary world, one that from time to time they do mock.

To lance, to joist, to bark: May anyone today resist the Stonewall imperium, (of June 28, 1969 right after I graduated high school), this recent farrago or confused heap of nonsense which wants to kill us? It was and remains an unhallowed event that so many doctrinaire bigwigs insist we must embrace; but, why? What ever happened to individual opinion? Who is it exactly who decrees that we must follow this foul path? These societal norms, orders, mores (not morals), are noxious and corrosive. I and you and many of the rest of us are told plainly that we must follow this debilitating attitudes even though we would prefer not to. Our private wishes are thus truncated, discounted, ignored. As if out of a molten sky we are instructed that it is no longer necessary to separate the sheep from the goats (Re: The Gospel according to Saint Matthew 25:32); however, precisely how do those in charge, those that propose and insist upon such a perilous course, deign to guarantee its long-term safety for all of us? And who are they (So arrogant, so imperious!) to so grandly and magisterially speak?

Clearly, if one disagrees with even one small part of the whole socially devastating package of bad ideas, one is castigated or insulted, behind the eight-ball, called rude names like "jerk" or "Nazi" or "bigot" (often their favorite moniker), or told to close the gob, to simply shut up and cork it. So much for free expression, for it has by this late date gone out the window, flown the coop. Such are the mores of our declining society that no one may speak out against this enervating mantra of devastatingly false values without fear of reprisal, condemnation, or penalty.

Diversity is all, we are lectured by unlicensed arbiters, these self-appointed social elites and bigshots. Perhaps they think themselves to be demi-gods or Merlin-like magicians. The consequences of this action of easy, passive acceptance for our culture, now and later, are essentially harmful, beyond a foible; further, that unquestioned acceptance of their errant dicta may well doom us; however, in today's realm of "tolerance" I am not allowed to say this without losing my job, receiving threats against me or my family, or lancing slanders against my character. Lately, all of those who have taken issue with the gay agenda have had their freedom to speak clipped or trimmed.

Flimsy changeable mores now run the show and it is simple and illogical foolishness to argue otherwise. For example, when President Clinton proposed the Defense of Marriage Act (eventually signed into law on September 21, 1996, a piece of legislation now debunked), three times his advisers asked the Department of Justice whether such a law was credible, legal, constitutional, and enforceable, and three times those advisers were admonished:

>--Go ahead. Yes. It is good law, a solid statute. Marriage can only be between a man and a woman.

Yet, today, not even a generation later, that law is roundly condemned and, fueled by quickly shifting norms, it was struck down by the silly Supreme Court on June 26, 2013. Though it is supposed to act unilaterally, the court simply caved to amoral pressure from the left, as it does so often nowadays. (Those nine like to cash their paychecks with the rest of us, but where was courage?) Still, mere laws of men have absolutely nothing to do with this debate, for it is what resides in men's souls that pertains, and those that argue about narrow legal questions miss the point. By the way, this is a federal question and not a state issue, as some maintain. Why? The internal combustion engine and jet travel mean that people may move across state lines. Thus, a lesbian couple "married in a lesbian friendly state like New York may move to Kansas where such faux unions are not recognized, and therefore that union may not be dissolved, quickly resulting in legal chaos, something which will bring smiles and fat wallets to many lazy attorneys disinclined since before law school to perform any real work.

Charges, sailors, infantrymen, we must examine with care how this amoral slippage, this fall from traditional values, has taken place. I am talking about how and why this normalization of homosexuality is a bad idea, one that will not work, no matter what we are instructed. The situation reminds me of all those Western of the 50s and early 60s (when society insisted upon moral rigor) where the sheriff says to the craven cattle rustler or wild gunslinger:

   ---You had better stop right there, pardner.

We take the hen's egg and then make the goose's egg go. Those dismantled who promote this errant life of same-sex frivolity ask only for trouble and disquiet. They tie a flaxen beard to the face of Christ, mocking both Him and themselves simultaneously. Hiding behind a veil of Christian piety and tolerance, they try to advance this unjust cause which can only lead to enervation and distress. In the midst of this rancorous debate, one must ask a very simple question of oneself:

Cinque Sortite: Five Assaults Or Sallies Onto The Battlefield

> ---Is this how a man ought to be? To be a homosexual, is that what God intends for us? Where is that written in His word, that I may see such admonitions for myself and so cross over?

Heading out on an olive-green motorcycle with only one carburetor, the one with the larger 4 gallon tank, the better for the longer drives across the basin, heading southwesterly across the wide Anza Borrego desert, in what used to be sheep country, but with scant gasoline in the tank, the cyclist assume that all will be well, that he shall not run out of fuel. Breathing the buoyant air around the Santa Rosa Mountains so rarely green tells the cyclist that all is well, yet he dreamt up this fiction from the mere sky, one without rain from heaven. This high tower perspective that he has adopted and which the errant culture now crams down our throats must cease, since it is one that announces to all of us, teenagers, kids, adults, those senile and bedridden, the young and the old alike:

> ---I am free to make up my own rules as I go along, and you must go along with it, buddy.

This is how we become trapped in an overwhelming matrix of sin, that oldest of words, and one still in play, despite what we are instructed. Thus, we repeat the missteps of our unfortunate misguided forebears who also thought they might contest and tangle with God, joisting with Him for supremacy. We must watch out that a black dog does come between us and our dreams, so that things may go wrong. They have already, since, like a bad or lazy farmer, they planted the rich seedbed with unwanted weeds that then did sprout. And, now frozen or trapped in sin, one cannot live like that since the resulting paralysis will get one nowhere.

So, all this having taken place under our somnolent eyes, as if we had been transfixed in a complete, perhaps drug-induced stupor, today we fish behind the net, missing the opportunity to help and save those are lost, though they may deny before an early death that such is the case. Throughout this errant chapter of our times, we have treated God with much arrogance and effrontery, thinking like any common simpleton, moron, or quisling, that we knew better than He. Does a larger pride than that even exist? Eventually all shall realize this compounding foolishness! Who knows why the geese go barefoot? There is a reason for everything, though in the beginning it may not be obvious. We must re-earn for ourselves a spiritual re-birth, one which would instantly repel, push against these harmful and destructive behaviors, though, given today's quicksand milieu in which we find ourselves, that resurrection likely shall not be soon in coming; and all of that dictates that the coming siege shall be a long and costly one, so brace yourselves for it, champions, underdogs, diggers, brace yourselves.

Many years ago, when much of this silly business of same-sex carnality was just nibbling at the edges, gathering to itself some small, incipient momentum, I, the grumpy retrograde uncle, sat down with a favorite nephew to pester him with a small, intimate chat. This was a scab, non-union employ that I was glad to take on. He had just graduated from an expensive and prestigious (so-called by the self-appointed arbiters of status and tradition) university in San Francisco, and, accordingly, I wished to discover if he had enjoyed and profited from those languorous and halcyon days far removed from the garish, money-grubbing world, and, too, whether his long four years in that decrepit Bagdad-by-the-Bay burg had in any manner, however slim, altered or tweaked his cultural preoccupations and moral viewpoints. To be blunt, had his soft college milieu lent to him its obligatory tolerance of the errant and perverse? I was especially curious to know if his normal manhood had been truncated by the overriding sexual tsunami which had so forcefully struck the city so many decades before. So, seeing in his young slim face a clear suggestion of my own, it quickly reminding me of my own now-fully-departed youth, I enquired of him:

> ---So, seeing that you lived for quite some time in San Francisco, that pre-eminent gay mecca, am I to assume that, given the cultural atmosphere of permissiveness there, you are happily a keen sympathizer of the gay movement, or perhaps, having crossed over another Rubicon, even a practicing bisexual? For, where the gate is open, the pigs will run into the field of corn. Do not be bashful, nephew, since we share the same blood, a similar genetic code. Go ahead and explain yourself, and remember that you cannot cod me in the least.

He had the good sense to blush a little at my untoward frankness, and then replied:

> ---I am somewhat of a friend to them in that I do not feel that they should be harassed, mocked, or made fun of. However, I am not bisexual, but thanks for asking, tasking. ('Twas a small, family

> joke, that.) But, it sounds to me, my favorite uncle, that you are pretty homophobic. So, prove to me that you are not. Can you do so now?

Instantly I was impressed by his mind. Why, clearly, he enjoyed, like I, the chatter of the wordy guns, the joisting at diction, the dancing thrill of debate. He also was a fighter, someone meant for battle. I thought how it was clear that he had honed his ability to debate, to riposte, to plan and carry out startling rejoinders, to conduct spirited sorties upon the veldt, and then to attack again onto the battlefield, fiercely waging any combat as if it were his obligation and delight, as so many of our clan had equally down all the days, earning his strength and wit, as I too had done, steadily at the knees of our stern and learned patriarch, his grandfather nonno, who would be my father. I responded:

> ---No. Simply put, no. I am not homophobic. Since any phobia (The word is from the Greek word, phobos, meaning fear, flight) implies a fear or alarm or dread, and I feel towards that mistaken and incorrect form of sexuality none of those things. I am not afraid of it. Do you know that the word is not in most older dictionaries, so rare was its proposition? No, dear nephew, I am not homophobic; rather, I dislike the practice of homosexuality, just as surely as I do not care for tomato soup, slovenly landlords, or crass tailgaters upon the highways. Here, know that I am not being mischievous or randy, but clear and truthful. Is that view of mine too medieval for you, not current enough for your most liberal views, now that you

have graduated from that fancy university? Which is it? Students in those places become malleable clay for the marauding propagandists who run the place. My dear relative, whose mind I admire, may I demur or must I be unhappily silent? I simply regard or gauge that the widespread practice of it as something which will bring, sure as eggs, eventual complete ruin to our people. Cor blimey, gee whiz! I would have to be a suck-egg mule to say otherwise! Too, I hold that the encouragement, to make it appear as something normal, something harmless and benign and innocuous, is plain malarkey, counter to biology and history and morality, the last of which stands for God's word, which we do disregard at our peril. If the current trend of acceptance, tolerance, and acquiescence continues, we shall be destroying ourselves as part of a complete moral collapse. But, nephew, today may I say any of this to the raucous crowd and not then be demeaned and branded as a throwback, someone scorned as a stupid rube, retrograde hick, or oddball crumb-bum, someone revealing unkind coarseness or bitterness to all men?

My nephew then stared at me blankly. Was he shocked at my frankness? Did he think me a callous idiot or worse? I could sense his mind turning, turning, since he had become silent as a stone or speechless; so I, the stubborn hothead and gaseous windbag, his uncle, continued on, saying to him:

>   ---I am one of those who thinks a sinful defiance abounds. How did this happen? What are the

underpinings, the justifications, for all of this? Answer? There aren't any, just rude instincts now untamed. How does anyone know in advance that these tactics of theirs will work. Answer? They don't, so, therefore, disaster awaits. Maybe I should just shut up and go away, as Neal Boortz says, but I cannot, since I hold that this attempted normalization of homosexuality is but a grim gosh-awful signum that we are going to pot, most quickly and speedily so; and further, due to my upbringing, I am one of those happy and recalcitrant dissenters who does not cotton to the new orthodoxy that is being insisted upon every day with growing force and velocity. No, thus, all is not "hunky dory", "A-OK", or "copacetic", as we have been sternly instructed to believe; no sir, and not by a hazarded long shot. Unanticipated problems stemming from this poppycock and hokum shall emerge and engulf, a little like what happened with the Mercury Program: No one in NASA saw the severity of the health shield re-entry issue until it was upon them in full force. Hindsight is always the more keen. These mad and putty headed practitioners of the same-sex agenda think that they are grand and swell, that they are leaders who are pushing the better envelope, but the plain truth is that they are simply deranged, and lost in the deepest wood of the highest trees and underbrush tangles. In dealing with these deeply forested issues, la selva oscura, in the middle of the way, which is one's life, one must always this question: What would happen if all men and all women did it? That pointed, at-the-heart-of-it question must be many times posed and then posed again. And good solid answers, not lame-ass evasions and off-one's-rocker excuses must be found. There one may find the answer. Do you see my point? Or am I just an out-of-it dinosaur, the slowest turtle, a hand-wringing louse who does not know that cruel and nasty time has simply passed him by?

My nephew, that day now so long ago, remained speechless and together, later on, we never spoke of the bosco same-sex issue again. Still, with that small conversation there began a longer debate within my mind which has lasted to this present day.

Marriage between a man and a woman has been a nearly universal linchpin of society since it spawned. It is the fountain or spring, la sorgente, from which the very idea of government flows. Not always, but normally, a happy constant union of male and female tends to produce economic stability and independence, and, most importantly, productive and balanced children. In silent and clandestine ways, ways designed by our Most Wise Creator, God, biology drives this union forward with subliminal pheromones that we are still coming to understand. Acting as glue, they drive a couple closer together, generating deep feelings of yearning, desire, and constancy.

Yes, as the talkative, arm-twisting promoters of homosexuality are so quick to posit, one does see instances of homosexuality in the animal world; however, such cases are rare, and last time I checked, they do not well perpetuate the species. Promoters of same-sex normalcy are everywhere in our culture now; they are always reaching (for a bridge too far?) for a justification for their errant actions; and therefore, as often happens when self-justifications take place, many of their arguments quickly become arch or extreme. Yet, the simple truth remains obdurate, not easily moved: Marriage was given to us by God, not so we would be made happy, but that we would be made holy; and that is because that institution, if it is engaged in properly and thoroughly, will foster forgiveness and compromise, both factors having little to do with happiness (that too-sought-after and elusive ruby), at least in the very beginning. And the other basic truth, the other side of the same Buffalo Head nickel is this: Zealots for normalization do not care one whit of fig or un poco for the Ten Commandments from which the prohibition of homosexuality springs. For those keen zealots those rules might as well not have been written on stone in the first place, since so little regard in some lavender circles is given to them. In our increasingly secularized and permissive society many wish to live without fetters of any kind, and also, they hold and assume that that is all there is to it, and that they will be no down-side, no final judgment, no unknown repercussions, no emotion or physical problems, or other disparate negative fallout of any sort. However, a thinking person ought to pose the nagging question: What if those holdings and assumptions turn out not to be true?

How did I come to this fork in the road, close to the bosco wood, where I so thoroughly departed from the rote track taken by so many of my compatriots? One must look to one's past, and how one was reared to understand how any moral position is first engendered and then held. Chief among the many influences upon me on this raveling question, in ways more hidden than direct, is the following story. My father was in the Navy during World War II, serving as a lieutenant navigator on transport ships in the South Pacific, supplying armaments and other necessities to combat troops closer to the front. At our dinner table in Manhattan Beach, California roughly 12 years later, my older brother told to our large family gathered there that a group of homosexual men, an enclave or grouped cult of them, lived not too from our house, on the northern edge of the town, in a place called El Porto, and that some of his high school friends used to go up there on Friday nights to beat them up, to attempt to squash or curb or punish their carnal rebellion against normalcy. Quickly, my father said to the family at the table:

> ---Hell, In the Navy back in the day we used to beat them up all the time!

My mother, a kind and most gracious woman not appreciative of such rough talk, grimaced at such coarse language, especially when it took place in front of the younger, impressionable ones like me. With her body language she told me that the strident words of my bellicose brother and father were not the right way to operate.

Yet, within my small mind a fresh dialectic arose out of the conversation that evening, one brought to birth by that debate, and one tendering the simple question: How should one lead a life? What does it mean to be a man, not a pansy? Indeed, should one lead the life of a homosexual? Can it be justified on the grounds of greater pleasure alone? Is it necessarily harmful, essentially dangerous? Will it lead to a life necessarily frittered away or demeaned? Will it work or perform well over the long haul, both for the individual and for society as a whole? What will the effect on our culture if this attempted harmless normalization (sic) in time holds sway? These questions began to simmer and bubble in my then pre-pubescent brain, though mostly, it must be told, my thoughts ranged to refurbishing old ten-speed bicycles, the French ones with cantilevered chrome rods to get the chain to change sprockets, or to precisely where on a basketball forecourt I ought to use the backboard for a bank shot off the glass as opposed to attempting a clean swoosh. Whether to beat up a homosexual was never my inclination nor does that sort of cruel pugnacity inform this tale. Therefore, let us assume that physical harm directed toward anyone for whatever reason is not a solid option. And let us also assume that we are all God's children, made in His likeness, however wayward are actions and decrepit our thoughts. That first evening of rancorous debate at the dinner table so many years age roiled my mind on this problematic issue, probing me years later to ask myself this simple question: Is it a good idea, especially for all youth, those on the cusp of manhood or on the edge of womanhood, that those young adults be offered for exam and acceptance the idea that homosexuality is normal, that it is without any danger, and crucially, that the proposition has no moral connotations of any sort? Due to the transformation of mores (not morals which remain fixed) our culture, in general, says today that to be a homosexual is as normal, fine, proper, and acceptable as to be a heterosexual. Further, after these degradations of the moral code have been codified, society claims that homosexuality is just another option that may be profitably pursued, or at least we are so told. And the point of this small study is to examine whether our culture, in so casually and blithely promoting this same-sex normalization, has gone off-track, off the rails, or completely bonkers haywire, broken, truant, and out of order.

Let us return once again to the battle front to examine the story of attempted normalization more completely. What a welcome chance we now are offered to delve more deeply into the subject! Clearly, in today's ransacked, threatening world, the choice of one's sexuality has become, at least on the opaque surface of things, one with no moral component. It is at this crossroad, this key nodus, that we must begin any discussion. Witless ideologues announce as if by fiat that the moral component that always surrounds sexuality as a protective cloak has been ostensibly removed, obviated, plucked out, and tossed aside. (By Whom? How? However, mere talk cannot accomplish such a thing. More later on that point.) These new pied pipers, misleading Rasputins all, announce that all sexual options and prerogatives are moral-less and therefore, essentially equal. These crazy notions are said with a straight face, and thus we swiftly descend into the gathering darkness. The compounding lie and arrogance of it all! With their reckoning, it follows, for example, that one day I may act as a heterosexual and the next day I might determine myself to be a homosexual, asserting along with Will:

---What you will or as you like it,

for it, your sexual choice, does not matter to God or to one's soul not one whit, smidgeon, or iota. Therefore, our cultural semi-gods (faux) a generation ago determined and spread the monstrous fib that profligate and unrestrained sexuality was not just a strong option, but an undeniable right for all. With reckless glee our leaders (sic) enthusiastically told us that such an unrestrained life, one which no cruel commandment might corral or inhibit, would hold no drawbacks of any sort, and nor would it pose any moral, biologic, or emotional risk. With the wave of a wand, the choice of how one might behave between the sheets was suddenly rid of all traditional doctrine. From that point in time onwards, we were instructed that no order from on high or on earth pertained, since one ought to be free to do whatever the current desire at that very moment dictates. Thus, the choice of one's sexuality became akin to choosing a certain flavor of ice cream at the ice cream shop: Is it to pistachio (my favorite!) today or mint chip (too sweet!). It does not matter what choice is made, since there is absolutely no moral component to the discussion, or so we have lectured and instructed for many decades now.

By extension (and all of these factors gathered themselves together, coalesced, and took place in a societal flash, in less than an eye's wink, and with a speed greater than that of any high speed automobile accident), many more surging bad ideas gathered: Blithely we were informed that all love was equal, that a single parent may adopt children, that children might be plausibly raised by two dads or two moms, and other distant far-flung configurations as well, namely that some households may have more than two adults acting as parents, ad infinitum. We have created a raging demon here, one which now lords over us, and the battle in which we are engaged is now fully upon us. We find ourselves in the midst of spiritual warfare, nothing less; that is, nothing less than a battle for men's souls is now being waged. Arcane illogical assumptions have sprouted quickly as bad weeds do in the spring. All of these divergent attitudes, divergent entirely from history's long reach, we were told to adopt without question, misgiving, or skepticism; and many within our culture did so, as they had been told by the lordy-lordy, imperious arbiters, presumably not questioning the long-term value of such assumptions. Did they ever ask of themselves: Would these actions over time help our society, or harm it? Yet, for many years naturally skeptical of quick assumptions (the short phrase "unintended consequences" comes to mind), I would ask myself: What is the natural wellspring for such radical attitudes? What event or events had to happen before such radical ideas might be engendered and put in place? And, most crucially, has not a harmful process of undermining of the divine already started? We see that a sapping or enervation of strength has been required before these startling, complete, and revolutionary changes in attitude could occur. Let us now study that word, undermine, since it means to weaken or wear away a base or foundation.

All of the cadre's earthquaking assumptions rise from the crowd, pronouncing to all who would hear:

> ---Do what you want! Everything is Ok if the desire is there! Starting now! Go! Join in the new pleasures!

Could those words only have been promulgated if many other hidden tremors had not rocked us earlier, building themselves to an unseen, yet greater, seismic force? Firstly, I understood that a treasured belief in God had to first mocked, then sacked. The assumption was made and then accepted that God neither made the universe nor rules it. Any benign order to the result was the chance of random chaos derived from an earlier Big Bang moment, or so the God deniers postulated. Any notion that there might be in the afterlife some sort of divine judgment awaiting and, afterwards, assignment to heaven or hell, was derided, castigated, laughed at. Here is the linch-pin: Once one declares himself to be an atheist, it is not a difficult long jump, but rather just an easy hop, sick and a jump, to say this:

> ---One may make up the rules as one goes along, depending upon the desire of the moment.

Simply put, if one is an atheist, it is inestimably easier to then declare oneself to be gay.

Secondly, then, as the number two does follow the number one, if there is no God, the Ten Commandments may be shelved, put on the back burner, disregard and ignored, that is, most of them. E.g., murder is still a prosecutable offense; however, that stricture too may morph in the future to a lesser crime, so strongly do mere fed desires now rule the roost. Remarkably, at least to a traditionalist like myself, this was a thing simply and swiftly done. Easily first, facile princeps. They, these erstwhile leaders of the homosexual movement to normalize that practice, nonchalantly declared that one of the commandments most difficult to obey and follow, the Sixth Commandment which tells us:

> ---You should not commit adultery.

that commandment, starting from the dreaded days of Woodstock of August, 1969, was now null and void; that it does not exist and has never existed accept in the souls of religious kooks; and too, that therefore sex had absolutely no moral component to it. It, they preached, was just like washing the car or doing the dishes, just distinctly more pleasurable. This was of course, a logical sleight of hand or head fake. By the way, stemming from this bad idea there rose a corollary, that adherence to any moral code was a blinding mistake only committed by nostalgic fools, throwbacks to a too-rigid, intolerant past. So, now, after all of these mounting shenanigans, we are in a devil of a fix, yet one that we have created for ourselves, stolid brick by stolid brick. Perhaps we should have listened to Tom Clancy when he tells us:

---There is too much bullshit and not enough fact.

Tom Clancy. The Sum of all Fears; G.P. Putnam's Sons; 1991

or to Senator John Kennedy when he says, speaking of the chaotic, Biden-created border mess:

---This is bone-deep, down-to-the-marrow stupid!

Senator John Neely Kennedy of Louisiana speaking at the Texas Mexico border in late March of 2021

As we circle the wagons a tad, afraid of the Oglala Indians just over the hill's brow, close by the Powder River as she flows north towards the Yellowstone, just now I muse that I may have the order backwards, that normally first one disbelieves in the commandments, and then one repudiates God. Perhaps it is the old case of what entity comes first, the chicken or the egg, the merlin or the magician? Most men do not set out abandon God. Man attains that unhappy station, that high level of rebuke, only by taking many earlier steps, ones that always start first with pride and then derision. Simply said, one thinks one knows better. If man ignores the rules first, then a later neglect of God may follow. If the second ordering prevails, and through untethered pride, a man decides that he may reliably forsake the commandments against sloth or gluttony or adultery, or, indeed all of them combined, overnight the Ten Commandments become the Ten Suggestions; and then, after having accomplished that desertion of the traditional norms and morals, that desperate man shall then be that much more likely to take the next unhallowed step which is to say to no one if particular:

> ---I may well live without God. I shall be then free to make my own judgments. Therefore, I do gladly renounce Him. Therefore, I now no longer need his Grace, nor His strength, nor His direction.

Thus, this abandonment of God and His word is made up of several mocking steps which, in turn, then join to form a disbelief in Him altogether. Rather than trust in God, asking Him for Grace, many people now place such a key thing, trust, only in themselves, essentially trying to set themselves up, implausibly, as individual separate and separated godheads. And evil, something sneaky, banal, subterranean, and something which always pollutes the mind incrementally, yet which never says clearly or loudly its own name, arises as a dense fog within our midst.

All of these events which fracture character must occur in discrete, traceable, and sequential form, although, since they are clearly part of Satan's work, and if a man is not paying proper attention, he may not take much notice of his slow, incremental disintegration whilst it occurs. Eventually in time, after all of these flights away from an earlier moral code have taken place, and after the very notion of a governing deity has been scorned, it follows that the issue of a moral restraint or impediment to ANY sexual activity no longer impinges, preys upon, or pertains to one's conscience. This goal of free sex so proudly forecasted by the progressive sybarites has been reached. We have been talked out of restraint by our own lack of resolve and too, by our complete inability to think clearly on these complicated matters. (The dearth of religious instruction in public schools may have played an evil hand in creating this cognitive inability.) Suddenly, or so it seems, a man or woman is "free" to do whatever he or she wants, no matter how errant, foolish, or disgusting. One is free to sample either the vanilla ice cream or the richer pistachio, or to sleep with another man (or another or another!) if he wants to, if that action happens to be that moment's fleeting choice. Of course, it is not a choice at all, since untamed and unguarded desires may often rule the man, as the Greeks did warn us so many years ago.

So, these phony and cultish Knights of Templar (sic), thinking that they are on some new crusade for expanded blissful carnality, and supposing that they may make up their own rules, they, like mutual minstrel pied pipers, lead each other around by the nose, armed to the teeth with these dangerous and pernicious marching orders. They think that nothing can go wrong and that they are free to enjoy the bodily glories of these new and expanding pleasures; nonetheless, these actions are an affront to God, who has gone nowhere, and to themselves, since surely, if the blind lead the blind, both blind people, due non vedenti, deux aveugles, shall plunge asunder into the gaping and receptive ditch which awaits.

With this new dictum of normalization, something which every day more and more we are forced to accept and bow down towards in false homage, as is said and remembered:

>   ---The cruel die is cast

Suetonius speaking to Julius Caesar on January 10, 49 BC with his troops about to cross la Fiume Rubicone just south of Ravenna

since, as is well known, he who eats fire, craps sparks. Here is the key: Before it was adopted by whole cloth, a careful exam of the bogus proposition of normalization was NOT conducted. And, after it was taken on haphazardly, willy-nilly, fast and loose, a predictable tempest was released. Steered by an ever more progressive and propaganda-fond mass media, most of the cultural elites took on the cockamamie dicta of the gay mantra unquestioningly, with all of its disordered, varying, and amoral rules. Soon it became important for companies and universities to hire an always higher percentage of gay employees as a validation to the outside world than the company was alert, spirited, wise, hip, with-it, or cool; in truth, those new hires were nothing more and nothing less than a blind paean to political correctness, that new social commandment above all others which today seeks to eliminate all free expression. In short, even though the notion does not hold water, normalization was pretty much accepted unreservedly; as if sent by a celestial messenger, a bad angel, this idea arrived out of the blue; we traditionalists were told to know-tow, cork it, and be quiet; and normalization was described in this sloppy way:

> ---No big deal, man, so don't be a downer. Damn! Cool out, will you?

and it was carried out in many circles with the same sort of bland and carefree insouciance that one might employ in a steakhouse in selecting a marbled Rib Eye cut over the slightly more plebian Strip version. And, at least on the opaque surface of things, in one fell swoop (a cliché that I have grown fond of) the nattering nimrods, the silly pleasure seekers, the agents provocateurs, the better orgasm chasers had won, and, as if overnight, homosexuality in our world became a growth industry, and one which would not be questioned.

Crying out loud, we should next be wise to retreat for a moment, even more tightly circling the wagons, for Pete's sake, and re-cap the dire and tenuous situation in which we now find ourselves living. As far as I am able to discern the history of this shift in mores, one fraught with danger and escapism, over two generations ago or about nine years after the invention of the birth control pill on June 23, 1960, at the phony crux in time at the foolish, dissolute party called Woodstock (from that unblessed day forward...) and nearly at the same time that recreational drug use was declared (By whom? By whom? By whose authority and what provenance?) to be irresistibly chic and absolutely harmless, this change in attitude towards homosexuality, this fundamental metamorphosis in many prominent circles had taken place. The quiet and astounded plebians were ignored, since the panting patricians held sway. Social forces much larger than any one person acclaimed this fact to be true and uncontestable, un fait accompli, something already done and accomplished, finished business, and a fact which could neither be truncated nor diminished. Those in favor of its normalization proclaimed from the mountaintop to all who would listen that homosexuality is neither evil, nor a sin; indeed, many proposed that it is fully normal, benign behavior, and therefore ought to be encouraged, if not sanctified. Therefore, to those in charge of this new cultural dictum or mantra, it followed that those who spoke out against it were ipso facto guilty of stern intolerance, retrograde intransigence, if not worse. The word went out quickly, as birds depart a tree, that no discrimination may take place against it, nor any cautionary words spoken, nor any punitive measures carried out. The accepted new line of thought on all sexual issues was quite simple and it is this: Do whatever you want, with whomever you wish to do it! The culture, my culture in a bold and unshakeable voice, told me that these new courses of action were a "viable" choice, to employ that cliche for a moment, some lame-ass diction, just a short phrase that even then 50 years ago caught my late teenaged ear. A "viable" option, I mused. But didn't that short word "viable" stem from the Latin word, vita, meaning life? For, even then I understand that anyone who chose to embrace these new homosexual practices would be to rashly court an expanding death, not a triumphant life.

Then, overnight, as if sent by carrier pigeons who knew exactly where they were headed, even more confusing and impossible messages, delivered with what for a time might have been termed collegial restraint, went forth among the populace. Traditionalists like myself, and millions of others, were told to comply, or else. When I allowed that by normalizing homosexuality:

> ---We are cooking our own goose! We are buying our own farm! We are committing suicide!

I was either ignored or castigated. When I said to anyone that:

> ---The enemy is at the gate. Civilization is at stake!

I was instructed to be quiet, demure, passive. Many dissidents from normalization were put in the unnavigable position of swimming against a strong tide of social forces egged on by a compliant, servile media. The new proponents of normalization, pleased as punch with themselves for their fresh captaincy, told, instructed, and well-neigh commanded us to accommodate ourselves to these new rules, our private misgivings be damned. Yet, right away, due to my upbringing, no doubt, it struck me fervently, as I am confident it struck many others, that such a belief, that homosexuality is normal, something to be praised and never, ever, condemned, that such a view contradicted and violated thousands of years of human history, for such a practice corrupts the soul, encourages trouble, brings sorrow, and corrupts virtue. Dollars to donuts, set your watch, it does not serve; it shall not work.

Yet, their consistent hectoring word went out as insistent instructions to the masses:

> ---Come along, will you? Listen to me: You must close your gob, shut your mouth, since there shall

> be among us neither malingering nor deterrence, nor any of your procrastination or foot-dragging moves away from our goals of a free and unrestrained and liberating sexuality.

Right away and all along, I saw bears dancing and people starving, their souls suffering and trapped in a darkening cave or buca of their own making, their own intent construction. Why in the hell tarnation would we ever conclude that this bad idea would work? Does our collective brain not function properly anymore? I knew early on that acceptance of such a harmful mode of action and being contradicted hundreds of years of human history, no matter what the present adherents might allege, for they are just trying to sell the soap. I understood instantly that adherence to such a course of action would tend to weaken the family emphatically, that key social unit which, more than any other factor, had buttressed society down through the ages. Quickly I saw that homosexuality's practitioners often equated love with desire, and affection with intimacy, and that many would never be faithful to anything other than their own building or ebbing desire. Instantly, I perceived the long reach of these fresh libertines, that they would try to enwrap and envelop all of society with these new fractious dicta. In a second, I sensed the many unrecognized dangers lurk around the corner and under the door, dangers that affront and antagonize pugnacious Saint Michael who tries to guard us if we left him; Saint Michael knows that these dangers are free to roam and prowl in greater desecration about the world, creating nothing put harm in their wake. Right away, I grasped the disconcerting and fundamental nature of these abrupt transformations about what exactly constitutes proper sexual behavior. I knew that it was not logical for any culture to make the case that it may wave an unmagical wand and thereby banish all sin. Far from it, I then mused, since sin is determined by God and not by mere man. And, what the dickens, there hangs the knife.

Here, in the middle of the field of battle, au milieu du champ de bataille, I do pray that you are rested and past raring to go, to join this combat against this common, low foe with eagerness and grit. Grit, grits, guts, homily holly, holy water grits, I mean grit: Got any? Whatever happened to that grit and, too, grainy gumption? To the merit of integrity? As Father James Altman of La Crosse, Wisconsin asks:

---How many real men are there?

From this point onwards we must have no malingerers, and no foot draggers. Real manhood does not accept acquiescence to this last sad social stroke of folly. We should be wise to ask and task ourselves: Who is your boss? Your desires, however uncircumscribed and fleeting, do they rule you every morn? Or, is that entity something outside of yourself, something which perhaps is God?

***

So, quite quickly back then, I had thought through all of these thorny briary tracings within the mind and asked these selva questions that did shoot and then scoot. And why not? Often, I would answer my own questions with another question and, again, why not? (Is some wit about?) The merit of one's integrity---does it possess any permanent value? Am I, or anyone else for that tatter, no longer free to think and to ruminate? When this normalization business arrived late to the dance, we were told by the ruling cultural elites, softies and snobs mostly, to act as tame as yearling lambs, to be terminally silent. Early, I had grasped that the normal and considered teachings regarding marriage that I had been taught in my youth had been dispatched by strong-armed bullies to oblivion; and I wondered whether that dispatchment had been wise? What would be the downside, the danger, and the detriment to it all? Today, may I again task the query from the mount, or must I close both the mouth and the mind? Am I an ignoramus or a rudesby to think these thoughts, to question, to debate, to go against the grain and uncautious flow? Was I then, or any other soft-faced youth on manhood's cusp, allowed to not play the sedulous ape? May I make up my own paltry mind? From whom might I procure proper permission? That is, may I or anyone else demur, protest, or simply step away from the culture's foul, dirgeful embrace? In the plainest terms, in this world of overpowering political correctness, of an ever narrowing First Amendment, can one speak? Ask? Think? Question? Or, do those that scowl and protest need to close their mouths, left to weakly smile or grimace at all the dangerous drivel that now passes for truth?

Once again, sailors, shipmates, aviators, we are engaged in a spiritual battle, and nothing less. Are you prepared for such a contest? At the same time, thinking of prescience, I wondered: What shall happen next? Following the natural law of unintended consequences, and after taking all of these faulty steps, what is around the next pernicious corner for our society? Where will all this lead? What new wrenching calamity is unforeseen? It shall depend on the fall of this house of cards. It is quite uncommon now to swim against the advancing stream. Will this new strange course, this easy embrace of the normalization of homosexuality, something which has never worked in the world's history, will it lead to some sort of broader moral cancer and decay that cannot then be controlled, deterred? Will we not shortly see the mounting death of souls? Will there not be a slow and steady degradation of character? If this normalization of the unnormal is the new rule to which all must adhere, and the regular family is thereby harmed and threatened, what shall take its place, besides chaos and enervation, depression and disquiet? Moral lassitude? Growing deprivation? The soul's corrosion? Thus, the pig is stabbed in the belly by its own brood.

Upon this campo di battaglia, if you allow it, let us now attempt another flanking maneuver. How could all of these prominent and obvious dangers have eluded us, unless we had not as a culture already slipped considerably into some sort of foul maelstrom or quicksand of mean, porous decay? For, how far we have fallen down the slippery slope of making up our own rules as we go along! We fill the well after the calf has already drowned there. By banishing and neglecting the simplest rules, we have put ourselves squarely in harm's way, with the crosshairs of the rifle trained upon our oblivious foreheads. Because of this monstruous foolishness that we have wrought, we are now in a place of the most severe danger, however, not one of repentance, locus poententiae, since we do not yet know truly the nature of the sin, and therefore at least for today, until we wise up, it may be neither studied nor forgiven.

Even in my own unheralded youth, I asked these same questions, mulled these same logistics, considered the identical strategies within the fight. Early on, I began to frame for myself these arguments against normalization, even as all of society (or so it seemed) pell-mell embraced it. Early on, these cultural princes and pompous queens told me to cram it. Common sense, my God through prayer, and a study of history, of where these dark demons had brazenly danced before, told me every day that sex with someone of the same sex would automatically lead to trouble, all sorts of compounding and wanton trouble. Faith and grace would fly out the window. (William F. Buckley writes the same thing in his book, Near My God: An Autobiography of Faith; Doubleday Press, New York City, 1997; recalling the Latin phrase: Propior Deo; Near My God, To Thee.) My ideas expressed in this analysis are not new ones, but old-fashioned, true ones simply stated one more time. And again, I wonder: With Eliot, do I dare to eat a peach? May one speak anymore? Can one freely exercise an open mind or must it be sedated? In our increasingly secular society, one which more and more mocks faith and the necessity of prayer, may I or anyone criticize homosexuality as something intrinsically harmful to the souls of those men or women who practice homosexuality, or must I retreat in the face of that culture's strong onslaught to cower in mute passivity? So far, the loopy cultural hucksters who run the show have told traditionalists like myself to simply see and watch and, more than anything else, keep our big mouths closed.

With wariness I must circle around this gathered entrenched enemy as a fit sniper or besting ranger might do, to calculate and devise the cleverest angle of attack. We are at a stern crossroads now, and saying that one is sorry does not get the job done. Warning: This shall be a long arduous battle upon the veldt. The truth is that we are surrounded by the enemy, instead of the other way around.

Cinque Sortite: Five Assaults Or Sallies Onto The Battlefield

We are thus like all paratroopers, aren't we, Jimmy? And the next question is: What stance, quale posizione, must we adopt today to win this looming battle which must not be postponed? How best to vanquish the enemy?

Well, now, so. Let us turn ourselves backwards in time to regard and re-assess the earliest skirmishes. At square one, here hangs the pot: We have engineered this carnal experiment for fifty years or so, for two generation's worth of time (It has been a hastily planned jamboree! A series of endless cuckholds prancing about, a bit like Ferrari's prancing horses, gli cavalli rampante! A silly sybarite's delight!); and, since one action or course will lead to another, whether it be a good dead or a mis-step, what may we conclude? The herring does not fry here; that is, things are not going as planned. We have a gaping hole in the roof and thenceforth the rains fall within the house, onto the red oak hardwood floor. The sow pulls the bung, meaning that sloppy negligence to the real rules of the joist shall be rewarded with disaster.

If one knows anything about immune theory, and, specifically, if one were a virologist specializing in the voracious mechanisms of sexually transmitted diseases, and too, if one were not afraid to use a little precious common sense in speaking up, in telling the truth beforehand, one might have easily predicted what then took place. What did those who pushed so vigorously for this new life (sic) think was going to happen, or did they not conjure much upon the future, only interested in this moment's tender eclipse? Perhaps at play was the understanding that those who ponder the future derail the pleasures of the moment, to live now. The truth is that AIDS arrived, just as any study of the history of diseases might have foretold! Of course, it did! It could not have been otherwise! It has killed millions around the world and enfeebled and enervated millions more. And what has been gained, beside an excess of bestial carnality? I have stumbled upon the following statistic from the Center for Disease Control:

> --- Men who have sex with other man are 44 times more likely to have HIV and 46 more times to have syphilis.

The Schwarz Report, Volume 51, Number 2 by Robert Knight. Sodomizing the Military, Part 1; page 5.

We have belled the cat, or carried out a plan both dangerous and impractical, all for the sake of a fleeting moment's gratification.

More, and unsurprisingly, this rise of unrestrained and experimental sexuality among both sexes has weakened the strength of the traditional family. Millions of young children and teenagers have been raised by single moms, many of whom are completely broke, and thus dependent upon the espanding and wasteful federal government for mere subsistence. Fathers are usually not around to guide and protect, to sternly counsel and advise. God's perfect plan, to have a child raised by a woman and a man, a mother and a father, has been tossed out of the window. For myself, I must allow, I had perfect parents, a kind and gentle mother, and a forceful, yet extremely fair, father. Many kids today are not as lucky as I was then in my youth. In particular, the role of the male in the household has been consistently mocked. As earlier stated, and foolishly, adoptions are now permitted by two gay men (indeed, just the other day I read that THREE male "lovers" were able to adopt a small infant, so one must then ask: Why not go for four?), two gay women, a single man, a single woman, or what you will. I feel sorry for the children who grow up in these alternative environments, thinking that their notions on sexuality will be compliant with the parents', and, in short, that they will most likely have a fully cockeyed, skewed, and unnatural view of the world.

Too, newer forms of other sexual diseases have arisen out of this biologic ash heap, a clear and predictable testament to our new, and unchecked promiscuousness. These new diseases shall have to be treated with as-yet unknown drugs, but can we not avoid the problem in the first place? Is it not preferable to not contract the contagion in the beginning, rather than to treat it once it has arrived?

And perhaps most importantly to this discussion, the rise and so-called normalization of homosexuality has meant that an innate sexual confusion has mushroomed: Many are transfixed by the possibility of being queer or gay, and some have decided to declare themselves as bisexual, or so they say. No doubt many think that this week, I shall be gay; however, next week I shall be a virtuous heterosexual. Bewilderment and bafflement spike, leading to unguarded anxiety, disquietude, and panic for many. After all, society and our disintegrating culture have told these youths on the edge of adulthood that homosexuality is but another amoral option, a little like taking a bath instead of a shower, or choosing to drive on a back road instead of an interstate highway. These perpetuators say this since they do not believe that sexual activity has any moral dimensions; and, in that view, they are decidedly mistaken. Further, they do not possess the authority to make those judgments. So, finally, we must ask ourselves, after that fateful and unconsidered step has been taken, what further compounding evil exists? And was this grand bodily experiment worth it, worth all the trouble, the loneliness, the consternation, the waywardness, the disorder, the discontent, the divorce, the depression, and the disease?

Evil: May I even say the word? Or am I precluded? Can I speak my mind? May I say anything about anything, or will I sure as shootin' just get canned and shown the door? I just do not think it prudent to laugh with the devil and to mock God. Who is telling me what to say, what to do? May I put on some armor? So shortly this country has gone to hell, as if on purpose. Nobody knows what they are doing! They say they do but they do not. The proponents have made a smokescreen, something full of plain hokum, jumped-up drivel, and false leads. What ever happened to the old idea that if you make a claim, you had better be able to prove that claim?

For myself, I shall keep an eye on the sail. Horse droppings are not figs. Evil and sin do exist, and in this world, they may be neither banished, nor discounted. Where is it written that one may no longer speak about such things? Has the mere possibility of evil simply gone away, disappeared as the self-appointed cultural elites so blithely argue? Of course, it has not! By what new cultural rule or standard am I no longer permitted to speak? This issue demands more attention, just as the meat on the stick needs to be basted. If I do not speak up, or seek to accommodate and pander, am I too not guilty of an evil? Acquiescence is demanded of all us now, without our having any say in the matter. The word comes from the Latin word, acquiescere, to remain at rest or agree tacitly.

Cinque Sortite: Five Assaults Or Sallies Onto The Battlefield

We live in a topsy-turvy jaundiced world; however, may I even say so? The herring hangs by its own gills.

So, gays shave the fool, us, with no lather. Like a false Merlin, they have tricked the world, pulling the wool over our occluded eyes, and now it is easy for them to sail auspiciously before the wind. Sometimes, at least briefly, fools get the best cards. They insist with no proof that all actions beneath the sheets are equal, and that, therefore, any evil or sin in the act is obviated, effectively disposed of or negated. However, how can anyone make that errant claim; or, rather, after having made such a fatuous pronouncement, how can they prove it? I do not hang my cloak upon the peg according to their wind. These folks are imperious and arrogant; they love their new-found, arriving out of the blue, power; they say everything is okie-dokie; they have made themselves out to be demigods; they foolishly conjure that they have the transcendent power with a snap of the fingers or a nod of the head to change the rules under which society operates, as if by zauber's magic or done by a sorcerer's apprentice. But the truth of it is that they have as much chance of success as a one-legged man does in an ass-kicking contest, or so says Christopher Knopf.

This sad day many of those lost ones who engage in homosexual practices will make the claim, one still unproven, that all love is love, and too, that all love is equal, and lacks any moral pertinence. Of course, it goes without decree that this proclamation is only meant to excuse or erase the sin. Further, some will make the even more ludicrous claim that posterior intimacy is a measure of a society's advancement and maturity. Though the obverse is true, if I say so to this new gay world, I am instantly labeled an antagonist, a retrograde, and an immature, hateful, or under-evolved fuddy-duddy. Clearly, to many involved in this once-subterranean world of gay sexuality, no question of evil or sin exists, since the world is shouted aloud to the heavens:

> ---I can do what I want, with whomever I want to do it with. I create no harm, and hurt nobody.

Through their own mock determinations, prodded by an increasingly godless society, sin has been banished to the back bench, and attendant shame and embarrassment as well. Since, they argue, God no longer makes the rules (but only suggestions...), these proponents of the gay life are governed more by shifting gay dating standards or freaky Grindr protocols than by the God's commandments. Do they own a conscience which works? Yet, all the while, one must ask: How can anyone who has cast aside the moral code ever accurately assess a future action, that is, whether it might be a good one or an evil one? Once the rules have flown the coop, how shall we govern ourselves? Who or what force shall guide that person? Personal whim, a passing word, mere fleeting desire, or coercive peer pressure would seem to have taken over from the directions of God.

Any building with wall cracks or a meager foundation will soon collapse. That notion ought not to be surprising to us, since the issue hangs like a privy over a ditch: It is obvious. Saint Augustine claims that sin is energy in the wrong channel; and further, he argues that evil is less a malicious presence than an absence of the good. Famously, he tried to find the face of evil and could not find it anywhere. In the gay world and elsewhere (e.g., big business, as in banking or the pharmaceutical and abortion industries), evil may be bland, blank, and opaque; usually, it does not loudly shout its name from the mountain's top; it rarely reveals itself as evil per se; and too, often, it is not shocking or tawdry, at least on the surface of things. Today's heavily relaxed moral standards tell big mouths like me not to bother, to keep quiet. We are given this dictum:

>---If I am not meant to be their keeper, I will let geese be geese.

Hannah Arendt (among others), speaks to:

>---Evil's charming banality, its commonplaceness.

Hannah Arendt's book: Eichmann in Jerusalem: A Report on the Banality of Evil; Viking Press; 1963.

Therefore, to win the battle, we must begin to grasp that the terrible thing about sin is that over time's incessant march, it may become "normal", or so it may seem so at first glance. And thus, the acquisitive banker does not appreciate his greed, the drug manufacturer does see the damage caused, and the abortionist does not understand that he has just committed murder.

All the while, though, unrecognized sin and evil enervate, even though those two words may not even be uttered. For, even if we do not know it, sin and evil sap our strength. He who has spilt his porridge onto the floor cannot well scrape it up again. Just as unseen predatory moths may devour a James Pringle plaid blanket, so too shall uncontested sin and evil shall devour a person and a nation. Through their corrosive attributes, sin and evil automatically cause enervation in the body and the mind, deprive our will of steel, and lessen our daily vitality, something that we would normally stoke, possess, and display. Together, they reduce and curtail our mental and physical vigor, like any common cancer and scary scourge might do. They put a rod into the spoke of the bicycle's wheel; they bend the nail, stain the tie, deflate the tire. Essentially, as both factors work in tandem, they weaken us and make us lax and lazy, like too much bad Scotch, or too much sitting around the house might do; and eventually, as any mounting and mounding weakness or debilitation does, whether caused by man or by accident, they shall destroy us in full, and that much I do know as an odds-on, true, sure thing.

Is it any grand surprise, then, that gay people tend to lead drastically shorter, truncated lives, and too, that they are inclined towards disease, depression and suicide? Is it not stressful for them to attempt to deny this cause-and-effect connection, to allege out of anxiety that it does neither pertain nor matter? That stress itself may lead to an even greater depression, or the onset of a disease that may have been lurking. Each must know in his heart (though he may not say so plainly) that such a life is like a hoe without a handle, a large ship at sea without a proper rudder. Deep down, in the quieter moments, they must sense that these painful acts erase the potential for a greater life; they rationalize away their sad choices to secret spots then left behind; and over time's ticks, they close their eyes to a way of life that is abhorrent and counter to God's clear, stated wishes for us.

We gnaw on the same bone determinedly. Still, may

we turn some, aver? May we join together on this warpath, upon this ravelling gauntlet since, unlike so many empires before us which have resolutely fallen, we have not yet lost the capacity to fight, although today that skill, one as important as any other, is surely winnowing, atrophying, and growing slight. Here is the inch pin, the pull to get the longest end: We are meant to bear children, though how rarely those simple words are today tendered to the public square. Our nation's birth rate is at its lowest ebb ever. If one cares to take a peek or gander at gender, puo vedere, anyone can easily see that we are all designed that way, as a sort of lock-and-key mechanism, to beget, to propagate, to produce offspring as daily as a fat, content hen delivers eggs. Women are meant to bear and nurture them, and men, to provide and protect them. How else might children survive and thrive in this fractured and rudderless world, if they do not have two persons of the opposite sex to guard them against all the sundry onslaughts, difficulties and diseases? God's plan, should we choose to accept it, is to be faithful stewards of the little ones, to take both kind and stern care of them always, and to guide and lead them more by example than by anything else, since those actions will always be the surest teacher. And so, when gays adopt the homosexual gambit, one fraught with danger, immediately they thwart God's judicious plan.

Thus, we are meant to be tinkerers at the edge of this miraculous act of creation (A new life arrives to the world!), in which we play a small, but crucial, part. As parents, it is our greatest job, tending to our children's welfare, to praise them when warranted and to chide them when that approach is needed; it is our job to provide food, clothing, moral instructions, laughter, and love. Over time a parent's individual desires may become secondary to this primordial biology, since, after all, we have already had our first full swings at the plate. (Even today, these words written two generations away from my childhood, I can still recall most keenly the deep love that both my parents had for me.) Children, in this great and good plan, one made by the most wondrous design set forward only by God, they necessarily take us out of ourselves so that we might care more for them than for ourselves, and in that automatic and natural process we thereby defeat, perhaps without even knowing it, the attractive vainglories of expanding selfishness, rampant ego, and foolish pomp. Through this miracle of birth and progeny, that greatest of sins, arrogance, is trumped without our knowing it. Once again, our mentor, Saint Augustine, tells how to think about the matter:

> ---Our bodies are shaped to bear children, and our lives are a working out of the process of creation. All our ambitions and intelligence are beside that great elemental point.

As long as we are having this discussion, engaging in this ping-pong, back-and-forth battle of vastly opposing views, consider for a ticking minute how far our society has veered away from this wholesome and necessary example, and specifically, let us study San Francisco, the City by the Bay. Quel beau lieu! What a beautiful place, all the white and pastel-painted houses standing as alert sentinels upon the steep hillsides, taking watch over the ocean or the bay in all directions! Everywhere she is surrounded by the sea, which can verge on the deepest Solent blue, almost a grey really, or which may shift in an instant under the glare of the penetrating sun towards the lighter shade of aqua, that color with a modest tinge of green. The air in the city is always fresh and bracing, buoyed by Zephyrus gusts that blow in from the Farallons 30 miles to the west outside the Golden Gate. My perfect parents lived there once, briefly, right before World War Two. Then, she, the city, was full of enclaves of ethnicity: First of all, the Italians and Portuguese many of whom came to fish the sea, the Irish, the Germans, and many Russians our west among the avenues, and down in the Mission District resided the bountiful Mexicans and others of Hispanic origin. There, then, there were so many chances for youthful fun: Fishing in the placid bay or out to the deeper sea on boats that would have plied from Fisherman's Wharf, and don't forget the chocolate factory there and the ice cream stores, the opera and symphony, los taquerias, the San Francisco Seals of the Pacific Coast League, Lefty O'Doul playing at Seals Stadium at Bryant and 16th streets, and of course, bucolic and expansive Golden Gate Park where my young parents, then only 25 years old, used to stroll on Sundays (Senza lavoro! No work!), pushing a pram carrying my older sister, Nanette. And, at that time, 1940, the city (E la meglio citta del mondo!) held nearly ¾ of a million people, and the schools and churches were burgeoning, overcrowded, stuffed to the gills with yelping, teasing, boisterous children.

However, just three decades later San Francisco became the nation's leading gay mecca, the epicenter of this emerging pernicious cult. Many homosexuals, realizing that there is always strength in numbers, were glad to move there, since that migration would help to establish a gay political machine. Many heterosexuals, especially the Italian and Irish, left the city for the less crowded suburbs in Marin County or the East Bay. The gay contingent took over the city quickly (mirroring what happened at roughly the same time when the progressive coalition seized power in traditionally conservative Vermont), like locusts do feed in a field of ripe grain; and soon, they were firmly ensconced there, snug as mealy bugs in a dusty rug, electing lap-dog politicians to do their improvident biding. It was soon evident to all that wild bears prefer each other's company. Many joined this burgeoning erotomania, arriving at the beautiful city from distant Iowa, Mississippi, or Wyoming, testing that fraudulent impulse that they had put in place, one cancelling or supplanting the very idea of God. So today in that city, the largest faction of the population at 35% states that "No religion" is their religion! Too, unsurprisingly, the number of children has declined sharply and today youth under the age of 18 represent only 13% of the population. Only the Chinese of the city have maintained a decent, replicative birth rate. Many Mexicans have been summarily forced out of the city due to spiraling housing costs, and so, they have taken their strong family and religious values to other nearby cities that are more affordable. Many grade schools and high schools, some established many generations ago, are now shuttered since there are not enough children with which to fill them. Today, it is possible to walk or traipse all over the city, in particular the Castro District, and not see one child. Homosexuals united there in faux marriages do not routinely produce children, since to do so is biologically impossible. This sad state of increasingly barren cities, lacking the happy whoops and cries of children, has unfortunately spread to many other cities across the land and around the world. Many active gays cemented to this errant cult have joined to a life fully outside of children;

and they are therefore bereft of those little ones, creatures miraculously made in our own likenesses, who speak to us of our own successes and failures, our vices and virtues, disappointment and triumphs. Apparently, they have not pondered these simple words from Godfather III:

> ---The only wealth in this world is children, more than all the money, power on earth.

Said by Michael Corleone in Godfather III, 1990; screenplay by Francis Ford Coppola and Mario Puzo

And that can only be because certain other factors, erotomania, stoking desire, common lust, have become more predominant in their lives. Absent God's grace, what force or dicta shall guide them? It is clear that many young men do not agree with Mario and Francis's assessment that children are key to a better life. This thing is easy to understand: Questa cosa e facile da capire. When a new parent first sees his new infant, fresh from the womb, we see a clean soul, a life untarnished by willfulness, me-first attitudes, and unrestrained desires. Later, inevitably we later witness in these growing youngsters, foibles, mistakes, and vanities, and then later still, perhaps some predilections for cloudy reasoning, stark gestures, foolish risk-taking, and snap judgments. As parents, we only wish them well, and we ascribe to them our own faded hopes and windmill-tilting aspirations; with eagerness and concern we watch their yearnings mature and fail, climb and collapse. We do not want them to find false friends, nor find pain in accidents or derision. Across all ages, sent by obscure, yet present, genetic codes, we sense our flaws in them, distinguishments sent by us to them under the cloak of dreams. Thus, parenting of children is properly a constant lesson in humility, that endless fount of all wisdom (Thank you, Socrates and Einstein!), and it is for that reason, one now largely forgotten and discounted by the young denizens of San Francisco, that the normal family remains a cracker-jack good idea, one invented not by man but only by God.

Adesso, basta! Enough already! Without anyone ever asking me for my slim thoughts, the definition of what constitutes real and legitimate manhood, something key to me and all other men, has been fundamentally re-written, re-formed, altered. Society, whose crippling corrosive mores now run the show, it has forced me in my belief system, and other men as well, to deflect and push back against these new, sour, curdling determinations. In the massive metamorphosis that came hell bent from leather from afar, we were never asked our opinion; but rather, we were told to comply with these new and enlarging rules. A prima facie coup d'etat took place overnight and folks like me and millions of others were told to clam up, shut the gob, button it, and to act impotent, subservient, and obliging to the new treacherous mores. Every day gay elites without proof of any sort maintain that the homosexual life is as dangerous as a peanut butter and jelly sandwich or a slow Sunday stroll in a safe park. And every day my children are presented with two vastly dissimilar models of acceptable sexual behavior, depending upon who is doing the talking, and as a parent the fact that the odious model is presented as an equal to the other (A simple choice! Vanilla or chocolate! Pistachio or mint chip!) is annoying, insulting, frustrating, offensive, reminding me of the phrase "to stick in one's craw". By the tickle, a craw is the stomach of an animal or a crop, a pouch-like enlargement of a bird's esophagus, a place where food is partially digested or stored.

In the meantime, in the midst of this swarming sexual milieu, radical feminism, frankly hateful of most men in general (that is, unless they are sissy pants or weak pansies!) has encouraged women to delay or even to foreswear marriage and childbirth, since, that misguided philosophy stolidly maintains that to have a happy marriage is to harm one's career, the new supposed nirvana. Women were taught that since men are such out-of-whack dogs, useless idiots, baying-at-the-moon horny toads; and many strident mentors coached young women that females ought to be childless throughout life; however, with these misguided orders, as Helen Roy, editor of The American Mind, points out, these women were told to eschew their own biology; she writes of:

> ---anti-natalist programming and biological denialism.

And she forecasts for those women who adhere to these errant orders an old age unsurprisingly devoid of children and grandchildren, and that they will be missing out on what she terms as:

> ---intergenerational female friendships

where a granddaughter might be nurtured by both her mother and grandmother, and vice versa, which is all part of God's wondrous plan for the greater family. This tactic of the left, to encourage women to be eternally barren, is part of the culture of death embraced by the left; birth rates have been dropping for decades; and it is an intentional, part-and-parcel technique of the left to destroy the family, to chip away at it, however that chipping away may be accomplished; with the goal being to have the godless state, not the loving family, bear the primary responsibility for the raising and nurturing of children. Thus, for many leftists the state is their new religion, although, of course, it is not a religion at all, but merely a form of government, for it does not speak of, revere, or even mention the divine.

In any case, as if overnight (but, as we have seen, these cultural maneuvers to transmute what is acceptable were as carefully planned ahead of time as any astute military stratagem), the old model of a faithful husband, a strong and sometimes stern father, a man who habitually delights in the beauty of his wife's body, someone who would scoff or think poorly of any man-to-man comingling, saying to himself and others:

> ---Ridiculous! A wipe out! No more peg boys! Trumped-up trouble! Meatheads all!

that model has been discarded, tossed aside, and replaced by a preternatural pretender intent upon obliging tolerance at any cost. Yet, we only get what we tolerate, as Father Mike Schmidt of Ascension Press predicts. Agnostics and atheists order us not to believe in God since to do so is to sell ourselves short, alleging that our path toward sexual self-actualization would be cut short by a faithful life. We are told by the ruling elites that all men must acquiesce to the idea of homosexuality, of bisexuality, and all the other variants of pleasure that now sprout up across the landscape; we are told to capitulate to all forms of political correctness; we are told that we must not speak out against the now-common sight of two men kissing, two men holding hands, two men adopting children, man-boy pederasty, open marriages, widespread pornography, and so forth, ad infinitum. We are instructed that the new, modern man must accept all of these misguided and disordered forms and phenomenon, and many more beyond them, even though they never have worked anywhere, and even though they are diametrically counter to past systems of belief. This new man is now in an awkward situation, suspended on a high wire above the gaping canyon below. If this new man disavows or disowns or points out the gaps in the hedge, the inherent defects in this tidal wave of normalization, how it shall neither work nor hold, then this new men (and perhaps it is you!) is termed a bigot or homophobe or uncharitable. Effectively then, the freedom of speech of those who still oppose normalization has been truncated or removed from discourse. Therefore, I have little doubt that if this small piece is published and happens then to receive a wider audience, the humorless thought-police shall be out for my neck; they shall hasten to have me canned if not tarred and feathered in the town's central square for such divergent expressions.

Yet, one persists, as one must. I have been directed to ask those questions that have not yet been asked, those that slowly come to mind during the course of any slowly evolving rumination like this one purports to be:

1. Why should I or anyone else have to countenance this devasting behavior which is so counter to history and religion?

2. Why should any taxpayer have to regard as normal and usual the presence of gay bathhouses who sole purpose is rampant, anonymous sex, and who attendant medical costs all will ultimately bear?

3. Why should any typical parent be required to accept the model of the worthless rake, horny lorels led mostly by a glowing hedonism when, at the same time, he tries to raise his or her children with the opposite notions of fidelity and restraint?

4. Why should we have to affirm society holding up the gay life as something noble and beneficial, as a tantalus to be sought, something to yearn for, when the majority of history confirms the opposite?

5. Why should we have to put up with, confirm, the next sad and cultish step in our culture's dissolute demise, that of a transgenders' so-called right to scare, deface, and mutilate their own bodies?

6. Why should we have to live in this sick and fetid atmosphere, a mean goat's environment that says, "Anything goes! Anything!" where detached, pleasure-filled sex at verily any age with either sex is de rigueur, customary, encouraged?

7. Simply put, why do we have to put up with any of this nonsense and what is the best way to end it?

In the midst of this mounting tragedy, one that we have created from scratch on our own, every day proper families try to impart to their children traditional and positive messages, one that pronounce that men and women are grandly different, that there are two sexes and

Cinque Sortite: Five Assaults Or Sallies Onto The Battlefield

not seventeen, that androgyny is a myth perpetuated by gender fluid fanatics, that men and women are mostly meant to be married, to live together singularly and lovingly as a loving, patient couple, and that sex is best left for the marriage bed. However, every day the errant culture pursues a counter indoctrination; it increasingly mocks that message of faithfulness, deriding those who believe in it fully and vociferously and from every mountaintop and dais; and what is more, it sneers and scoffs at traditionalists for believing in them; and its leaders tell our children loudly from those same mountain tops that we traditionalists, not they, are the puppet tantamount fools! They employ the tactic: Turnabout is fair play, using turn table. Because of the growing decadence and coarseness of our society, daily a young daughter needs a mother's calm and thorough sex education briefer to counter all the lies, falsehoods, and propaganda spewed by that ill society. However, should not that little girl not be allowed to have a carefree youth? Is not the cart in front of the horse? Two deceivers speaking sotto voce to each other always keep their own advantage in mind: That is, the Fox and the Stork do dine together. Don Vito Corleone asks this of us all:

---How did things ever get so far?

The answer is that, while driving, we were not paying proper attention to the twisting road, and so we nodded off to the Land of Nod with the motor running and our sleepy hand on the wheel, and obviously we are about to go off the high side into the weeds, brambles, and roadside tangles. Since it was deflated, we did not use our faith as an armor against these growing atrocities against the soul of man. So, in studying this doomed-to-fail attempt at normalization, we must again ask ourselves: How did it happen? The answer is pretty simple really. You gather together a group of people, an anti-God contingent or force to be sure, a battalion whose faithless members do not believe in any sort of an afterlife, in judgment, essentially in a God who rules over us all, and then we traditionalists got sleepy as they began to run everything.

But, in stepping back some from the fray, how do these errant soldiers upon the veldt, faux crusaders for normalization, know for sure that normalization is a crackerjack, killer-diller idea, since, as the pesky logicians instruct:

> ---When one makes a claim, right away one must prove it.

How do those who are so strongly anti-religious know for a fact that there is no God? Is that statement of theirs not just another rash guess or faulty conjecture, something that they wish to be true? Their saying so does not make it fact. We must examine even at this late date the premise of their argument, for if it is faulty (which it is), the entire building shall collapse. Most proponents of normalization assume there is no God, but how do they know this to be true? Clearly, this is their predictable and foggy-minded assumption, an idea dreamt up out of nothing but air and one that does neither hold nor last. I remember the conversation between itinerant handyman Homer Smith (Sidney Poitier) and trading post owner Juan (Stanley Adams) from the 1963 movie, Lilies of the Field, when Juan tells Homer that he, Juan, considers prayer and religious beliefs as a form of insurance in case the East German nuns for whom Homer is helping to build a new chapel out on the arid Arizona desert are correct in their belief that there is a God. Though it is not a true or deep faith, Juan tells Homer that such insurance is a small price to pay to avoid eternal damnation.

Also, it is a surefire, uncontestable fact that we humans have a marked and fallible tendency to talk ourselves into things, into keen pickles or the darkest jams, into some pretty thick and deep messes, simply because we can, since we have the free will and opportunity to do so, especially if via a paucity of prayer, we lack God's grace which is there all along if we deem to ask for it. (Re: The Gospel according to Saint Matthew 7:7-8.) Simply put, when someone is off track, they don't realize they are off track because they are off track. What bank robber, having grown up in poverty, does not think he is entitled to rob a bank? What adulterer does not think he is correct to sleep with his neighbor's wife especially since she has been flirting with him like crazy and since his own wife has been a lousy, snappy, shrewish on-the-rag grump for weeks? All about us now, we see proud and unashamed "Cafeteria Christians" who think it perfectly acceptable to pick and choose which rules needs to be adhered to and which rules may be casually discarded or neglected. When a young person joins to a false belief system like the cult of homosexuality, unintended consequences rear their ugly head all 'round; such is the entrapping nature of sin; perhaps that first false step into treachery and greater darkness is made to be part of something, to join a cult, or to get rid of some dissatisfaction with life; however, those steps will only grow the sin and not erase it; they will only lead to depression, desperation, and perhaps suicide; and as Matthew once again tells us:

> ---But the children of the kingdom will be thrown outside into the darkness, where there will be weeping and gnashing of teeth.
>
> The Gospel according to Saint Matthew 8: 12

On the other hand, acceding to a life of prayer, that young person would have been much better off in following the words of Saint John:

> ---Zeal for Your house will consume me.
>
> The Gospel according to Saint John 2: 17

Saint John tells us to pray, else we are lost. No matter how much some may yearn it to be true, one cannot be a real Christian while behaving as a homosexual, or, for that matter, behaving as an adulterer. Witness the moral gap in the hedge of that serial profligate, Hugh Hefner, who did little else but destroy marriages across the world, including many of his own, all done for the ascendancy of demon lust; for if that primordial instinct is not contained, but rather under the urgings of our erotomaniac society grown and enlarged, it shall be the victor over any man's soul. How many times these illogical statements are uttered as if they were cast-iron true! One may not feign ignorance or protest that:

> ---I am special. I have these yearnings. It is harmless enough.

Cinque Sortite: Five Assaults Or Sallies Onto The Battlefield

Such a young person on the edge of the cliff, instead would be wise to ask himself:

> ---Does God have the right or power to dictate to me what constitutes proper sexual behavior? Or, in the midst of my sexual wanderings, is it up to me to decide what path in the darkest wood is correct?

These gay elites who want to rule us and that society has lately so blessed (sic) with this obscene imprimatur, it is obvious that they are just making up their own bedroom rules as they go along; unrepentant tricksters, they join only to a life of growing desire and ascending pleasures; and to try to justify themselves they in that deviant course are supposedly looking for meaning; however, so wanton are these ways, so removed from God's grace, they shall never find it, nor any lasting peace.

***

One of my clever and valued cousins aptly reminded me lately of the oldest story---of Adam's loneliness when he was first put on earth, and how God, when he beheld that loneliness, gave to Adam a woman, Eve, to complete him. They then did cleave to each other in the sense of "adhere, cling, to be faithful to, or to stick fast". Recall these words from Saint Paul's Epistle to the Romans:

> ---Love must be sincere. Detest what is evil. Cleave to that which is good.
>
> The Epistle of Saint Paul to the Romans 12: 9

To further cement couples' loyalty to each other, in His surpassing wisdom God put in place the matrix of sex as a kind of biologic glue or cement, and in particular, sex-engendered, aroma-based pheromones, which are strong biological signals of attraction, fidelity, and, yes, ownership. Thus, when couples are long separated, it is often in the mind of both the scent of one for the other that is the key to remembering the other. As we understand, God never told Adam or Eve that they might plausibly migrate or drift to another; instead, he told them that they must be faithful to each other, even onto old age when the sexual impulses might have dulled some.

Eve would be a constant helper to her husband, Adam, not that she would be subservient to him (as many shrill feminists of today would have us believe), but, going back to the original sense in the Hebrew, that she would be his equal, and that she would complete him, just as Adam did complete Eve. Over time, guided by biologic instinct and by the notion that their unique union was something blessed, something very special, a compact that had to be guarded and treasured and protected, they procreated. Yet, Saint Augustine tells us that human sexuality had been wounded or damaged by original sin, and thus required the redemption of Christ for that sin to be erased. But, what if that redemption is not recognized? That is the question for today's demeaning, debased, dissolute culture. Yet again, I cannot imagine that sexuality to Adam and Eve was ever a dominating factor in their lives; but rather, it was a natural and simple circumstance that they shared to demonstrate their deep love for each other, specifically to bring a joyous constancy and fidelity to their union.

However, today, Jasper, Sunday soldiers, suffering

Cinque Sortite: Five Assaults Or Sallies Onto The Battlefield

cats, hard-as-nails sailors, let us look around. Sex is everywhere! Millions of men and women are just plain Jane crazy, raunchy crotch hounds, hopped-up horny toads. So, today, yesterday, and tomorrow, sex sells soap, cars, carpet, Venetian blinds, double-glazing, motorcycles, pancakes, you name it. Its role in our lives has exploded for crass, mercantile reasons, and sex has become hugely overemphasized, all done for the almighty dollar or pelf, the green. I read somewhere that half the hits on the Internet are to search for pornography, something which only harms the normal biological instinct for union and procreation. Mostly to make money, its sublime purpose---to allow married couples to express devotion and affection for each other, and also, at the same time, to bring new children onto the earth---has been exaggerated way beyond all reason, summary, or description. More than anything else for the purpose of this discussion, we have all been advised (Informed! Told! Instructed!) by today's runaway culture to grow always ever larger that sexual impulse, to seize upon that normal, simple, and benign instinct and make it always bigger. Therefore, we ask for sex to do far too much in our lives and are then disappointed when it cannot carry the water, that heavy load or impedimentum. Despite what many now may think, and perhaps disappointingly for many young men or women who "consider themselves" to be gay, sex is actually a small part of life and not its nexus.

Aboard Lee's loyal Traveller and retreating some upon the campo as a flanking maneuver, we can see that many gays are foolish, proud, or misled enough by older mentoring peers to conclude that desire equals love. They believe in this fallacy because ruling elites in our society have told them to believe it, and the younger ones, on the cusp of making that awful leap into oblivion, always do what their peer group, not God, says. Thus, faithfulness to a wife is no longer praised in our society; indeed, now the opposite, we are hectored, is true: 'Tis better to be Johnny Appleseed than anyone else! Since desire will normally fade some with time, those so trained by society's unwatchful dogs, under constantly retreating mores, now excuse themselves from all loyalties or fealty, and then feel compelled (Properly schooled! Proudly instructed!) to seek new mates of any sex with whom to couple and cavort. What is it that that soft-in-the-head dope Woody Allen says, perhaps only half in jest?:

> ---Being bisexual increases the chance of getting a date on Friday night.

I am speaking of a new kind of indoctrination: It is good and just for anyone to be a fervent rabbit, a fever head, a Jane crazy or piccolo player, someone who with practiced habit jumps from bed to bed. And over practiced time, over-arching and always stoked desire can easily frame and then dominate those lives. The Greeks have told us thousands of years ago that one may easily become a simple slave to passion. May I say that it is not good to be a slave? What innocent soul wishes in the beginning to be dominated by the dominator? So, naturally enough, as the progression of the impulse grows and distends, some live only to experience that sharpest, keenest pang of lust! Thus, in scarce two generations, calmer notions of fidelity and constancy have been tossed onto the street like last year's tired tee shirt. And too, that idea that any love may deepen as couples age together, even as their physical attractiveness, to outsiders, declines, that idea in our culture is diminished and rarely discussed, and it is certainly a factor neither promoted nor praised.

From my tone here throughout, it is clear that I believe that the homosexual life needs to be repudiated, and also, correspondingly, that its normalization must be forsworn; otherwise as Cormac McCarthy writes:

> ---We can't stop what's coming.

No Country for Old Men; Cormac McCarthy; Alfred A. Knopf; 2005.

And that strongest of words, repudiation, it here needs to be studied and implemented. Repudiate is from the Latin word, repudiare, meaning to "reject, cast off, to put away, divorce". Further, this phony and corrosive idea, one pushed by the ruling media elites that we somehow in the name of tolerance we must, as they tell us:

> ---Put up with, suffer, allow, permit, tolerate, endure, and bear

their agenda, that notion of theirs must be combatted and fought against by all means needed. If we do not contest normalization and then in time vanquish it, I feel the deepest anxiety, the strongest foreboding for our society's survival. Normalization is not something to be just regretted as unfortunate; it is not something to be kindly debated, cautioned against lightly or casually; rather, it is a pernicious seismic shift towards distress, depression, and darkness that must be battled vigorously since it is the embrace of a sin, something which can only cause woe and enervation and separation from God. And, flowing from that observation, all of us need to confront the uncontestable fact than God is in charge of things, not mere man.

Now, some will say that I am just having a cow, that I am a Nervous Nellie, and that I would be better off to just live and let live. Those folks tell me in their next breath as a sort of order or command that I must employ the following words while confronting the growing call for the normalization of homosexuality:

> ---Condone, look the other way, give a green light to, pardon excuse, forgive and forget, remit, sanction, countenance, stomach, accede to, nod at, endorse, tolerate, more (for there are a lot of words available to us to describe simply being weak).

Yet, I maintain that this normalization is the wrong path, praising wrong and false values. We have put in place factors that can only lead us all down the road to darkness and deprivation. The road many have followed is an affront to common sense and to God, not necessarily in that order. (By the tingle, throughout this discussion, I am condemning the sin and not the sinner, since the latter job is not mine, but God's.) We are now in a position of great distress, which is to say that our backside is already on fire, though we may not know it. For far too long, we traditionalists have sat on our hands and waited, sat on our hands and waited, gazing at the sunset, perhaps thinking the smoke from this issue might drift away; more, we have wasted far too much time just gazing at the stork, rather than doing something, say, decrying, evangelizing, exhorting, praying. And yet, even now, at this late date in this moral backsliding, there is reason for hope, and hope for us all. Why? How is that possible?

As usual, the correct answer is right under our noses; and it sits across from us at the table: Man's free will. That is, we are free to run with the goats or not. Here it is best to simply quote Sirach who says these things far better than I might say them:

> ---When God, in the beginning, created man, he made him subject to his own free choices. If you choose you can keep the commandments; it is loyalty to do his will. There are set before you fire and water; to whichever you choose, stretch forth your hand. Before men are life and death, whichever he chooses shall be given him.
>
> The Book of Sirach 15: 14-17

Thus, for all of us, the end of the contest, the endless joisting upon the veldt, draws near. This sad and arrogant experiment for normalization, a sad choice fraught with the deepest dangers, this prideful and foxy asking-for-trouble decision, this clear contravention against all natural law, biology, and the preponderance of religion has never worked well before, no matter what the disinherited, disordered, depressed dissidents may allege. And most assuredly, it is apt to do much harm. A blind man, uno cieco, could sense that, even if he be sightless. Why should it not harm all of us now? What has altered or morphed so that an old and tired DC-3, this too-heavy plane, should suddenly be able to fly over the steep Sierra Madres from Oaxaca to Puerto Escondido? Nothing! Zilch! Nada! Had not the

Greeks and then the Romans also pursued this most errant and lascivious course? Did it not there and then also lead them to ruin, abjectness, and dissolution? Take a look at the pervasive acceptance of common homosexuality at Britain's so-called top universities between the wars: Might not that soured, corrosive atmosphere have played a part in that nation's stunning lack of preparedness for World War II? Cowed by errant impulse, her peoples were so diverted, so distracted that they had lost track of the ball. And how exactly did that happen? Whence did that flow?

Instead, let us remember that we are still free to make good choices. God gave us this freedom which we must put to good use. We are still free and unencumbered to embrace older values or truths that actually do work well over many decades' time. Anybody can see through an oak plank if there is a hole in it. We must, accordingly, and if we are to save ourselves from the keenest enslavements and desires, revolve backwards some, pivot, or turn again toward that oldest idea that sex is truly best relegated to the happy confines of the marriage bed. (As a baseball zealot, parenthetically I must mention that "happy confines" was common parlance to describe cozy stadia, that is, before the ugly "cookie-cutter" parks in the name of more money took over.) If we do not so believe and so act, sexual confusion, raging coarseness, mounding dissatisfactions, and rampant new diseases shall enter the room and stay there squatting for quite a while. Our society, and especially the gays, have made sex to be some sort of harmless bedroom sport, when it distinctly is not. And once we have gone down this road to perdition, how do we then ask evil to leave, to depart? Shall evil be glad to go? How do we ask these sins to leave us alone? Why have we made sexual ubiquity to necessarily be a good thing? Why have we thought it right and proper to be led around by the nose by surging desires that shall never be met, by those strong subterranean currents, like some underground river, say the Henderson of the Nevada high ground desert, or the Timavo of the Karst coastline, currents which shift and move, shift and move, and which turn in endless cavatappi corkscrews, like that same Carsoline river which turns back again upon herself? We must return to the concept that all decisions, including but of course not limited to the sexual, carry with them as so much heavy baggage a decidedly moral component, despite what proponents of the homosexual life and many other sybarites may try to allege. Everything, however, finely spun, comes to the sun. Surely such a mundane notion cannot be called startling or a surprise. And we accept again, returning to the prior high ground, the notion, drawing it to us like a favored talisman or the most sacred of relics that, firstly, heterosexual marriage is part of God's plan, and secondly, that sex is a kind of beneficent dessert from God for heterosexual couples, so that they may be drawn the more towards each other in pleasured faithfulness and fidelity. It is something special, and not to be eaten all the time, else one would get fat, gordito, gros, or grasso, around the middle, for, as is well known, one cannot live on mousse or cannoli alone.

Even a blind man (and yet again, perhaps he more than any other...) can see that our culture is at a precipitous and challenging crossroads. Shall we continue to kill ourselves? Steep cliffs and mean escarpments alone surround us. The darn thing is we have only ourselves in the crosshairs of the rifle, as if on purpose. Of course, we are in deep trouble and the gravest danger; of course, we are! How could it be any other way? I fear a fall, a deeper fall; however, it cannot be, non puo essere. The health of our nation, our world, are at stake. If a patient as a nation is in the hospital, it teeters on the edge of this rampaging, corrosive disease; but, due to the rising swamp of propaganda all about (It is OK! It is OK! Don't worry, stiffy! Go with the flow, dope head!) the condition remains not well recognized; and therefore, it may not be properly treated. The ruling elites of the cultures, self-appointed zealots all, tell us that 'tis fine to be same-sex wanton and lustful, to grow desires ever larger; however, is that course possible or wise? Might not the desire begin to rule the man? What say you? These deceptions ought to be uncovered, to shine clear to the sun in the light of day. I can only say any of these things since I know that the sin remains the same; it does not go away after we wave a wand in the air, no matter its aspect in darkness or, coached by our errant elders, our altered and false perspective of it.

Too, as the battle for men's souls wages on, twisting and turning as all battles have done since the days of Olympia and Thule, from the days of Hastings and Bannockburn, we willy-nilly grant new, presumed, and groundless rights to those who praise, sanction, and promote the normalization of homosexuality, always inventing out of whole, clean cloth fresh allowances and engendering deeper transmutations of our culture. Somebody should pose the question: What if this embrace of the errant is a colossal mistake, a huge failure of judgement that will harm us both in this world and the next? Is this the road we ought to take? All of this is much more fundamental that we can now know.

Meanwhile, apropos of nothing, the courts, those supposed denizens of justice and of what is fair and just,

Cinque Sortite: Five Assaults Or Sallies Onto The Battlefield

the courts are stacked to the gills with progressive, left-leaning, activist judges who acquiesce if not lead all these untoward actions; indeed, some observers may allege that these misguided areligious judges lead the fervent charge onto the battlefield, onto the champ. Elected officials who believe in harmless normalization (a non sequitur if there ever were one), they have spent the past few decades appointing judges whom they understand from prior assiduous study will be friendly towards this jaundiced, off-the-trolley track, enervating cause. A pack of wild wolves has taken over the shepherding of the flock. And justice is thus quickly traduced, truncated, and tossed aside; and in this quick process (Be quiet, will you? Be quiet!) thousands of years of history and religious doctrine have been ignored, obviated, disregarded. Therefore, more than anything, we act dumb and speak little, acting as if the Ten Commandments had never been writ.

Mark clearly, battlers, soldiers, legionnaires, happy combatants all, this decision: Granting homosexuality a hallowed place in our society has made a seismic shift towards welcoming disaster. We ought not to encourage such a foul practice. The issue is like a large, but sloppy and out-of-true, framing of a considerable house about to be hit by a vicious wind when not fully stable: It shall not stand, but collapse upon itself. The beams of it shall be loosened, the dowels once in place shall fall to the ground, the nails will retract, the joists and purlins will slip, the angles of each frame to the other will pinch and be suddenly all out of whack; this house is our society which has stupidly embraced a widespread unfastenting and loosening of the important sexual strictures, those things once closely held and taught, which then did serve well to guard, constrain, or control what was known as acceptable sexual behavior. Opposingly, this new rule of unrestraint demanded by the cultural elites and smarty pants, the ever-present know-it-alls, this absolutely foolish move to try to make homosexuality (and other deviancies) normal, this new dictum from on high, from the crackpots, from the servile, from the lust-ridden, from the pederasts, from the godless and fully secularized, this new order is a mistake, an egregious error, a pandering feint which shall take all of us down fully to our knees, and which then shall make us all prostrate upon the ground, and perhaps only then shall we think to ask God for forgiveness. This new rule of unrestraint, where pretty much anything goes, stems from our increasingly godless world, from always heightened desires, and a political correctness which has run amuck.

This political correctness, our new faux religion, steals my tongue and yours in one fell swoop or breath. The First Amendment has shrunk, if not atrophied away all together, since it is a mere muscle like any other; and therefore, if it is not daily used, it shall soon waste away to deflated tissue and dust. That is precisely where we find ourselves: For lack of use and by skyrocketing intimidation on all fronts, free speech, for which our forefathers and mothers fought so many wars, that asset of open discourse is daily shrinking, if not gone altogether. For, consider again that if this small sortie or sally onto the battlefield, one of five imprudent thrusts, were to be printed and disseminated widely, the strong bet is, dollars to donuts, captains and seamen alike, Dilbert, dingleberry, that I would lose my paltry job, and tout de suite, quickly, or adesso. (Aye, matie; but if one door closes, another shall soon open, or so says Bell.) At this late date, I say bring on that dismissal. For far too long I have

Cinque Sortite: Five Assaults Or Sallies Onto The Battlefield

been afraid to say any of this; up till now, I am embarrassed to say that I have had a broad yellow streak down my back; but today, no longer. God alone guides these few words. Sometimes I feel as if we are already on a solemn sailor's death watch; and we are gathered together as weakened vice consuls ignored and flabby from booze on the morn of Los Dios de los Muertos, or The Day of the Dead. We regard this sad play quixotically, blinkingly, since I fear that with all men of the sea, we have had far too much to drink and therefore cannot think clearly, with any real lucidity; and with every passing day we view the steady approach of our own eventual demise as if it were happening to someone else. Malcom himself gives to the right questions: How? Why? And who among us at this late hour wishes to fight?

As well, all the correct answers are right in front of us. They have always been there, even if we did not see them. Perhaps we have been distracted by mean coercing manipulators during this sleepy march of Gabriel's sheep to the cliff. For, again, here is the nodus: The nuclear family is the bedrock, the foundation to any nation, and I do not mean, two fathers playing at child-rearing, or a single mother (go find a man, sweet sister, they are around), or any of the other obtuse permutations now passed up as normal and proper. At the hands of unchecked sexual experimentation and delight (always faux and fleeting), the family, like the one I was luckily born into to, has suffered innumerable tremors, shocks, jolts, cross back body blocks, sharp and harmful blows to the head, i colpi alla testa. A subdural hematoma comes to the fore, the mind. How shall it survive? How much further will we, idling watching the tableau in front of us to play out, allow it to be tested? All my resting and prone legions: May you now awaken? How much more time shall it take before all those who can may move to the better action, to save this nation from this precipitant drowning, this spreading corrosion, this growing cancer? How much longer will it take before we may grasp the need to shore up the creaking, poorly fastened house before all the rising waves and the lashing winds do rise to best it, to raze it to the ground? Thus, from this day forward let us refuse to bow any more to society's flawed imperative that homosexuality is normal and fine, harmless and fun. And the only weapon available for those of us who oppose the elites' tribunal is to no longer accept this most common and dangerous course; instead, we must explain exactly how all will be hurt, and propose another, earlier course, one which has been in front of our eyes all the time. On the other hand, to continue to be lax and tolerant, to continue to allow broad tolerance for homosexuality, advocating its normalcy and wider adoption throughout the whole of the world, that so-called tolerance shall only push our culture even more rapidly onto the road to perdition, that condition or state of being fully lost or perduto, perdu.

So, perdu, perduto, lost: It is a short word that never goes away. Over the years (tears?) I have seen or become acquainted with many homosexuals, or those disquieted ones unhappily "on the fence". About their faces uniformly I have detected both distress and discontent. Their eyes always tell the same tale: A confused wandering that shall never cease. Right after any sinful act, an act not part of God's plan, the long and unsuccessful attempt at self-justification after that act immediately begins; however, that attempt shall not be victorious, no matter how strongly the justifier wishes it to be so, since the sin remains, like a predominant, brooding Suribachi above Iwo Jima. Often,

I have noticed, their eyes shall avert anyone's steady gaze. I feel sorry for them, since they look like foxes trapped in a strong chicken coop after devouring the chicken; therefore, they are about to get caught and slaughtered. Many do not sleep well; they sleep with a lingering fitfulness and a constant thrashing about, and not like winners but like losers. Paraphrasing Josef Goebbels, they seem to think that if one tells a lie long enough and often enough, that that lie shall become the truth, though that be not true. Since it is in the natural perogative of man to do so, many will defend themselves, though Seneca told us years ago that such is always the wrong course. In the midst of being lost or at sea, many will be overly dependent upon their peer group for support and beneficence, and they will rely upon like-minded fans or mentors who shall attempt to buoy and bolster each other in a false, lying rapture. It is an itinerant vagrants' club of which I would not choose to be a member. Some make a concerted effort to seduce the younger ones, those still innocent, for it is best to snag them when young as they do then possess the greater gullibility. (Such a thing happened to Neal Cassidy at the age of only 15 in 1941 in Denver at the mischievous hands of a much older, horny provider). Still, their eyes to me seem to be opaque, unsettled, glazed, as if they belong unwillingly to a stubborn and tenacious cult. A fundamental folly rests at the core of this issue, as they have chosen a road distinctly away from God, rather than towards Him and His merciful grace.

Too, there is never anything casual about sex, even so-called casual sex, since the sexual act by its very nature always impinges on our very core, our subconscious and unconscious. These sexual libertines, determined experimenters in demon lust, have proposed a set of new rules that hold no credence: Their errant rules cannot be believed; they shall never be granted a calming peace, since It is always a mistake to live a lie. These lost folks seem fixed upon "having a good time", whatever the blazes that means, yet they could never be termed "happy". Perennially distressed, this lavender mob, they are never satisfied. Disordered, they contract rare and virulent diseases, many resistant to drugs. Disquieted, they die early. Depressed, they never experience the joy of children, the only real wealth in this tarnished world. And eschewing the divine, because they were years before told by their leaders (sic) to do so, they live solely in this sorry world, not the next, and yet, they routinely are unhappy and rarely at peace, though they may never say those things aloud to themselves or each other. And might that not be because:

---Only God makes me happy

as Roberto Clemente's mother once said? Yes, it is true.

In examining and turning over and around this long moral question, to look at it from all angles, studying it as one would a rare Waterford crystal vase or decanter, one like any other, to study it under the brightest light, to fondle it in one's hand, to see how it reflects the light and closes down upon the darkness, vanquishing it, one needs to again ask one salient question, the kind of prescient thing my father used to say to me when I was but a child, one which poses:

---What will happen if suddenly everyone does it?

Cinque Sortite: Five Assaults Or Sallies Onto The Battlefield

Note the proper use of the present tense, "does it", since this contest is still being waged. Gays may allege that it is over, that it is normal and fine and fit and proper to be homosexual, but that is only their clever negotiating ploy, one among many in their arsenals of attack. The answer to that question is to fully gauge and assess whether it is part of God's plan, and only then can one determine whether the gay course is a proper one. Any careful study will conclude that the homosexual life is contrary to God's plan. These dissidents all stretch the truth to suit themselves, as all men have done through the ages to try to justify lousy behavior. As Bartholomew Malleck writes:

> ---Satanists willfully reject the truth because they prefer the wickedness.

For neigh on two generations now the progressive secularists have been promoting and glorifying alternative sexualities of various hues and stripes, as if it were as harmless as a new type of soup or soap; and that sad promulgation has even infected religious organizations, those spiritual armies that are meant to tell us what is right and what is wrong, to such an extent that many high up in the hierarchy, bad priests to put it mildly, actually seem to be advocating for homosexuality, always speaking of tolerance, diversity and dignity, rarely speaking to the morality of the issue. Many of those clerics who ought to know better, priests who have spent many years in study, confoundingly now push for the normalization of homosexuality, and in so doing these errant apologists mock God. They are not coached by God, but by the devil whom they have allowed into their souls. In refusing to enforce moral standards these lax and lazy, uncourageous, and soft-headed priests are actually part of the problem; they are condoning lives of death, not of life; and when they condone and accept sin these bad priests are cooperating with evil, nothing less.

Beyond that sadness, there is building proof that active homosexuality, something contrary to God's law, has well permeated the priesthood, especially at the higher levels. Regard the debacle of now laicized McCarrick: For how many years did McCarrick use his diocese's New Jersey beach home to attempt to seduce young impressionable seminarians? How many of his complicit compatriots must have known the scandal that he was up to? How many of these spineless priests, when confronted with clear evidence of McCarrick's sinful behavior, looked the other way? And regard the closure of the local diocesan seminary here in western New York, a once holy place founded before the start of the Civil War, but now a most unhallowed place that had been before its closure a hotbed (please excuse the pun) of homosexuality among the seminarians in training for decades! It remains to be seen whether the Church will rid itself of these fawning apologists, these false prophets, these appeasers of the devil. Some say that a schism will take place within the Church, with the traditional believers going one way, and the purple, pro-normalization crowd going another, all to the growing displeasure of a watching, unpleased, and very angry God.

For fifty years now, suave persuaders of the left have postulated that they control morality, not God; however, the simple truth is that they wish to throw out the old standards and sanction a new licentiousness of their own construct; and increasingly that lame message has been tolerated, if not embraced by soft-headed, acquiescing priests. In recent years, as a kind of arch capper or new, nasty wrinkle, these same bad priests have begun to agitate for the easy acceptance of transgenderism, on top of the normalization of homosexuality.

By the same lax coupon, what if every heterosexual husband acted like Lothario, Priapus, or Don Juan. Le Marquis de Sade? Hugh Hefner? The point is obvious and odious and must be said clearly out loud: The cultural world is collapsing upon itself, now intent on its own suicide, upon its own self-immolation. It is like a tent with no center pole or an osteoporotic body with too little calcium in its bones: Both shall soon collapse. Under the leering threat of political correctness, and with the First Amendment diminishing every day more and more by the hour, we seem determine to give in to this cultish madness, introducing a rising cancer to the entire populace; a runaway contagion results with a flashing celerity, a little like my clear memory of seeing runaway mustangs sprinting across the high desert of northern Nevada near to Battle Mountain.

The resulting moral conundrum that we find ourselves in reminds me more than a little of the tactics of Tazio Nuvolari, the racecar driving Flying Mantuan from the 30s. He may have been the most skilled and, therefore, the fastest driver ever to have lived. Once he was asked how he could drive a "barca" so fast. He responded by saying that he was always either accelerating or braking, that is to say, that he never coasted or drifted, never. He knew that to progress and win he always had to push and prod the car to her fullest. (As is well known, by the tick, all beautiful things: Mountains, rivers, automobiles, ships, more are female.) And so it is with our temporary and fractured world: Always we are either getting better or we are getting worse. It is impossible to coast, to drift, to rest upon one's laurels. In the face of these sins denied, in the name of treacherous tolerance or desire untethered and unfettered, we think that it is possible to coast, to make excuses, to look the other way, to ignore, to act as if nothing corrosive or devious has happened; however, it is not possible to do any of those things, since the sin remains stubborn and obdurate, though these days that stark word is so rarely uttered.

So, for now, unless we as a culture wake ourselves from this spreading, self-induced, and crippling slumber, unless we recognize this endless sin and regard it as such, calling it by its real name, not for the first time either, unless we renounce it as harmful and dangerous, unless we begin again to speak assuredly and with no protective hesitation or kowtowing, our society will continue its downward path, a fast spiral into mean oblivion, no matter how strongly its proponents engage in practiced denial. After these 50 years of wanton experimentation, of prolificacy and abdication of our religious past (Sex as Sport! Sex as sport!), is it not time to say simply that it does not work? Is it not past time for children to be raised by a loving mother and father united in fidelity to each other? After this time of phony tolerance, is it not time to say that the sin remains? After this time of coerced perdition, is it not time for all of us to again be found? And after all the advertised surface fun, is it not better to be contrite and penitent and to ask Someone who knows a heck of a lot more than any of us for advice. For, as Saint Mark writes:

> ---This is the time of fulfillment. Reform your lives and believe in the gospel.
>
> The Gospel according to Saint Mark 2: 15

Cinque Sortite: Five Assaults Or Sallies Onto The Battlefield

Or read the prophet Hosea who says:

> ---O Isreal, come back! Return to your god! You're down but you're not out. Prepare your confession and come back to God.
>
> The Book of the Prophet Hosea 14: 1-3

Battlers upon the campo, and to reconnoiter or circle back, as is lately said, a close reading of these thoughts will dictate that they might equally been entitled, beyond "My Supposed Homophobia", "The Currents Depths of Sexual Confusion", "The Seduction of the Innocents", "The Consolations of Matrimonial Loyalty", or "How One Loses One's faith: A Step-By-Step Primer". This rubric cube has many sides, and the house has many corners, a few of them oblique, and some of which are not fully square. These issues are all part of one infinitely larger discussion, a small sliver of a greater piece of labyrinthian timber. At the core, again the only pertinent question must be this one:

> ---Who makes the rules, God or man?

And what is the point of crux of that punctilious question? Or, where is the heavy timber, to continue the house analogy. It is this: God gave us the Ten Commandments out of a calming love so that our lives would be vastly easier once we absorbed, embraced, and followed them. Before any of us were born, God understood that the sexual impulse, once aroused and abused, might be scat overwhelming, that those mounting desires might swamp us and ruin our better character, and that not all actions between the sheets are equal, as so many servile toadies of today pretend and proclaim. God tells us that there is proper sexual behavior, and improper sexual behavior, just as there are safe, and unsafe, ways to operate an automobile. Why should this simple concept be so shocking or foreign to us? Why should anyone have to conform to this new, strident, divergent, just-introduced status quo, one which tells us simply to be quiet and play dead. Instead, for those who still listen and pray to God, we are taught by Him that it is distinctly not sport, as the debased culture so often announces; 'tis a lie too often told. So, whence does our steep fall from grace, la caduta dalla grazia, stem or emanate?

That fall from grace which is all around us now in all men flows immediately from that oldest and most ignoble of sins: Pride, which is the catalyst for any separation from God. It is abject pride that tells us, dictates to us, that without penalty or derision we may no longer obey the rules set forth by God, that instead we make construct out of the clear blue sky some crazed dicta of our own, and that there will be no "downside" for such renegade, haughty actions. It is abject pride that whispers in our ears that God no longer counts, pertains, or love us. It is abject pride that fuels the "reproductive freedom" cadre, fascists intent upon selfish abortions. It is abject pride that postulates that anyone, and not just God, can make up the rules as he goes along life's twisting, turning path. And so, it is only abject pride that tells us that homosexuality is not a sin. We have wiped our backside on the door, or treated something lightly and nonchalantly, when we should not have done so. Starting with pride as the catalyst, that is, thinking that we know better, we commit a sin, and in that errant action we insult Jesus Christ. We offend Him and our friendship with

Him is thereby harmed. All of this is not complicated, but really quite simple.

However, if one is no longer prideful, a certain relaxing freedom may emerge, the freedom of obedience once one recognizes that a life lived with a simple modest adherence to the commandments (And I mean all of them, Dilbert, all of them!) leads to a less stressful, more peaceful life; and also that given that allegiance and fidelity, one will no longer be always buffeted by the constantly changing winds of one's own untamed desires, or by the mores of a decrepit, every-day-worsening culture bent upon the craven enslavement of its own people. Indeed, absent God, those desires and those mores may easily rule us all! Why did we ever begin to think that acceding to unguarded or perverse desires might be liberating? Truly, the opposite is true since constantly growing desires lead to a full mockery of freedom. What foolishness! These are ridiculous assumptions fraught with ill feeling and illogic! Thus, we toss feathers into the wind, working fruitlessly. Jean- Paul Sartre wrote many years ago, after having himself forsaken the idea that there might be a God:

---Man is condemned to be free.

From Jean-Paul Sartre's Lecture, "Existentialism is a Humanism, 1946

Today I wonder why he did not recall in the next breath the enslavement of the Greeks and the Romans (and many others) to unleashed, rampant desires? By the tingle, how do I know all of this well enough to write about it? Because, after time and many of my own wayward mis-steps, I have seen firsthand the failures of this prideful experiment, one that has been tried by all men from the beginning of time; but more than that, I have finally vanquished within myself abject pride and in the same instant have finally begun to trust God's word more than mine, and certainly more than society's morphing prurient dicta; I now know that often my eyes have been imperfect, myopic, occluded, glazed; and with his Grace from prayer I ask Him that more acute eyesight might come my way, and also for greater strength and direction, asking:

> ---What would You have me do now, Lord? What is Your next step for me along the path?

As we foot-soldiers tromp upon the edge of the battlefield, the pulverized dust rising up about our collars, always close to the view of the growing, vicious, hand-to-hand fighting that is all around us now and which shall never abate, and once God has been taken on as our leader, one particular idea must be proffered or put forth so that all of us, if we have the deep druthers to do it, may hold it firm, that hard rock of an idea, quella roccia dura di un'idea, and then, once again, hold it up to the nearest, clearest light, to examine it for unseen faults and cracks and fissures. And this is it: That waystation idea, or the temporariness of all of it, that our life here is but a brief and testing one; that we should be always ready for renewed conflict; that we must confront mean adversity and then surmount it; that we shall all be here for but a brief time; or as Shakespeare speaks through Prospero in the Tempest:

> ---These are actors...were all spirits and are melted into air, into thin air: And, like the baseless failure of this vision, the cloud-capped towers, the gorgeous

> palaces, the solemn temples, the great globe itself, Ye all which it inherit shall dissolve and, like this insubstantial pageant faded, Leave not a rack behind.

William Shakespeare; the Tempest; Act IV, Scene 1, Lines 1879-1887

Therefore, all those that live only for this transient world, who doubt the existence of judgment and an afterlife itself, who therefore fear no judgment of any sort upon death, whether it be stern or kind shall make no difference, those nonbelievers wrapped in sin would have said at the outset, to commence or jump-start the incipient disaster:

> ---What the hell! There is only this world and none other. I might as well have some fun while I am here. Carpe diem, or seize the hour!

It is no chowder then that these hinds fall with little majesty from the ox onto the ground, or drop into harder times. On the other tangle, those believing foot soldiers who suspect that there shall be some lilies in the field with the great unknown, death, after the heart ceases and the blood in the body stops its thumping and coursing, or some sort of other after-the-fact, considered reckoning or counting-up, are much more inclined to guard their behavior; they know in their already decaying bones that at the end there shall be a tallying up of some sort; and in turn they know enough in those bones to trust that the commandments might have been placed here as an assistance or an aid, l'aiuto, to all of us, rather than as a hinderance as they have been uniformly painted by the rakes and big-shots who attempt to run the morals (sic) of our world. These once misled and now misleading mentors usually think that they can bend the rules or just make some new ones. Oh, the arrogance and effrontery of those so loose in the bean.

The next step in any true life is to recognize the sin on the face of it; and to say that it is not a good idea to be a slave to any hedonism or vice in this world, a place increasingly dark and dangerous. It is forgotten common sense to say that a man should go where he should not be tempted. Instead, corruption rules the world and we move towards darkness. Unspeakable evil, cloaked and disguised as good, grows an aggressive atheism. We must confront the darkness in all things. Satan has set up a counter church, one devoid of divine vision. We must say to Satan:

    ---Get off my back!

Even Christ in the desert says:

    ---Save me from the traps they have set up for me.

    Psalm 141:9

All of this is corrigible or incorrigible as we alone determine it. As a counterpoint, and as a rebuttal, we know in our hearts that a return to the family is key to the salvation of our society, one now bent on its own destruction due to persistently lousy decisions made. After a time, those bad choices exact a stern price, I do warrant. Otherwise, our society, such as it is, teeters on the brink. It is not my job to condemn others, but to condemn their chosen life, and to demonstrate how dark and dangerous it is, and how it automatically kills the soul and embraces death. May I, tasking again, without coffee spoons, Myrtle, do this or must I, confronted by wave after wave of political correctness, bite my meagre tongue? Tacete! Taci! Cork it! Accordingly, once more, we must always regard the sin and not the sinner. We must study history for her probable, kind suggestions. We must achieve a better quality of thought via prayer and by using calm logic for someone else's benefit, and by always asking these sorts of pointed questions:

> ---What have I not yet considered? What else may possibly or probably go haywire? What will likely further happen if more and more lost and confused people, men and women both, join this popular cult, one blessed (sic) by the fawning crowd? And, why would we ever stupidly assume that this clear and obvious transgression upon both God and innate biology would ever work?

Any clear and serious study, as these brief words have attempted to be, will bear witness to homosexuality's failure in our world of both the past and the present, and that its normalization that is being crammed down our throats and that we daily see advancing, under the false guise of tolerance and accommodation, is but a Trojan Horse, a wolf in sheep's clothing, a soiled ruse or feint of clever tactic to embrace today's happy Satan, to refute and rebuke our patient God, and especially to kill off as fully dead or exterminate the family.

So, as common foot soldiers or pilots, trenchmen, piperoo grunts, pick-and-shovel boys, non-brass hat yearlings, we must not hang fire, dither back and forth, and pace in circles like sick hound dogs, but instead:

>   ---Hazard Zet Forward: Despite hazard, move forward,
>
> The motto of Seton Hall University, founded in 1856.

For now and in the meantime, as Doctor and Saint Luke would have it said, nel fra tempo, what ought to be done? (Luke 3: 10) Two things come to mind and most quickly so:

1. Develop further and propagate widely the idea that the normalization of homosexuality will not work, that is shall never work, and that its obverse, that it shall only cause deep inner distress and manifest disquietude, that "weeping and gnashing of the teeth" notion (Re: Luke 13:28), the greatest of inner turmoil. As a usually forgotten point of fact, insist upon the key notion that homosexuality in today's iteration of it is primarily culturally induced, not biologically determined. Remind people that wide acceptance of homosexuality as quite normal is a nothing less than a repudiation of ancient Christian dogma. As a practical matter, homosexuality has been and will continue to be a rotten ronchie, a hulking failure of the will, or a simple fiasco if one wishes to hear the Italian word for it. These sailors who so sail are desperate men and women, common desperados, clutching at straws and in the drink, that is, they are lost at sea or up the creek without a paddle, near-to-drowning and without a Mae West life vest beside the sinking ship, and soon they will cast off the last anchor. Perhaps they shall never see clearly, thru God's kind grace, their own past missteps. Perhaps too, they will never

grasp that what is so insidious (from the Latin word, insidiosus, meaning lying in wait for) or entrapping is this fact: Once the sin has been committed, the primeval psychology of the trap-handed sinner, eternal Quisling to himself, lost lam men all, he shall as one footstep marching forward follows the last, deny responsibility, alleging to himself that everything is A-OK, on the up, copacetic, tickety-boo, and just a raise-the-wind joyride. After the sin is made, impious self-justification instantly rules the mind and motive. There are not certain of the truth; indeed, many, perhaps most, do not care one whit or ransom about it. This phenomenon is part of the evil of sin and how it frightfully, stealthily, works, and worms its twisting way into the deepest sequestered corner of our souls. The mechanism of sin! For, it is natural for the sinner to deny any and all wrongdoing. These are times akin to those of the vicious Nero of Roma; we inhabit a world in the grip of similar evil. The world is missing something, and it is not a higher percentage of homosexual unions that shall save us. And perhaps, it if to be hoped, that at some point in the future that he who had been locked into this trouncing evil will look upwards for Someone to lead that person through the gift of Grace back to grounded land and to grateful safety. If they were a regiment of paratroopers, perhaps part of Operation Dragoon of Southern France in August of '44, maybe the flying fortresses would give to them some needed cover, so that those doughboys might depart the hidden swamps and lower mere lands, leave the twisting hedge-row country for some high ground on the steeply rising side of Sainte-Victoire Mountain, and in that course no longer be a portion for foxes. Yet, how in common blazes' name shall that unlikely metamorphosis ever happen? By some strange tincture, trace, or vestige? No, by simple prayer, and that fact leads us to the second job that awaits.

2. With only simple, merciful love in our hearts, we must pray for these errant men and women, those that over godless time and with much assiduous practice, have taught themselves to be raunchy sybarites who are:

---Constantly hunting, never satisfied by their adventures...eternal prowlers, tireless sexual adventurers.

> As the poet Paul Moran describes Marcel Proust in Journal Inutile, tome 2: 1973-1976.

We are all known by God and completely loved by Him, everyone of us, no matter the state of our soul. Such a thing is a miracle! All slaves need to be set free. We must pray (we are commanded, not suggested, to do so) that the dissidents will turn away from this callous life which does so assuredly destroy the soul and which promotes the sexual factor beyond any proper measure or reason, and too, and equally, which singlehandedly destroys and decimates the family. Most of us (not that we are superior, but with eyes wide open) with common sense and a modicum of graceful faith know that if any man is a sexual adventurer, one who is bent on continuing with that lascivious life, that he necessarily shall sadly be excluded from the more sublime side of life; he shall be by his actions excluded from the mirth of life's feast. Thus, sin is once again seen as deleterious, a word from the Medieval Latin word, deleterious, meaning to harm or injure. Those caught in Satan's web must turn away. But will they listen if they hear the words:

---Fall on your knees! Fall! Hear the angels' voices.

And will they understand that victory is achieved when only one man is saved? For, as Saint Paul writes:

>---There will be glory, honor and peace for everyone who has done good.

>The Epistle of Saint Paul to the Romans 2:10

And:

>---For just as through the disobedience of the one man many were made sinners, so, through the obedience of the one, the many will be made righteous.

>The Epistle of Saint Paul to the Romans 5: 10

As we pray for those who have gone off-track, haywire, and who are now broken, confused, or despairing, though they may not say so, we understand that their return to the fold is, at least, a 5-step process, and too, one which must be carried out in the right sequence, a little like how a pilot of a jet readies the big bird for take-off from the runway:

1. The sinner must recognize the sin,
2. He must pray that he shall vanquish it,
3. He must resolve to renounce it,
4. He must make some sort of penance or restitution, and finally,
5. He must stride out in his new world with God's grace at his back and no longer be loaded down with such heavy baggage as grievous sin upon his back.

Numbers 1 and 2 may be interchangeable, since the debate is the usual one of what comes first, the chicken or the egg? Perhaps prayer is needed first, so that then the depth of the sin, one which makes us estranged from God, may be truly seen for the first time. In any case, throughout this whole process of resurrection and renewal, the sinner, about to be one no longer, must know that God in His infinite compassion loves all of us, every one of us, fully, unconditionally, and forever, no matter how deep the evil or constant the sin.

And, so, by a merciful and loving God, all of us soldiers and wingmen have been given these new, precise marching orders. Indeed, with regret and disdain, some may term it a morning headache or bugle call. We have not been paying proper attention, sailors, soldiers, so, now it is past tender time to evangelize, to say no to evil (re: death), to get the lead out, to sound off, to go to the mat, and to earn our wings. We must no longer pass the buck, shirk our shoulders, or shrug it off, saying that it, this crass normalization, it is really nothing to worry about; the lying proponents have said for years that we would be better off to calm down, which makes sense since all wars, like this one, are about deception. No: For years now, we have been too calm, too passive, too sleepy headed. No sir, not by a yardarm! We must put on our war shoes, the heavy boots for the long field slogging across the campo and veldt that lies ahead. We must no longer be calm, but vigilant, decrying death-making evil whenever and wherever it is beheld. We must say to the off-the-rails proponents:

> ---Says who? Says who? Who do you think you are making up these new lousy rules? Because of you, we are all in a tight spot. This is just a booby trap. Tell me, are you some sort of crap king-in- waiting and we just did not know it? Who put you in charge, mama's boy? Who gave you the charge to make up your own rules, malarkey man, mallet head?

Again, we must learn to pray for those that commit this sin, one which like all sins separates one from God and His Grace; let us pray that those trapped in this dissolving and hurtful life will begin to recognize the extreme waywardness of their ways, how it shall never lead to anything good or noble, and that in living this life, one brought to prominence and the fore by a declining culture, every day they do push themselves, separate themselves further away from God. Coached by misleading, once misled, mentors, they flail away at unseen demons since all the time they are surrounded by Satan's mirage and ghost; these practitioners attempt self-justification (even though Seneca, once again, tells us not to do so), yet that gambit of conscience-soothing does not work in the least and never shall, for even in the dim of the night, in the dark night of the soul, one's prodding, pushing conscience always knocks softly upon the heavy oaken door. That action may be termed what James Joyce calls:

---the agenbite of inwit.

James Joyce's book Ulysses, Episode One: Telemachus, Shakespeare and Company, Paris, 1922

He speaks of the recurring remorse of a conscience in proper tune, that it never, ever, goes away, that it never stops the tapping upon the door of the soul, no matter how much one may wish it to desist and stop the pounding, that tapping, the knocking upon that door. A good conscience never stops; instead, it nags. Whenever I see gays committed to that life of death, I once more see, ascertain, and sense the deep and profound, long away hurt in their shrouded eyes, a very deep and unsaid sorrow that never goes away, diminishes, or departs; too, I regard the tangled sexual confusion and the full absence of any real and patient joy.

I am reminded of the utterly lost Samaritan Woman in the Gospel of Saint John (4:4-26). She has had five husbands, and now lives with a sixth man who is married to some other woman; Jesus offers her the healing waters, but is she willing to take it and reform her life? Sometimes, these men and women with their hurting eyes seem to ask me for solace, some sort of benediction, a kind word or phrase; however, I cannot give to them my blessing since that is not my job, nor do I possess a scant of that redeeming power; instead, I can only pray from them, with constancy and no superiority or derision, that they shall soon turn away from these harmful, ruinous ways forever. There is no doubt that in proper, devoted time, as they pray, they shall reach a new peace, one found through Grace, since as Saint Paul tells us:

> ---Guard the good deposit that was entrusted to you---guard it with the help of the Holy Spirit who lives in us.
>
> The Epistle of Saint Paul: 2 Timothy 1:14

And if they ask for my tinder thoughts, I shall say to them:

> ---Man proposes, God disposes.
>
> Proverbs XVI: 9

All men have been given by God a free will to change on any chosen day the route through this tangled world, should they choose to implement that component within their character. We all can select a new path, a new road through the thickest forest. Illusion may be very powerful, or so says Bolt. Still, whoever freely admits a betrayal, especially a betrayal of Christ? In the beginning it is always an over-reaching pride that drives all men, including myself, to sin, by thinking that I am better than God, that I know more than He does, that I know a priori what is the best course to follow, and without asking for His Grace through prayer to better ascertain the best choice for that route.

Two things I have learned during the course of this small composition: It is better to approach myself objectively as one midway on the road of our life, or:

> ---I found myself within a shadowed forest for I had lost the path that does not stray.
>
> Mi ritrovai per una selva oscura, che la diritta via era smarrita.

Divine Comedy, by Dante Alighieri; The Inferno, Canto I; Completed in 1320, a year before his death.

That is to say, I must learn to regard myself from outside myself, to see if I have made progress or have been only fooling myself with compounding delusions, lousy excuses, and foolish evasions. This is called using one's conscience for the good, and, like anything else, to do it right takes practice.

And secondly, that it is better to approach those bent upon the homosexual path, determined to shun God's path and to join that cult which always descends toward Hades and oblivion, more with abiding love than with mocking censure, since that former course will produce the more fruitful tree:

> ---For as through the one man's disobedience the many were made sinners, so also that obedience of the One many will be made righteous.
>
> The Epistle of Saint Paul to the Romans 5: 19

To be a better Christian, I must put myself in the shoes of the transgressor and imagine what it is like to be so lost, to be on that awful road to perdition, to be without real joy or patient peace, to be in that terrible place where sin abounds and entraps and engulfs; yet always the way out, simply to be free, to lose the sin forever, is always possible since Grace exists, but first of all, that Grace must be requested. Even Christ was tempted during His forty days in the wilderness. His tempter was Satan:

> ---Jesus said to him: "Away from me, Satan. For it is written: Worship the Lord, your God, and serve Him only."
>
> The Gospel according to Saint Matthew 4: 10

As we round the last corner on the way towards home, the finish line, again I must make a stark confession: I ought to have written this small piece, my measly two cents' worth, many years ago, since as a lowly follower of Saint Michael the Archangel, it was my assigned job to do so. I did not do my job. I have been slow and tardy, weak and procrastinating. After all, I was raised to fight against evil. I was always taught that if I saw something wrong that I must immediately fight against it, do something about it, and not to pause to dither, loll, twitch, or twiddle my useless fingers. Perhaps I have had a broad yellow down my back all these years, but that is just another lousy, lame-ass excuse, isn't it? For too long I was silent and passive, only watching the slow death of a culture. As Saint Catherine of Siena writes:

> ---Spread the truth in a thousand voices. It is silence that kills.

As this battle for souls is joined, we must stop our past passivity and timidity, the acquiescence and looking the other way; instead, we must become fully adult, stronger Christians, much more forceful and powerful. C. S. Lewis tells us precisely how this contest must be fought, that is, if it is to be won:

> ---As Saint Paul points out, Christ never meant that we were to remain children in the intelligence: On the contrary. He told us to be not only 'as harmless as doves', but also 'as wise as serpents'. He wants a child's heart, but a grown-up's head. He wants us to be simple, single-minded, affectionate, and teachable, as good children are; but He also wants every bit of intelligence we have to be alert at its job, and in first-class fighting trim.

C. S. Lewis; Mere Christianity; Harper Collins; 1952; page 77

Anyone who pleases God is already victorious. And God does not abandon such a person, nor shall He ever. All of life is a choice, since God gave us that thing called free will. Am I acting like an avenging angel? It is not for me to decide, but rather, to do. Intimidation and coercion have been used to weaken my resolve, to soften, not stiffen my spine, since this is how cultural wars are fought now. I just think that the homosexual life is the wrong road, and that it shall only lead anyone who takes it to desperation, depression, anxiety, and estrangement from God, as all sins do. One fact is clear: It is not possible to be a Christian and a homosexual at the same time, no matter what the lavender mob may decree so assuredly from the mountaintop. Today many well-respected leaders of the church are attempting to twist the words, in effect, to sanction homosexuality, to say that it does not carry the weight of sin with it, to say that is fine to practice that abomination in life, to allege that it is not contrary in the least with God's plan for us.

For most of my adult life, these idiot appeasers have been dancing with the devil for decades and the net effect of this compromise with sin has created three conditions within the people:

1. Confusion,
2. Dissolution, and
3. Enervation

These prideful, better-than-God actors on the stage stretch the truth for the gain of the moment, and I say again that they are wolves in sheep's clothing, Trojan Horses intent upon vanquishing the city once they are safely within her walls.

Today many leaders in the church promote a secularist modernism and also, contrary to dogma, foster a false catechesis based on at least four fronts:

1. Contraception, accepted in 1965
2. Divorce, accepted in 1969
3. Abortion, accepted in 1973
4. Homosexuality, accepted in 2015

when the Supreme Court by a 5 to 4 vote overturned the Defense of Marriage Act. The near-universal acceptance of these four false catechesis, as told by Church Militant, are now leading us to a full Moral Collapse (April 19, 2021).

It should here be noted that the sage and prescient Doctor Charles Rice (1931-2015), for decades a professor at Notre Dame School of Law, pointed out of all of this years ago. Professor Rice knew that our general acquiescence to these false teachings presaged faith's collapse, and represented the first chink in the armor of the faithful. He writes that the general acceptance of these four false truths, with barely a vigorous or healthy discussion about any of them within both the clergy and the laity, that passivity acted as a catalyst towards an unbenign acceptance of relativism, which in turn signaled the beginning of the gradual erosion of true faith. Further, he writes that while Pope John Paul II wrote Evangelium Vitae (published March 25, 1995), that encyclical proposing the old idea that life is sacred, and that parents using contraception are essentially acting as arbiters of death, acting as gods in determining whether a child may be conceived and live or not, that treatise was largely ignored by the church and people at-large, and thus a culture of death began to arise all about us. Thus, slowly and subconsciously for many, we have entered into a wicked place. If we are to be rid of that wicked place, we would be wise to further study Doctor's Rice's brilliant analysis, one that step by step charts the decline of faith in our culture.

An Augustinian priest who instructed me in high school and who later dropped out of that order has spent many decades consoling and feeling sorry for homosexuals, trying to gain dignity and respect for them, when he should have been quietly praying for them, telling that they were loved by a merciful God, and urging them to renounce the monstrous sin. For decades now too many of these soft-in-the-head, mealy-mouthed prelates have spent way too much talking about tolerance and forbearance, and not near enough time talking about separation from God and judgment, or what used to be termed back in the day "the wages of sin".

Too, an extremely prominent Jesuit priest (who shall remain nameless) who strides upon that world-wide stage with his errant voice has been telling us with sneaky guile that it is basically OK to be homosexual, and further, that same-sex marriages ought to be blessed within the church. Also, for decades and unbelievably, seminaries, holy places that out to be about prayer, meditation, and learning, instead, have been rife with closeted homosexual behavior, led by wayward seminary leaders who are by this late date expert at grooming young men to become practicing and content homosexuals. All of these attempts from these wayward dissident apostates (and there are dozens more) are rankly seditious, treasonous, contrary to the Catechism of the Church, and therefore must be thwarted, for they will only lead to greater consternation, and more "weeping, and gnashing of the teeth". For too long passive watchers of these declines in behavior, we traditionalists who adhere to the true faith have in that very passivity lost all moral force. As a once Christian culture, we have lost track of who we once were and accordingly, it is no surprise that we find ourselves deep in the middle of Dante's dark forest. We have been killing our culture as well as offending God, and too, riding ourselves of His needed Grace. We would be wise to consider the Latin phrase:

> ---Perto et Praesto. I stand firm and I stand first.

And, more than anything else, we would be wise to recall these words from the Prayer of Saint Michael the Archangel:

> ---Saint Michael the Archangel, defend us in battle. Be our protection against the wickedness and snares of the devil; May God rebuke him, we humbly pray; And do thou, O Prince of the Heavenly Host, by the power of God, thrust into hell Satan and all evil spirits who wander through the world for the ruin of souls. Amen.

In the last forty years I would be remiss if I did not mention another other obvious and odious trend, that the world is fully flooded, inundated, and awash in pornography, only sold to make dirty money and to grow larger the vice (Its crafty managers say: Do not restrain yourself! Do not restrain! Enjoy! Enjoy!). Constantly, trendy modernists and agnostic secularists sternly tell us that pornography is good for you, so indulge, indulge, and give in to that pleasure and make it grow. In the midst of this cancerous milieu, nobody seems ready or able to ask the obvious and important question:

> ---What is the long-term effect of this insidious embrace? What shall it do to one's soul?

This sort of bent addiction has never been tried before, but one can guess the results, that is, if the eyes are open and the ears clear. We now have teenagers (and younger!) who with the click or tap on their cellphone can access the most twisted scenes; however, can that be good and wholesome for the growth of a person? In truth, the so-called porn industry is but a sad transmutation of God's sublime plan, that a man and woman might unite and stay together, with sex used as an occasional glue for the more solid joining. However, in today's abject, ugly, off-track, and coercive world pornography has taken the firmest hold, and many people become addicted to it, not realizing the quick and coarsening damage it does to one's sensibility. Even so, the porn industry is full of "performers" who are beset by drugs, depression, distress, and suicide; yet also, miraculously and through vigilant prayer, some "adult actors" have managed to leave it behind since with passing time and constant prayer they have fully understood the incalculable damage that it automatically does to one's soul.

Employing that famous red herring tactic of all debaters and as a last-ditch and feeble effort, some stubborn apologists for homosexuality allege that Jesus never addressed the issue of homosexuality; and that, therefore, we should be free, unhampered by any doctrine or dogma, to make up our own rules in this regard (So intent some are in their arch illogic to upset the rules of God!). And here I would be remiss if I do not acknowledge the writings and teachings of Voddie Baucham, Junior. Preacher and Professor Baucham guides us to the simple idea that marriage can only be between a man and a woman; and further, that marriage is God's beautiful design, and that there is none other; that God working as the three-part Godhead of the Father, the Son, and the Holy Spirit is the author of that marriage; that man would justly need a female companion throughout his life; that the Bible is one story that does not vary; and that this sacred christening of the idea of marriage, not the sanctity of same sex unions, stems from these simple words taken from Saint Matthew:

> ---When Jesus had finished saying these things, he left Galilee and went into the region of Judea to the other side of the Jordan. Large crowds followed

> him, and he healed them there. Some Pharisees came to him to test him. They asked, "Is it lawful for a man to divorce his wife for any and every reason?" "Haven't you read," he replied, "that at the beginning the Creator 'made them male and female,' and said, 'For this reason a man will leave his father and mother and be united to his wife, and the two will become one flesh. So, they are no longer two, but one flesh. Therefore what God has joined together, let no one separate."
>
> The Gospel according to Saint Matthew 19:1-6

Therefore, as Preacher Baucham clearly points out, man alone simply does not have the right or authority, the power or provenance to make hallowed same-sex unions, to sanction homosexuality or any other various deviancy, and nor will he ever; and try as I might, nowhere in the Bible can I find any passages saying that a man must find another man with whom to spend his life. In other words, advocates of the homosexual life justify that position by making things up, by lies and distortions, by breeding future propagandists who will make the same flawed speech into their futures, and by touting a declining society's lousy mores instead of our past society's true morals. In truth, though the practitioners of the same sex life do deny it, scoff at it, and mock the notion, Satan is everywhere around us these days in our disintegrating and dissolute world, sending messages of entrapment and seeking to ensnare our minds and souls in the anguish and enervation that all sin brings. I am reminded of these words of Saint Paul:

> ---But I am afraid that just as Eve was deceived by the serpent's cunning, your minds may somehow be led astray from your sincere and pure devotion to Christ.
>
> The Epistle of Saint Paul to 2 Corinthians 11: 3

Therefore, especially in this increasingly corrupt and demonic world, always we must be alert and vigilant, much more attentive and ready to move, as all sailors and soldiers must be, for the corrosive work of the devil never ceases. Rarely does he say his name, and often, he remains hidden, sequestered in the shadows. Therefore, as Saint Mark tells us:

> ---And what I say unto you I say onto all: Watch! Stay awake!
>
> The Gospel according to Saint Mark 13: 37

This conflict between the forces and good and evil then is a just another battle, one like many others, and we would be wise to gird ourselves for the lengthy siege ahead. At last, finally, I am anxious, fidgety, and hopeful for the fray that awaits. And that's the truth! Always the devil is busy and never rests. In this fight which shall only expand, we must take no prisoners, and to do that we must be filled with determination and grit, resolve and endurance. To accomplish that, we must first further cement our own friendship with Christ; also, we must have a full belief in Him. As we round the final corner and finally head to the train station at the end of the line, we would be wise to consider these words from the Book of Revelation:

> ---I heard a loud voice from the throne saying, "Behold, God's dwelling is with the human race. He will dwell with them and they will be his people and God himself will always be with them as their God. He will wipe away any tear from their eyes, and there shall be no more death or mourning, wailing, or pain, for the old order has passed away.' The One who sat on the throne said, 'Behold, I made all things new'."
>
> The Book of Revelation 21: 1-5

These words bring to mind this simple idea: That daily, fervent prayer to God is necessary, not optional; however, so often in our increasingly secularized world, that notion gets no play, no play at all; further, we are told by society's imperious and pompous elites that we are not servants of God, and that we do not need to ask God for strength and direction; but alternatively, that we are independent demigods free to choose our own path, however dangerous, corrosive, or fracturing it may be. However, the truth is the obverse, that we are not gods, but instead mere humans made in His likeness, and that all of us need a functioning, working conscience, something which, through God's mysterious Grace, must be re-honed every day, just like we must continually eat properly and do calisthenics and bicep curls in the gym to make ourselves stronger.

For near to certain, as I adjudge it (though, who am I, who am I? Less than a flea, smaller than dust), we are in our last days, close to a total moral collapse, near to the end days of fractious disintegration and utter mayhem. All children, including my children, are now raised in a world that has deemed with no authority that the same-sex life is but another option; and it that perverted capacity, society has fully circumvented my authority as their parent and guardian. New and even uglier unimaginable depravities now arise, with more to come, doubtless. Everywhere, we have turned our backs away from God; and, what is more, routinely we shun and mock Him, for, once a man declares oneself to be an atheist or agnostic, as we have seen, it is an easy hop, step, and a jump to begin making up one's rules, without God's tempering hand to guide him. Practitioners within this same-sex cult that is all around of now, which is painted as something normal and harmless and fun, they have tried to wave a wand to relieve the sin of its burden or curse; yet, obdurately and as we have witnessed, the sin remains fixed and stubborn, like a far-off Montana mountain that looms upon the prairie high into the sky. Indeed, the more it is denied, the greater that sin rises. Therefore, we would be wise to consult the words of 2 Timothy:

> ---But mark this: there will be terrible times in the last days. People will be lovers of themselves, lovers of money, boastful, proud, abusive, disobedient to their parents, ungrateful, unholy, without love, unforgiving, slanderous, without self-control, brutal, not lovers of the good, treacherous, rash, conceited, lovers of pleasure rather than lovers of God---having a form of godliness but denying its power. Have nothing to do with such people.
>
> From the Epistle of Saint Paul to 2 Timothy 3:1-5

Don't those stark words exactly and precisely describe our ugly world of today? If these words are read widely and take hold, perhaps in a pig's eye, it shall one day in a distant morrow be writ of me:

> ---Let the first budger die the other's slave. And the gods doom him often.

Marcius speaking to Aufidius in William Shakespeare's Coriolanus Act I, Scene 8, Line 5

By what the heck! I shall enjoy the castigations and whoops and hollers, the more the better, for they shall bring me and all other dissidents from the modern realm a growing strength and a greater vigor.

What then is next? Luke, pray tell, my leader, what then must we do? So, now, after having done those two things, decrying the normalization and praying for those who engage in it, towards what beautiful city on a hill must we march, that is, where is the next fight, or for what result may we hope? Also, once again two things arise from the pulverized dust and most speedily so, saying:

1. I hope that all those confronted with the foolish power of this descending vice shall in constant time denounce it, as many have done, and instead grasp the full and miraculous extent of God's love and mercy. I hope that they listen well to Him when he says:

   ---Yet even now, says the Lord, return to me with your whole heart, with fasting, and weeping and mourning. Rend your heart, not your garments, and return to the Lord, your God. For gracious and merciful is he, slow to anger, rich in kindness and relenting in punishment.

The Book of Joel 2: 12-13

And I hope, to finish the story or to close the circle, il giro, that we shall again read and further study our beginning and wisest mentor, Saint Augustine, who too was once beset, plagued by these mounding sins of the flesh. There we shall learn with his guidance once more that each temptation mastered shall make us stronger. Otherwise, he might not have written our concluding lines:

---We make a ladder for ourselves out of the vices when we trample them.

But, still, the close reader may scold and ask: How improbable! How unlikely! Then, what must be the exact mechanism by means of which this fundamental transformation of any average man's soul may be engendered and then fulfilled? Yet, 'tis easy and facile and not a thing to be long discussed or much debated. Here is the only answer, and our Second Hope:

2. Grace. Grace it is. It will come into a man's soul yet only if it is asked for. It shall not happen alone. It must be asked for. We must first ask. We must ask for it with resolute hearts, firm resolve, and plain eagerness. And, once it is asked for, then it shall flow towards us, any of us, no matter our prior debasements or pride or callousness, like a strong river flowing downhill off the mountain, one

> unencumbered and unchecked. We should be wise to not forget or dismiss, discount, the strong force of those salving waters.

For, more than anything, and with neither derision nor insult, we must pray for these disordered men and women, that they shall renounce this wayward, prideful, unsafe life in which they are ensnared and which shall only lead to distress, discontent, and depression. What is their best path to renewal, to salvation, to saying goodbye to the seductive enslavements of evil? Pope John Paul II has the clear answer when he speaks these words to those in the firmest grip of sin:

> ---The greater the misery of the penitent, the greater God's Divine Mercy.

The Pope wrote his encyclical, Dives in Misericodia, publishing it on November 10, 1980 and also instituted Divine Mercy Sunday, underlining the fact that God loves us all equally and fully, something that may be hard for most of us to grasp. God wants all of His prodigal sons to return home. Again, the Pope understood that God's merciful grace is free, but that it first must be requested.

There is always hope, even for the abject and miserable, those trapped in this awful sin, for as Saint Augustine, who himself went through a terrifying descent into evil, only to then rise up above it, writes:

> ---How I wept when I heard your hymns and canticles, being deeply moved by the sweet singing of your church. Those voices flowed into my ears, truth filtered into my heart, and from my heart

surged waves of devotion. Tears ran down, and I was happy in my tears.

Earlier, Saint Augustine had himself studied these words from Saint Paul, as a catalyst for his own re-birth, the better for his own soul's resurrection and to finally retreat away from the tenacious and tentacled grip of sin:

> ---Let us walk properly as in the daytime, not in orgies and drunkenness, not in sexual immorality and sensuality, not in quarreling and jealousy. But put on the Lord Jesus Christ, and make not provision for the flesh, to gratify its desires.

The Epistle of Saint Paul to the Romans 13: 13-14

Yes, there is always hope, even for those who have for decades led this destructive and anxiety-causing life apart from God. Divine Mercy will arrive, but, again, first it must be openly and truly requested. Let us recall the well- known suggestion: Ask and you shall receive (Sant Matthew 7: 7). As Pope John Paul II said at the Shrine of Divine Mercy in Cracow, Poland on June 7, 1991:

> ---Those who sincerely say 'Jesus, I trust in you' will find comfort in all their anxieties and fears.

There is nothing more man needs than Divine Mercy, the love which is benevolent, which is compassionate, which rises man above his weaknesses and to the infinite heights to the holiness of God.

First, the sin must be acknowledged, and then a

confession must be made, both of which can only take place if Grace is near. As is written in the Acts of the Apostles:

> ---Turn to God, that your sins may be wiped away!
>
> The Acts of the Apostles 3: 19

So, then, all you wayfarers, sojourners, sailors and soldiers upon the heath or ship or congested, bloodied battlefield, all of you rangers and paratroopers and legions gnawed at by festering wounds, growing fear, or encroaching diseases, let us at the last close by recalling the simple words of an old hymn that you may know already:

> ---Through many dangers, toils and snares, I have already come. 'Tis grace has brought me safe thus far. And grace will lead me home.
>
> Amazing Grace was written in the late 1700s by John Newton (1725-1807), a slave trader prone to drunkenness, revelry and profane living.

As a directive to myself, yet one as an admonition also shared with you, should you wish to receive it, I give to myself this clear instruction, lest any of these prior words be too harsh or scolding. Jesus tells me, and all of us:

> ---I give to you a new commandment: Love one another. As I have loved you, so you also should love one another. This is how all will know that you are one of my disciples, if you have love for one another.
>
> The Gospel According to Saint John 13: 34-35

And finally, we all must pray the aforementioned prayer to Saint Michael the Archangel, his special, strong prayer, for aid and determination and vigor in this battle against the normalization of crass homosexuality, to slow and then stop that attendant moral collapse, a vanquishing which must be fully accomplished, for the peaceful future of the world and countless souls' salvation does depend upon that victory. Please know that public opinion will never be our manager in this fight against corruption, and further, how others gauge these efforts is not important; for what is matters is only that this forlorn sin goes away. As Saint John Vianney writes:

> ---Do not try to please anybody. Try to please God, the angels and the saints. They are your public.

For far too long we have all been yellow-back cowards, afraid to speak up. Here I speak to myself. Now, through lassitude and laziness in many circles, homosexuals hold sway, but they can only be that powerful with the passive, sleepy consent of the people. Now, finally, while our culture teeters on the brink of a full moral collapse, it is time for all of us to speak, to protest, to pray, to love, and to lead.

So, (And I say this to myself as well!) quit being a sappy lobster, stop the sitting around and lollygagging, the finger-pointing and the dithering and the endless rocking back and forth, get your detail together on the double, chop-chop, follow the true Papasan only, and with tireless Geronimo as your model know that there are so many long battles to fight and so much more difficult work to do, and finally, that all of these efforts need to be carried out now, pronto, adesso, as there are today, just at this very minute, so many suffering souls who are submerged in the deepest trouble.

NB: The Netherlandish Proverbs were used throughout the text, to bring us backwards in time unwittingly to another age, another distant time and place, when proud evil equally strode the world.

DUGRI: INTEGRITY OR THE IMPORTANCE OF ONE'S WORD

>---Lies will kill you quicker than cancer, quicker than booze.

From Husbands, a 1970 film directed by John Cassavetes (1929-1989) from his screenplay

>---The Truth, Helen, is always the right answer.

Amon Goeth speaking to Helen Hirsch in Schindler's List, a 1993 film directed by Stephen Speilberg from the Thomas Keneally book and the Stephen Zaillian screenplay

>---Why can't you give me a straight answer anymore?

Michael Corleone speaking to Tom Hagan in The Godfather II, a 1974 film directed by Francis Ford Coppola, from a screenplay he co-wrote with Mario Puzo

>---Prevarication: The Latin word, varico, means I straddle, and prevaricor means I go zigzag or crooked. The verb, says Pliny, was first applied to men who ploughed crooked ridges, and afterwards to men who gave crooked answers in the law courts (can you imagine?), or deviated from the straight line of truth.

Dominic M. Martin

> Brewer's Dictionary of Phrase and Fable;
> edited by Ivor H. Evans; Cassell Publishers,
> Ltd.; London, 1981; Page 891

> ---You believed that stuff? How could you think such a thing could ever happen? If you have something to say, say it. Does the first Amendment even exist today? How can we love each other if we do not first tell the truth?

Faced with this dilemma of the truth, whether we should speak it or equivocate, mislead, and connive, we should ask ourselves, or perhaps it would be better to say, task ourselves, with this obvious question: Why does near every message get garbled in that simple transmission? Here in the middle of the sea, in the center of the battle, it is always another story, right, Wolfie? Often, folks who demonstrate a dishonest selfishness (saying that if I am happy, the world is happy...), they insist upon calling everyone outside their privileged sphere a friend, when they distinctly are not. Use your head, said not for the first time. Faced with these prevalent gaps in the hedge, growing holes in the wall, so many missing files and more, it is clear that we need to invent or adopt a whole new language, an entirely different manner of speaking, since falsehoods build, just as old milk shall grow sour. For a better, cleaner life, lies must be banished, chased away, and all evasions eliminated; however, one wonders, given man's innate proclivity for simple, easy fibbing, whether such a thing is possible. So, we shall now speak of smiling birds of a feather, and to do that well, we shall need to go back, as usual, to distant childhood, those days when we first learned to speak the simplest truth. For this bargain, good people only are required. So, let us begin to describe precisely how one ought to speak.

As a boy, I can recall once being caught in a jam or mean pickle. When caught stealing a warm oatmeal cookie just out of the oven, those baked for a charity and not for me, and after having sneaked a couple, I was tempted to lie to my loving mother, to tell a fib, to, as the resident corps commander, mislead my troops into mean oblivion. On the other hand, and in the back of my head all the time, I remember how both my parents persistently used to warn and caution me with the two reasons why one should never lie:

1. To tell the truth is always the right thing to do.
2. If one tells the sterling truth, one does not have to carry the burden of having to keep straight the lies!

However, as a man goes grows older, it may appear to many that lies become more and more necessary, fully essential for success; yet, how is that so? How that creeping slide into prevarication commences is the point of this small tale.

If one is unlucky enough to have a practiced fibber as a parent, it is much less likely that a child will be inclined to tell the clear and open truth. One thief begets another. Many years ago, I had the trying experience of working with such a colleague whose father was not honest and whose son, unsurprisingly, also turned out to be fundamentally untruthful. Earlier I had played some basketball with him, and I had noticed how on the court he was likely to cheat, to call a foul when there had been none, and the like. Later, in our many business dealings together, he would rarely tell me the full or, as it used to be termed, "unvarnished" truth. Thus, his speaking was more theatre than truth. In the main every day his aim was to create illusions and cast aspersions upon others as a form of one upmanship. Daily, he spoke to advance his own private cause, usually a financial advantage of some sort, though he would never say so outright. Sometimes, after he let loose with a yet another fake and phony whopper, I would ask myself:

> ---What put that notion in your heard? Where did you find those disjointed words?

He never defined his terms or spoke with precision; instead, he held things back, as if playing a game of five card stud poker late at night while sipping good Bourbon neat. Always he spoke in a kind of private code, a jesting and bantering and feinting one, full of misleading quips and hard-to-discern asides, muttered utterances whose real meaning anyone would be unable to ferret. This shell game with words was his convenient friend and he never wanted to get rid of it. His was a shell game since he never came clean about anything. Over the years he had practiced bloviation to create a cloud of confusion, contradiction, and deflection, and he enjoyed obscurity, obfuscation, and any clouded thought. He liked to keep things "loose", and he did not like being pinned down. Over the long, unfortunate years that I knew him, he was intentionally abstruse, resistant to clear comprehension, and he played with words as if his diction, his choice of words, was some sort of obscure, sequestered game only played out within his own head. He liked to make the other man or woman guess his meaning. A listener might try to read his opaque face for a clearer meaning and only see his occluded eyes blink. He thought communication was his private game, and he was the main marionette in charge. Therefore, I and the others with whom he worked could only guess at what he meant; and it was this deliberate inexactness that he used to create a daily advantage.

I imagine that he must have perversely enjoyed this sloppy mode of speaking, since he saw his listeners, including myself, squirm with questions, confusions, and hesitations. Maybe that stance of his and our reactions to it made him feel proud or powerful, that he was the joker guy in charge in his endless power play with flier words. In sum, he rarely if ever said what he meant, nor meant what he said; and for that simple reason he was simply a pain in the rear to work with. He loved to create verbal chaos. He enjoyed and luxuriated in the con, the easy swindle, the full-of-hot-air deception, the hurrah's nest of confusion, and the nasty kettle of fish resulting. His was a lame game of subterfuge and deflection, implied yet ungranted inferences, and large issues left unsaid or unclear. Over time I came to regard him as someone untrustworthy; I did not trust his words; and I gradual saw him as a gyp gunman or buffoon, like a corrupt sheriff of the posse out chasing the bad guys who should not have been appointed to that high position in the first place. He certainly was not a trusted gentleman whose word was routinely solid, nor an honest businessman with whom one might reliably conjoin finances. He thought nothing of telling tall serpentine tales, always to his own cloaked advantage. Gradually I learned to limit my time with him, since his words could not be taken at face value, but rather interpreted fuzzily under varying shades of light. This whole vexing story still angers me more than a little, makes me blanch and wonder, even today years later as it is put down to paper since I ask myself this simple question:

>---What the heck ever happened to people being blunt, frank, sincere, and open in expression?

Now that some decent time has passed---luckily for me since I no longer have to wonder or guess at the meaning of his many words---I understand that his fraudulent, dishonest, intentionally deceptive way of speaking has become the accepted norm for discourse; hence, this small tale arose. Today, my business colleague's faulty and untrustworthy diction has become the more common mode of speaking, as predictable, normal, and regrettable as dirty snow in late March; and concomitantly, forceful and direct language has retreated, disappeared as the waves crashing upon the shore then do retreat and disappear back into the sea. Here are a few keys phrases that should signal to all of us a thrust towards the unfaithful word or phrase:

>---Let me be frank...

or, its equally odious cousin:

>---Quite frankly...

or,

>---Now we know...

or:

>---Some would maintain...

Cinque Sortite: Five Assaults Or Sallies Onto The Battlefield

or:

>   ---It remains to be seen

And if someone within earshot says this awful word:

>   ---Empower

do right then jump off the jeep, run as fast as you can away from whomever said that word, and dive for deep cover, I am telling you right now, for you are about to get bushwhacked, clobbered, or assaulted from behind.

Upon hearing such odious phrases (and, yes, there are hundreds, no thousands, more of them) all listeners must watch out for the fibs and distinctly so, since what will follow in the speech shall be lies upon prevarication, deceits upon deceptions, menacing mendacities, and other forms of constantly curving untruths or what used to be called horseshit before we got too big for our britches. Thus, the model of proper speech has changed utterly. And today, anyone straightforward is thought of by those that condescend to lead as some sort of looney tune rube or rustic, a bonkers renegade perhaps, and someone forever set apart from our modern and "more civilized" society. And pray tell, Benedict, flim-flamers, Quislings, hokum merchants, why is that? The only response is that our standards for the truth have changed, slipped, morphed, and not for the inveterate good. Here is the key to this unbrave new world that we have made for ourselves: A man's word is no longer thought to be important or crucial, his obligatory bond with others in society, and something that every day must be done or accomplished in full. When was the last time you heard this sort of talk?:

> ---We shall live up to our side of the bargain; however, the next questions is, Will you?

Regretfully, that mode of clear speech is quite rare today.

On the other hand, it is deemed or judged normal, proper, and fine to prevaricate (such a lovely and melodious way that repulsive word does roll off the tongue, as if it were meant to be said all the time!); amoral arbiters all around us now tell us it is fine to lie, to fib, to deceive, to equivocate, to fabricate, to finagle, and to fleece, as long as some keen gain might be achieved. How many words we have in the dictionary to describe an untruth! By these weak standards, those today still eroding the more, my fibbing business colleague is really quite average! Why, many grifters would probably regard him as a typical chap, a regular fellow; and then they might task us with the next logical question, one that follows as surely as 11 follows 10:

> ---What is all the darn bother? What is all this fuss about?

It is common now for many speakers to relate only, say, 80% of the truth, yet to omit the most crucial 20% of the nugget, and all the while to act as if the whole solid truth had been uttered. This is how one plays games with another man, or pulls the wool over. Oh, to play the hooded, four-flush fox; 'tis normal now! This is an adopted or acquired habit of mind, something gained or earned by rote over time, a bit like a certain gesture about the face, like Muhammed Ali's slow scratching at the chin, or how one gains skills at the piano by practicing scales for long hours. One is not born with these hoodwinking skills of deception and disingenuousness, but learns them later on and only through long, assiduous practice. We are speaking here of simple duplicity and treachery, something craven and manipulative. Yet, remarkably to someone from birth surrounded by straight speaking, short sentences, strong Anglo-Saxon words and imperative commands, as I gaze about and adjudge the scene, this new foul custom of speaking, that is, to be clear:

> ---Always talking out of both sides of the mouth at the same time so that the meaning is not clear

that loose and lousy way of speaking is now the new and "proper" standard. Everyone does it, you see. It follows then that there are too many weak, conditional words of doubt like:

> ---Might, could, should, perhaps, maybe, possible, likely, may, if,

and hundreds more since their use leads to the sacred goal of plausible deniability. Today in the business world lying is the keen, preferred model, something de rigueur and expected; moreover, lying is considered a snide form of adult machismo, and its stock-in-trade: Secrets, are used constantly to cover up the ever-present mistakes or a more nefarious sleight-of-hand. Therefore, many people (and not just our pitiful politicians!) lie pretty much all the time and get away with it; because on this long custom, some no longer know how to tell the simple truth; and then, they lie some more since it has become a habit and they have become gradually pretty good at it. Their faces are generally mordant and do not disclose the ongoing subterfuge. Upon the stage they only act the part of the honest man. They can do this since they do not believe that words, or actions for that matter, have significance or real consequences of any sort. Many of these adept interlopers, laminators, kinsmen in intentional obstruction, would no more assume that words matter or have any real consequence than they would claim that pigs could fly, or that a fleet of cats might march in unison. In any case, over the past few decades what constitutes proper verbal behavior has altered in a fundamental and unhealthy way.

And for this to have happened, Lancelots and Genevieres, we must have fully shut our eyes and ears, a most foolish thing to do when surrounded by connivers. Since I have made such a claim, the sharp reader is correct to ask for some proof. Returning to the definition for "connive", the word stems from the Latin word, connivere, meaning to close one's eyes. We have closed our eyes and ears to the endless spin, the ubiquitous propaganda, the false speech that surrounds us now. For years now, in the face of mounding duplicity, a different and false way of speaking, we have closed our eyes to frankness and candor; and, instead, have accept lousy pablum, malicious exaggerations, and mistaken theories all entirely without question. We elect presidents who have not told a word of the truth in years; they are beyond the pale; they are those who routinely mislead, who with no smirking parse what the word "is" is, who speak not to tell the bare wood truth, but to build coalitions for greater power, to placate and calm possible adversaries, to shift responsibility away from themselves, to promote confusion, and to evade confrontation, something which might possibly harm their own unique political fortunes. Of course, the best liars, those who are the most practiced at it, are the politicians from all of the parties, since to speak only for miasmal effect, to create a shifting mirage of misleading words, to make a word salad, that is their common, practiced stock in trade. For these word stretchers, spin is all. These are practiced liars; like with so many other things, playing the piano or fielding ground balls on the baseball diamond, they have become adept at fibbing, stretching the truth, engendering out of whole cloth rank, feckless inventions, using red herring and straw man attacks and many other tactics to advance their case. And because we no longer recognize truth, we no longer search for and elect men of simple integrity.

By the stubborn truth seekers still among us, all of the above cannot be long debated. How far we have moved away from the diction of brusque Teddy Roosevelt, who often seized any chance to extinguish guile, to lance hypocrisy, and to deflate the pompous. Here are a few quotes from him that point to his use of simple, strong language:

> ---Keep your eyes on the stars, and your feet on the ground.
>
> ---Believe you can and you're halfway there.
>
> ---Complaining about a problem without proposing a solution is called whining.
>
> ---Nothing in the world is worth doing unless it means, effort, pain, difficulty...I have never envied a human being who led an easy life.

His fresh, firm, and direct manner of speaking today seems to us as if it came from another planet. His clear, forthright diction is so different from that of the slimy, self-pleasing sycophants of today, who are mostly untrustworthy toadies and deft grifters, and who employ neither lucidity nor precision. Perhaps it would serve us well down all the days to study for a time how we have become so indulgent and accepting towards our self-serving, full of malarkey leaders (sic), and how this new, drastically lower standard of speech might have arisen.

Machiavelli in Il Principe alleges that we are correct to say whatever it takes to secure a goal, to use whatever diction or inflection or facial gesture or straw dog attack might more seamlessly achieve a happy conclusion. Thus, though they would not announce it, most habitual liars are essentially clever egoists, thinking that:

---If I am happy, the world is happy.

Our world is now chock-full of such dreary selfish types. Often, the usual rationale for telling a fib is closeted self-interest. Especially in the political world, a crate full of crazed cats, lies uttered blithely and at the right moment may lead to stupendous wealth, the grandest of riches in this temporary world of ours. To this cloistered ilk, content in their constant prevarications, secure in their stern derision for the truth, it is just fine and peachy-keen to alter the stated facts to fit the circumstance. For proof of this large claim, please consider these three moments of history: Monica, Benghazi, Watergate. Plausible deniability is all, but first it is best to create some sort of smokescreen, to detract attention from the real foil. And for ourselves, we

Cinque Sortite: Five Assaults Or Sallies Onto The Battlefield

no longer know how to recognize real leaders, competent, reliable truth tellers; instead, lately we seem to specialize in electing "suits" who routinely fib, those weaklings who lie all the time, those grifters who chronically think:

    ---I would be better served if...

But, doesn't the smallest child who just pinched a tasty, soft macaroon from the ceramic cookie jar do the same thing? Doesn't the planning commissioner who negotiates an underhanded quid pro quo with an equally sleazy city councilman do the same thing? Doesn't the president who one days says that the United State will not be militarily involved in another country and who the very next day orders an attack on that same country do the same thing? For, this business of lying, it is something one practices, and after a few years of trying, one does become quite proficient at it.

And, now, because our societal standards for the truth have slipped so thoroughly, this nasty, trashy, subversive habit of lying is all around us now. It is like some sort of air-borne bacterial disease like Legionnaire's, or perhaps some sort of insidious, sneaky virus from which one may not easily escape. As a child one may learn from "friends" that a small fib is excusable, and thus the predacious race toward falsehood commences; then, selfishness begets the taller tale or the runaway story, hyperbolic and exaggerated, and then another and another. Lying becomes a nervous and unconscious habit, like the way a dog circles his bed before plopping down upon it. Yet, in this corrosive process, that necessary and common link between people, the assumption that I may assume that what you say to me is unvarnished true and vice versa, well, that important linkage, is now blocked, impeded, truncated. It all started when we first put up with simple baloney, ostrich falsehoods, ordinary claptrap, silly pablum. So, it then follows that the end result of any lie or evasion is a primordial isolation for both parties, both the liar and the one lied to, the deceived and the man deceived; and therefore, a man is left alone in the darkest, obscure woods, to once again paraphrase Dante. And, by further easy extension, John Donne's philosophy:

> ---No man is an island, entire by itself; every man is a piece of the continent, a part of the maine
>
> John Donne, Meditation XVII; Devotions upon Emergent Occasions; 1623

by these practiced fibbers that philosophy is discarded or tossed aside, and made ipso facto irrelevant.

Now that the sad stage is set, now that it is recognized that truth telling has become rare, now that deft deceit and lying are nearly required for temporal success, let us reckon, if we choose to do so, how can things be made better? Or, are circumstances sterling and preeminent just as they are? Is everything as it should be? Those questions may only be asked after one realizes how dreadful this state of affairs is: Seven billion people on this good, green earth, each going after each other, angling for an advantage or ploy, trying to wrest power from others by deceit and chicanery, speaking to achieve what is individually the most fortuitous.

Many years ago, the most prescient writer, George Orwell, AKA Eric Blair (1903-1950), spoke about all of these things. He knew that language is power, that totalitarian

Cinque Sortite: Five Assaults Or Sallies Onto The Battlefield

elites, bigshots all, would try to use twisting words to form propaganda which in turn would turn men's minds inside out. He understood that whoever controls the language, wins the battle and then the war. We grasped that words by charlatans and con artists would be re-defined on a daily basis to achieve a temporary political gain. He predicted that an audience that had been lied to long enough might well enjoy being lied to. He warned that lies change the receiver's unconscious in ways hard to ferret or describe. He was fearful that lies might one day be the order of the day. He knew that false speech could be used to make null and void the past, so that history might be re-written in a new light and memory obliterated, thus stripping our youth of purpose. And he forecast that the end result of this twisting of the language would be a loss of individual freedom and perhaps a failure of a free government to be replaced by a growing tyranny, which is precisely where we are today---on the verge of losing forever our right to free speech, to be replaced by doublethink, newspeak, political correctness, thought police, big brother, and woke consensus. Orwell speaks to all of these issues and nuances throughout his oeuvre and, in particular, in his famous essay entitled "Politics and the English Language" (1946), a work detailing the importance of clean-cut lucid language, and a slim volume that should be required reading in every high school in the country, that is, if I had my druthers, that is, if I were the bird colonel in charge. After tall, a bird colonel is better than a bird brain, or at least, so say Mayes and Landon. After studying the prose of Orwell carefully, any reader will know how far we have slipped from the dictional standards he so precisely and thoroughly laid out for us in our use of the language.

To improve our use of words, prompted by Orwell and so many others, we would be wise to regard the thoughts of the Israelis who have a very special word that we ought to know about and study. It is the word:

---Dugri

and it refers to the highest standards of honesty, integrity, accuracy. Balashon, the Hebrew language detective, translates it as:

---Straight, true, proper, suitable, honest, good (person).

If more dugri informed our choice of words, the world would be a better place. Yithak Rabin (1922-1995), the 5th Prime Minister of Israel, possessed much personal dugri and displayed it daily. He was no equivocator, no alibier, no interlarder, no shirker, and no simple oiler. He spoke the truth as he saw it and was not a fan of sea ooze, or worthless talk. He was not a chiseler, nor a lam man, nor did he pull rank. He knew how to mix it up and was not afraid of a fight. He had no use for phony, trumped up explanations, nor did he like trial balloons or misleading evasions of any sort. He was not one of those who liked to shoot the breeze. He spoke straight from the shoulder but knew when to stow the gab. In other words, he was probably quite different from those around him, those who cottoned to consensus, focus groups, and diversity. Perhaps without surprise, all of Rabin's laudable, common sense traits got him killed. On November 4 of 1995, he was assassinated in Tel Aviv just outside the City Hall by an extremist fanatic using a semi-automatic pistol. Why? The assassin had opposed Rabin'

Cinque Sortite: Five Assaults Or Sallies Onto The Battlefield

signing of the Oslo Accords. Rabin's yearning for peace in the world got him killed. Still, the point of this short tale is simply this: How much better off the world would be if these positive and simple character traits of Prime Minister Rabin, lucidity and conciseness, were more common, more accepted, more expected, and more demanded? This is a simple idea and, therefore, not one to be faulted or discounted.

In the wink's eye: Whether questioned or not, is it not better to throw the beer cans, once drunk and down the hatch, away from the front of the vehicle, to come what may, as one barrels or high wheels it down the moon-lit highway? Is it not more friendly and fortuitous to come clean and, thereby, to always come up smiling? To care less than a fig or fico or flick for mean consequences? To fiddle and dither less, and to speak forthrightly more? Festschristless, is such a tantalus thing possible? To do otherwise, I fear a muddle, or what we see now, where the leader smiles before he lies and then smiles after he lies, as Dan says about Joe. Now all the same birds smile always whilst they insert the sharp lance to the receptive kidneys, looming self-interest being all, tangential acumen goose to the gander, or Old Tom's twisted tongue. Don't these inveigling birds sometimes click their teeth too?

To say precisely and exactly what you mean and to not mislead---what an arcane, out-of-date concept! It is one which must be more practiced in our scattered, disordered, lying globe. Nowadays it is easy and common for our leaders (sic) to lie, thus creating a phantom narrative, a phony story; they intimidate, bully, and lie to achieve their only nirvana, power (for most of them are fully godless, though they shall doubtless allege the opposite); knowing

Dominic M. Martin

their Orwell, they love mob justice since it means that quick pivots may occur; and too, they change their story as often as you or I may grab a new pair of socks to start the day, and, since there is today absolutely no memory, since that key function has evaporated into the mist, nobody holds these intent connivers to account. This lousy habit of sloppy speech must be got rid of, just like how a good and careful dentist extracts a rotten tooth from the jaw and then throws into the bin. Most people now speak mostly for effect, like an experienced actor might upon the run-amuck stage, to create or stir to life an image, to engender a faux and transient emotion, to feign fair weather when a mean storm hasten just beyond the escarp. Such useless fardel might well get us into some mounting trouble. However, one must probe, what do you tink about tall of liss, Ollie?

Many of today's phony gutless wonders who purport to lead are not telling the simpler tale, but inventing, embellishing, omitting, or forgetting the most essential nugget, all done to better serve their lusty and growing mercantile. At some point in their youth, they would have joined a club of fellow fibbers, the better to further their ascendancy up the tall ranks of power. Then they went to a fancy college, perhaps of the diseased Ivy League, not to learn, but to network with the other social climbers, to grease their way up the money ladder. These shuck-and-give hucksters, inveterate inveiglers and their ilk, have gone into politics where they have taken over, conquered, the spoken word. Our mode or manner of public discourse has morphed into something repellent and not to be trusted, since it is now full or, or coated with, the sticky slime of deceit. Most aggressively, these political actors have simply hijacked all speech. In all things they lack tenacity and so their opinions are fluid and changeable, sometimes flipping overnight to better fit a new situation. In their speech they are far past the real, well beyond unchanced omissions---take your poison tallymen, barge polers---and so, we small-potato private and bosuns soon then enter this liar's misty labyrinth, his crooked pergola of half true jests, his tainted maelstrom of entrapping and twisting fibs, the common world of the poking and useless rejoinder, the wink and the nod, and the covered brow. And so, they say to us bewildered ones who only long to trust:

>---Of course, I will get back to you soon. Why don't we do lunch?

instead of saying, as Mel Brooks writes:

>---Call me when you are famous, OK?

This lousy manner of speech has taken over the world, and not for its gain. Disordered motives converge and meld and fall apart as all fragile faience must, but this happens before its time, battlers, before its proper time. This habit of untruth, now so common about the land, makes unhep slaves of us all. We begin to serve the lie its dinner while we ourselves go hungry. All go unserved if lies predominate. Why not avoid the double-faced sin in the first place, Excelsior, and work towards the higher level? Durst? Ejecta? Fib? The gills move.

For a laugh or tickle, Myrtle, Rex, something we all could tiddle use, consider how frequently, ubiquitously, most politicians prevaricate. (But not good old Teddy who is long gone!) Why, to lie is their stock-in-trade, their natural modus operandi! To spin, to weave, to placate, to mislead, to blame the chap not in the room, otherwise known as the triangle---these tactics and more do serve them well down all their days, as Davies says. These grifting shirkers would never say:

> ---The thing is, kiddo, if you make a promise or a pledge, you must fulfill it. You got that, buster?

or:

> ---If I say something to you, you can take it to the bank.

or:

> ---I only deal in straight goods, partner.

Today's new breed of liars want to control all events and all people. So, as if their speaking is a practiced and dedicated artform, they jest and twist and avert and concoct and equivocate, thereby creating a brand-new fiction from the fact. When these coin robbers steal from our convenient till, our national wealth, how could it have been otherwise? Of course, these lousy leaders lie; of course, they do! They wish us to slide toward tyranny, and when we passively put up with their falsehoods we do aid and abet that abnegation. The totalitarian left engages in runaway word play every day, and since there no longer is such a thing as memory, they get away scot-free and nonchalantly walk down the road.

Oh, if suddenly the preening prevaricators, prissy patsies all, told the truth! Perhaps some benevolent deity, seeing that slide towards tyranny that is all around us, he

Cinque Sortite: Five Assaults Or Sallies Onto The Battlefield

might take some proverbial pity on us and control their tongues so that each fresh word out of their gabbing gobs from that tick of the moment onward would be fully, wholly true. How wonderful it is to so chance the dream! Why, then there would be no more unbelievable assertions, no fake stories, no more unfounded whoppers of deceit and intrigue, no more fake shenanigans, and no more pathetic and disgusting mendacities! How different then the world would be, Nash, how different, indeed; however, I bet that better cliffhanger is never written.

Doubtless, much of the responsibility for being surrounded by these lousy lying leaders is ours since we elect them. We join in the swindle, and the obfuscation that results. Why can't we better recognize honest truth speakers? I suppose that is a skill like any other, like skeet shooting or flying a kite, where one becomes more skillful at it over time.

It used to be that we expected leaders to tell the truth, and most did, or at least more than today, where lying is well neigh required and no big deal. Please consider the painful case of President John Kennedy and the Bay of Pigs fiasco of April 17-19, 1961. Earlier, before he was elected, the generals and high-level operatives in the CIA masterminded the invasion on the south coast of Cuba, they thought it could not fail, and they believed that once the attack had commenced that the president would do anything to achieve victory; however, the president was amiss in that he did not study the invasion thoroughly enough before giving his tentative go-ahead; immediately, once the battle had commenced, he got cold feet and pulled the Naval air cover, thus dooming the assault to failure. Afterwards, the admittedly green president admitted responsibility and confessed to the American people that he had made a mistake, a serious mistake. This honesty endeared him to the American people and his approval skyrocketed once he admitted to the error. Would a leader of today be as honest and forthright as President Kennedy had been? I think not, since our manner of speaking and truth telling has changed utterly. Instead, we have leaders who are practiced liars, who are very good at lying because they have been doing it for years. The adulterer who cheats on his or her spouse, and then denies the affair through 20,000 or more lies, that cheater eventually becomes adept at such massive, soul-stealing prevarication. They learn to hide evidence, omit the key point, engender distraction, and use camouflage to cloak the essence in a mysterious shroud. Or, as Sir Walter Scott writes famously and well:

> ---O, what a tangled web we weave when first we practice to deceive.

Sir Walter Scott: Marmion: A Tale of Flodden Field; Canto 6, Stanza 17; 1808

One lie begets another, and soon enough the liar gets trapped in a sticky, complicated trap of his own making.

To conclude this study, I must return to my childhood and explain how these ideas about the importance of honesty first entered my prepubescent brain: My parents put them there! And here's the untall tale: One day when I was around 13, my dad caught me in a lie. Yes, it was about something stupid, and isn't that the way it always is? I soon learned that my dad had an ear for lies like cats have a nose for fish! For, within less than second, he glowered at me, and exhorted:

Cinque Sortite: Five Assaults Or Sallies Onto The Battlefield

> ---Now your life is going to get ugly. And how bad is up to you!

Immediately and clearly very angry, my father strode out of the room. So, within seconds, the stern, almost vicious, upbraiding began. For many weeks, he only glared at me in a hostile stare that would have melted anyone. He never looked at me directly, but askance. He did not speak to me for close to two months, and when I walked into a room, with mocking derision, he would walk out of it. When I said:

> ---Good morning!

to him he acted as if I were speaking some other language. Finally, after that very long time and feeling thoroughly mortified, I said to him:

> ---May I speak with you, dad? I am sorry for the lie. I am stupid. And I will not ever do it again.

Instantly, he pressed me:

> ---What was the lesson you learned, dingleberry? Are you going to forget the lesson? How many days will it take before you completely forget the lesson? Will you carry the message with you into your later years, lummox? Put that in your mess kit, buster.

I told him that I would always remember the lesson, even after he was long gone and pushing daisies. But from that day forward until he died, he put me under always greater scrutiny. From time to time, he would toss out admonitions like these:

> ---If you don't give me the ammo, I can't fire the gun.
>
> ---A man's word is his bond to another, do you follow me?
>
> ---Learn to avoid people who trade in lies, since they will bring you under the wheels of the bus.
>
> ---I want concrete results, not stupid intentions!

And a couple of weeks later, in those halcyon days before the simple ethos of uncontrived honesty was abandoned, I as a big-eared youngster heard my old-school, stern, but fair father bellow on the phone to some mendacious business fellow back East, with my dad saying, no, yelling, shouting:

> ---Listen. If you lie to me, Benedict, you lie to yourself. How can I ever trust you again? How, you bootlicking bastard? What exactly is your word of honor? What? Answer me not like a Norman.
>
> No more smokescreens or evasions, do you follow me? Answer me, cobweb, baron, ace. Don't you know what plain English is? If you think you are going to pull one over on me, think again, grease- ball!

Cinque Sortite: Five Assaults Or Sallies Onto The Battlefield

As a tad hearing his strict and severe words to the guy trying to trick him and too, thinking back to the day he caught me raw and red-handed in my stupid fib, I never forgot the clear and clean words that he always used; and I resolved that, if I did not want to get tossed into the hoosegow again, I better learn quickly how to speak like him, to use short sentences and strong verbs, and to always pursue and chase bare lucidity, and not confusion and misdirection.

As the years went by, my father continued to study me closely, that is, once he had asked me some sort of a tindering question. I know now that he daily wanted to give me a test, or to start some sort of fire, or what is sometimes called a conflagration. He was very good at starting conflagrations. After he tasked me with a question, he would stare at me evenly and intently; he would stare at my pale face with a fevered concentration that, even further backwards in always receding time, he must have used in studying the smudged maps of the Anzio beachhead where he had been posted and fought during the war.

Sometimes then, on a daily basis during those teenaged years, as he fairly grilled me, examining me closely, relentlessly, for any suggestion of a parsed falsehood, some damn lie or evil omission, he would get a weird look in his eyes and lapse, slide, collapse into this crazy Anzio argot of his, as if that foolish battle in the wrong place had returned and it was once again the Spring of '44. Often during those interrogations of me he would launch into some Army slang since, he must have thought, using those ancient, recalled words of war would compel both of us to begin to speak more truthfully, to use less cant and bunk, those twin things which pretty much pass for speech today.

Do you think that that assumption of his was a correct one, one that would "hold water" to use his apt turn of phrase? Surely by now you must have an opinion on the matter.

One day in the summer of my sophomore year, before I could drive a car and as I was periodically going through short bouts of eruptive acne (well warranting the moniker "Mr. Pizza Man" from my less charitable classmates), my father handed me a small, baby blue pamphlet or volume entitled: Propaganda and How to Recognize it. As he gave it me, he said:

> ---This is serious business, son. You must be able to recognize propaganda, so that you can better fight against it when you get a little older. Remember this: The truth is the truth, something immutable and constant. Morals are morals, not mores. Morals are made by God, not man. Lies mean you can't tell the truth anymore and that is when real creativity dies; and that is exactly where we are headed, string bean, that is if we are not there already. You must find a way to always tell the truth, tender foot, so that it becomes a habit that never goes away. You got all of that, bud?

So, after that exhortation I read the book, but some of it went over my head a little. Some of the passages I had to re-read several times; but some of the ideas I did remember and are ones like these:

> ---When the propagandist has his way, up is down, and wrong is right.

Cinque Sortite: Five Assaults Or Sallies Onto The Battlefield

>---If can you re-write history, you can next eliminate the past.

>---The free exchange of ideas in Hollywood is dead, since the people running that phoniest of places are money and power-hungry, amoral, leeching, arrogant buzzards.

Often those days, my dad and I would talk about proper speech, and how to initiate it, and then how to later protect it. And usually in those conversations he took on the hunched posture of a soldier. Since it was summer his face was tanned the color of a dark walnut as if he had been on some sort of soldier's long tromp, and yet, he was entirely unwrinkled by the sun. By then lost in thought, his mind was then ranging backwards, and his stern brown eyes, guarded by the deepest brown eyebrows thick and furry, would then accost me, but they also tended to me and watched over me gently. As he so tightly regarded me, scrutinized me, inspected and probed as if he were on graveyard watch, I had the strangest feeling that my dad was a first cousin to the equally tanned Generalfeldmarschall Johannes Erwin Eugen Rommel, that brilliant man originally from Heidenheim in the Kingdom of Wurttemberg, then part of the German Empire, and the one general who had pushed Bernard Montgomery's troops all over the sweeping sands of North Africa. To my young ears during those discussions, my dad had smoothly taken on a tinge of the Swabian accent, as Rommel had also possessed; yet here, I now do wonder, was my memory faulty? Was it telling me some new lie? Still, then and now I do wonder:

> ---Did my father descend from the same strong rigid stock as Rommel? Did he? Were they related?

After all, when I was still in high school this might explain my father's occasional fierceness, his pugilistic dedication, his rigid dedication, and his steadfast determination. All through those teenage years my dad was always testing me by firing question after question at me, like a .30 carbine @ 750 rounds per minute leaves the M1. By asking so many questions on a million topics and then waiting for my answers, he wanted to know if I would stay completely true and honest during the barrage of questions, taunts, and whistles. This habit of mind was something that my father considered crucial for any man. As Rommel too had required of his soldiers, dad wanted from me only words straight from the shoulder, the real skinny, with no foggy embellishments or silly exaggerations. He wanted short words and short sentences, only full of active verbs, and not weak passive ones, if at all possible. He was trying to make sure that in a couple of years I would not turn out to be a doofus rookie, a lying leech, part of the lying rabble, or a simple idiot. He was as pushy as anything, and investigative as any Marine or resistance platoon leader might have been out on patrol, and not fighting in some little pissant war, but a big one, which would be the one that would count. So finally on that day so long ago, that day when my dad reminded me of Rommel on the lookout and ready to pounce, that day when I even today swear that his voice had more than a trace of the Swabian angle about it, my father ended the discussion of words and fighting, of fighting and words, by saying to me, most emphatically, almost plaintively:

> ---Listen, sprout! Do you know or consider Campania? Aprilia? Lipini? I landed with all the other guys at Nettuno of the deep blue sea like all the other flagrant and home-sick soldiers of the 5th Army, conscripted or volunteered non-shirkers (since that is what you did back then), and now I am just a silly shit on a shingle, another know-nothing, foot-slogger gorm getting shot at by Smiling Feldmarschall Albert Kesselring and his 14th Army, like all the go-to-the-mat-for recruits and the other greenie Sad Sacks trying to find the way to the darn Valmontone Gap. Where is it? Is it past the Fiume Rapido and the Fiume Garigliano, or is it beyond the Volturno further to the south, towards my constant cobalt friend, the ever-present sea? We did not have time for a swim, to take a dip in the ocean. Aye, at least back then it was a good thing that we had tenacious, untiring General Lucian Truscott on our side, and that, in turn, means that we were lucky, darn lucky! Did God give us that luck? Or, do all soldiers make their own luck? Answer me, now, doofus! Do you follow me? In any case, we must break out! We must do so and now!

All the time as he spoke, and then later on throughout my later teenage years and then into adulthood, he was studying me sharply, keenly, looking for the smallest falsehood, the slightest prevarication, or even a hint of that most despicable thing: Conniving. All through those years, he was testing me and grooming me in his own intense, foot soldier's way to be a simple, ordinary truth teller. And, whenever he comprehended that there was even the tiniest chink in my young knight's armor (for these fatherly inspections took place quite often), that I was telling the most harmless cock-and-bull story or the most insignificant canard, then he would chastise me and explode with a long string of invectives. There was no way he was going to raise his son to become a common grifter, a lying weasel, or blame shirker; no way in hell or blazes; and he was going to make sure damn sure that did not happen! Whenever I even came just a whisker's close to a fib or obfuscation, any fuzzy speaking, he would decry this adolescent foible and the resulting loss of manhood (for he said that real men tell the truth, always), telling me a dozen times, for donkey's years, haranguing me, that lying was simply wrong, and how the endless trouble that any lie would get me into would last shave longer than Nettuno's cobalt sea. He was demanding that I only spoke the truth, just as he had demanded of himself and his fellow soldiers of the 5th Army that they should reach the Valmontone Gap 22 years earlier. In this commission, he was like any other battalion leader, or paratrooper, or, especially, any submarine commander, indeed, anyone else in charge who is supremely pressed for speed and unity of purpose, someone who must demand the whole truth all the time because, as Wallace says, in the battle they do not have any time for bullshit. He knew that liars railroad others and pontificate, always putting themselves in the best light, and when they malign and demean others, they reduce themselves to less than whole. He meant what he said and said what he meant, and his word was always his bond. He knew that the battle to tell the truth was like any other battle, one that would always be long and arduous. He knew that liars want chaos so that they can collect and conserve power. And he knew that once the lies start, they

Cinque Sortite: Five Assaults Or Sallies Onto The Battlefield

only proliferate, and that they spread faster than hundreds of tumbleweeds rolling across the salt-laden high desert scrub brush land north of Winnemucca off of endless U. S. Route 95.

As it turned out, from that day forward, whenever I screwed-up and chanced to fib (which was not very often after all that upbraiding and scolding!), my dad sensed it right away. He could tell when I was just thinking about lying! He understood and wanted me to understand right away and forever that this lie-telling business was a serious character flaw in anyone, that its incipiency in me had to be destroyed and eliminated, that it had to pulled out of my mouth entirely by the full root and then destroyed; that, otherwise, it would rot and abscess and prematurely destroy me and all for whom I cared, that any lie would make me forever enfeebled and enervated and decrepit and a big, stupid fool before my time, more quickly than any disease or unkind fortune, that its venal ugliness would compound automatically ten times or more inside of me, every day doubling to a hundred times its prior size. With his intense brown eyes shrouded by his thick brown eyebrows he told to me that any lie would make me sick to the stomach and in the brain, that it would burden and harm my soul, that it would make me overnight, whilst I slept, a dingbat errand boy or skirt lackey or sissy pants fellow, a mere footman or stupid toady to every fib I ever might have muttered, since, he said to me that day now so long ago with an almost maniacal glint to those eyes:

> ---They never go away, these damn demon lies. They never go away! Never! The thing is, kiddo, if you make a promise, you had better keep it. Do

you hear me, buster? When you make a deal, will you live up to your end of the bargain? If you don't, I'll know, even if I'm already gone, even from my grave. Do you follow me, son? Do you now?

POSTCRIPT: A QUICK TOSSING ASIDE OF THE HEAVY DUFFLE BAG

---How can I help? Tell me exactly what to do.

---I know one thing, my friend: Siamo retardo. We are late. Very late.

> In the middle of the night two sentries are talking while standing watch upon the fort's broad rampart overlooking the valley and what shall be the scene of tomorrow's battle.

---No poor chicken ever set the price of an egg, that much is for sure, since only people, not hens, are in charge of things; yet, sadly, most of us are bull dukes and dumb as anything.

It was a dark, long night in the middle of winter in 1944. Outside the soldier knew that it was cold, very cold and gelid, and he could see that the dry snowflakes swirled in light, bouncing, circling flurries in the night air, buoyed upwards by the occasional sirocco that blew down upon their camp from the North, from the two mountains, Monte Artemisio and Monte Peschia. The soldier could see the snow clearly through the window of the barracks because of the long, strong, temporary floodlight that lit the yard that surrounded it. He thought how it must have been a couple of weeks since his right calf got shot up, and just a couple of days after his release from the makeshift military hospital at the small church in the village of Conca.

The achy pain from the wound which was still healing and the stitches that pulled when he shifted a little in bed had awakened the soldier. The soldier was glad that the wound had not gotten infected and was not even a little puffy or red, even though the conditions in the church's hospital in Conca were less than desirable, and that made him a little proud since it, the lack of infection, told him even in the middle of the night that he was strong. Too, the soldier knew for sure that he was damn lucky or fortunato that the 88 millimeter bullet from the German-made Mauser could have easily shattered, cracked, or nicked one of the bones of his right calf, the tibia or the fibula, but rather it had embedded itself deep into the thick gastrocnemius muscle where it had resided until some greenhorn rookie doc lassoed or yanked on it, extracting it out of that pulsating, bloody muscle using a half-sterilized needle-nose pliers or vise grips, or what the fancies call a surgical forceps. The soldier knew that soon, maybe tomorrow, he ought to go to another church to pray for always greater health, perhaps at la Chiesa di Santa Maria della Salute towards the northeast in Venezia, in Dorsoduro to be precise, but since the fighting was still raging, wild, and vicious, he understood even in his foggy state that such a visit of healing for the moment would have to be postponed. Finally, the tired soldier wondered how many Hail Marys he would have to say to avoid catching another 88 millimeter bullet, especially one to the heart or head.

Afterwards, he could not be sure of the exact time that had gone by since he was still groggy, dazed from getting wounded and also some drugs they must have given to him to combat the pulsing pain and his brain was not as sharp as it ought to have been. Yet, here in the middle of the night, in the middle of winter, in the middle of the battle all around him now, he would neither despair nor grow despondent, no. All the other soldiers around him in the barracks were asleep and he could hear their muffled breathing as a low rush or hum, like soft waves crashing upon the seashore, and also, from across the large room an occasional chough or spontaneous sneeze. It had only been a couple of days since he got out of the hospital. It was a good thing that it was night and the other soldiers were asleep since he did not wish to speak with any of them. Maybe in the morning he would, but for now he needed his sack time. He knew that in the morning still a long way off that there would probably be dozens of new, eager, greenie recruits that would want to chew his ear off talking about nothing.

In the gloom of the night the soldier asked himself whether he needed to pay some just, due, proper, and expected homage to the porcelain god, the library, to micturate, to pump ship, to urinate or to pee, but in the end he knew that he was empty of all yellow water inside his tummy, and he was glad for that since it was dim and grey and hard to see inside the barracks and he did not wish to go across the room, maybe tripping over guy's duffle bags or clumsy, tangled, sprawled boots underfoot where and when, a little like how a 4.5 M1 interrupted screw shell tries to get off the ground and find the enemy, the Krauts, he might have pitched himself forward out of control, maybe conking his dago testa head sideways and hard onto some other guy's bunk.

The tired soldier could have come from any battle, any war, since they are all the same. Since he had been there for close to three years now, he was washed out tired, beat up, and damaged goods. There along the

Lazio coastline, it had been a very long siege, longer than any of bigshots, the brass hats, the flat asses, the great ones, the chair jockeys, had foretold. Like all good soldiers who do their job he knew a screwed-up, botch-job, slapdash operation that moment he first had laid his eyes on it: FUBAR, and there was never any better word to describe it, no, sir. The Italians use the word, casino, meaning chaos, but it amounts to the same thing. He had seen first-hand all of the turbulence and confusion, the loud and incessant chatter of the guns, guys getting killed with suddenly blank looks on their faces, all manner of parts flying off, fevered blood puddling everywhere, and then the hasty, wild retreat towards some sort of lousy bivouac or temporary sanctuary. In the middle of the mess he wondered what bozo or jackass was in charge of this ronchie dippy jamboree! The whole thing had been a green hornet and had not gone as planned, not by a long shot. From the get-go, the soldier knew in advance precisely how it would end: Lousy. And that is simply because this soldier, like all the good ones, had understood and studied the lay of the land, the topography, and from that extrapolated to the battleground instantly, and therefore could predict just like Major General John Buford, Jr., had done on that key, last day of June in 1863 at Gettysburg, since that seizure of the high ground meant probable success. So, the tired soldier asked himself: What if good old, sharp Buford had not seized the high ground first?

The soldier tried to go back to sleep but could not, so he got out of his top bunk carefully, trying to not make a ton of racket for the other soldiers grabbing doss all around him, and he stood next to his bed being quiet and just thinking since there was nothing else to do. He thought to himself:

Cinque Sortite: Five Assaults Or Sallies Onto The Battlefield

What idiot thought beforehand that they would fight it out and win a battle on such soft ground, in the middle of a fetid swamp? What a dumb ass! Not a snowball's chance of success, pard. Can any of these clueless brass hats even say the word: Malaria? The jerky dumbbells had made us clay pigeons, sitting ducks. Had it been Churchill or Clark or maybe some other lame-ass bonehead that made the call to land at Nettuno? So, Operation Shingle had been another pompous governor's disaster and had put in place for all history to see and study for ages to come that ugliest of words, one suggesting all clownish failures: Anzio. The soldier was like any other normal fellow, here a trusting and trusted prophet or scout, who knew when he was about to step into a rusty beartrap that would clamp hard and suddenly around the soft tissue of the ankle; and all through the long war he had been blessed to forecast with Napier's accuracy when things would shine brightly and clear, or when they would go sharply pear-shaped, sideways, or south. That skill is simply what used to be called cleverness, before that word too became corrupt because the wags in charge had begun to use it way too often, whenever they spoke to each other when trying to impress.

In a way the soldier was glad and smiled to himself that he had got shot in the leg since that way he could step away from the fighting for a short respite without being called a cursed malingerer or slimeball shirker; and too, it must be admitted, at the impromptu hospital in the tiny church at Conca he had been transfixed by this busty, red-haired nurse with the very white teeth from Indiana, asking her many times in his growing fog of pain and clouded distress when they might be able to grab a meal together, maybe the next time she got hungry for some kind of cena or supper, until she told him laughingly to be quiet and sot off; still, all the while he needed a break from the fighting, though he knew that the war would not be over when he returned to it, not until the last bullet had been dislodged and the final Kraut either had been made either a prisoner or a corpse.

Earlier, in the day before this night, the tired soldier, worn out and fatigued like any other foot soldier would have been after this long contest, a tad languorous after this long, poorly planned engagement with the Hun, with the Boche, the Krauts, he as a small potato buffeted by term-less and clueless solons who knew nothing of fighting, after his long meandering trek on foot from Conca, he had arrived to the barracks thirsty as anything, parched, and craving some gallons of good cold lager, some buckets of beer, suds; also, a soppressatto dagwood, hoagie, or panino from Campania together with some slices of nutty and melted Provolone, would have done nicely, that salami of the people that is pressed down upon us, but in the middle of a war, besides fighting, the soldier's only chore is to dream and he knew that there would be neither sandwich nor beer, nor close to them; and as he had walked in and spied his top bunk, more and more limping a little on his gimpy right pin, he had been happy, just duck soup happy, to toss his heavy duffle bag high into the sky above his top bunk and then to see it land softly on the exact middle of the brown Italian wool blanket with the three crème stripes at either end for a total of six, covering that bed which would serve as his nocturnal home for who knows how long into the uncertain and tenuous days of the future; he was happy, of course, as a by-product of constant, fine effort, not as an admitted goal, and glad

Cinque Sortite: Five Assaults Or Sallies Onto The Battlefield

since over the three long years of the war the duffle bag had gained some pounds with German pistols, silver, trinkets, jewelry, leather belts and wallets, and a good handful of fine quality silver watches, and thus had become a growing hinderance to any soldier's speed or what might be simply termed an impediment.

In the middle of the night, and since there was nothing else to do, and since his mind would neither calm nor settle, he thought of the singular from the Latin, impedimentum, that one thing by which one is entangled, slowed or impeded; yet in the plural, addressing himself for a moment as Cervantes, he recalled that impedimenta is any piece of traveling luggage, awkward baggage, and especially in military language, the word means the baggage of an Army man, hence, in this case, his, his heavy soldier's duffle bag, now filled with the grim mementos of war, souvenirs of the killing he had seen and participated in for close to three years now.

Confined to barracks, the soldier knew in his head that the small composition of retaliatory ripostes, sorties, or attacks, both the singular as well as the plural meanings of the word were at work and play: By completing this last trek, this final assignment, our soldier, il nostro soldato, was spent, weakened, almost fully used up. He sure could have used some deep doss. Yet, even in his tiredness, he was content since always he had done his job (via work, not wishing, Miguel, but work), and with almost delicious fatigue he had been happy to at last heave, or too, fling upwards, the military baggage, the heavy grey and dusty duffle bag high into the sky onto his tired soldier's bunk, always asking himself the soldier's common question:

>   ---Where is my common commoner's sleep? I could sure use some, McCoy; but, where is it?

The soldier stood near the edge of the bed, looking at the top bunk and the medium brown Italian wool blanket where he had been trying to sleep, hearing the snores and guffaws and farts and, thinking of faraway quim and distant lungs, the small moans of his fellow foot sloggers all around, and he thought in the middle of that long night, surrounded by those given the gift of sleep while he would have to beg for it, that it was a darn grand, good, and provident thing that he had gone through Basic Training 3 years earlier at Camp Edwards on Cape Cod, since there they only fed you city cow, chipped beef also known as shit-on-a-single, and dried, pithy, and undersized oranges from dreary Dinuba or poor Parlier. He knew now that the lousy food had toughened him up more than a little, getting him ready for his current deprivations. There, sometimes, braggingly on Sundays, they served up tasteless cuts of beef, tough, gristly, and fatty all at the same time. Also, too often the rookie soldiers were offered insipid and drecky, old salt, bean soup full of lardy Manteca, vieux sel, and cipolle conserve troppo a lungo, or onions too long stored. There too, he had met Drill Sergeant Matthew Hayden whose constant, haranguing, barked orders right away had made the soldier tougher, allowing the duffle bag to be less of an impediment, just a tad lighter upon his lean shoulders. Any heavy baggage like a duffel, the soldier thought, must be properly transported, held aloft above the ground so that it shall not graze upon the earth. If it is delivered to its destination without damage, my duffel should serve me well down all my days, or so the tired soldier again thought, pondered, as he stood near to the edge of the bed, his right calf still aching, staring at the six crème stripes upon his Italian scratchy wool blanket, his mind still a muddle from the pain, the drugs, exhausted from the long slog of the day before, spent from the lack of sleep, and too, beset by the fear of the morrow, that some faceless German might slay him in less than a second. He understood that it was his immediate job to impede the caustic itinerant German's march to the implacable sea, those oceanic waters that see all while doing little to change things, with the soldier knowing that if their fighting is not as vigorous and full-throated as Hayden had instructed and even today expects, that then the war shall swallow us all whole down the gullet, as if we were mere tadpoles or guppies, playing in the hard sand at the edge of the sea. The soldier thought how Hayden had sure as anything delivered on his promise to make all the soldiers scampering and fleet, more resilient and able to pivot, and too, to always, in every minute of every day, expect a battle and never run from it. Thinking backwards in time, as one does especially during war when there is plenty of disconnected, spare time to do so, the soldier remembered back three long years ago to the last speech that the gruff and grumpy Hayden had barked at all of them, just before they were to ship out to the waiting war, steaming east on transport ships out of the Bean Town, also known as Boston:

> ---Listen, my little rookie mamas' boys, my job here at Edwards has been to make you into lean and mean fighting machines. I know I have done my job as commanded by my superiors. You must never gain the belly if you are to know how to fight the enemy. You must be razors, and also you must assume nothing. Be ready all the time. If you are alert and mean and fully fit, you shall a better

> chance to return home. That is all there is to say. Go with God, every damn last one of you, and I mean that straight from the shoulder. Vanquish the Hun, subdue the Boche, and achieve full victory!

The soldier was glad that he could remember Hayden's words so clearly, every one of them and in the right order, now that he was at Anzio and in the midst of this messy, endless combat, since they had already helped him, and he knew that they would do so again someday soon.

Of course, immediately, turning to the present, the sleepless, exhausted soldier, like any other infantryman might have done, a real gen and not a double-bottom bloke but one full of normal Anzio anxiety or the jitters, he asked of himself, while still not stirring from the edge of the bunk, standing as rigid as a statue, so rapt in his reveries, and wondered:

> ---How important is this storm, this siege between the swamp and the sea, this poorly planned, dithering attack upon the Boche? Is the goal of the brass hats, who do never do any real fighting, attainable? I know that the operation was not well vetted, but was it at least sanctioned, or by God sanctified? What more am I prepared to do to accomplish the mission? What kind of world will it be if the Nazi, and not the Allies, are victorious? Not a good one, Rosenberg; that's a lock, Levine.

The tired soldier knew that he is thinking more than a little wacky since he was so slogging tired and on edge, his mind making this night on the bed's edge a nutty, nocturnal Anzio walk, jumping and twitching from this to that, all

Cinque Sortite: Five Assaults Or Sallies Onto The Battlefield

done to dodge Kraut shells, shells that did want to kill him. He was glad that he was among guys dedicated to the cause of besting and burying wild man, crazy Hitler; too, he was happy that he was not surrounded by a group of Hessian mercenaries, since in that foul instance, your heart would not be in it, and doing it for dough is a paltry bargain. Also, he knew that he joins with many other soldiers in being an unpleasant arse, a fly-in-the-ointment to the higher ups who had not been strong sticklers for detail and had not thought this damn thing through; he understood he was an albatross around thousands of leering necks, a ball-in-chain, a bottleneck or choke pea. Hell's bells, someone had to do it. He argued against all passivity and loitering, slouching and dithering, and railed against the tacit side's claim, one silly and unwarranted, that all is well and swell and tugger neat which clearly it is not. The tired soldier recalled one of his favorite quotes from the Bible, one that his mother had given to him nearly twenty years ago:

> ---The wicked flee when no one is pursuing, But the righteous are bold as a lion.
>
> Proverbs 28: 1

The tired soldier like to remember that quote from the Bible that his mother had given to him, since whenever he recalled it, he felt strong inside and all the more ready for war. One must be ready for war, all the time. And so like all soldiers who aim to be good, he knew that it was best to Tom Mix it up, to question the stuffed shirts, to always squabble and question, to fight like a whirling dervish when that was needed since such fighting always makes, generates, more energy for itself; he had to toss the duffle bag skyward and then forget all else, forget it all, but only to further engage the enemy with quick viciousness, always to further engage the slouching enemy, so that then a proper battle may then be fought and victory achieved.

Too, the tired soldier, whose perpetually stirring mind could not embrace gracious sleep, whose brain would not still, he thought how it had been the gruff Hayden who had guided him all along, who told him in his ear, just the other day while being treated at the Conca chapel's tiny hospital, to get the hell back to the front, and pronto, chop-chop, the better to bush back upon, deter, repel, and vanquish the unrepentant Hun. Those words were a good and provident thing, the soldier thought, then recalling his Drill Sergeant's first words to the squad upon their earlier arrival at Edwards as a sort of bookend to the just-remembered last words. Daily, ever since that first exhortation, the gruff Hayden ever since that first training in Massachusetts had been whispering in the soldier's ear, telling him what to do, to be fully stalwart (a word most rarely said nowadays!), to get off his rear and pivot, to better best old Hans. It would not be a cake walk, no sir. The exhausted soldier, in the middle of the night and still not able to sleep, recalled the very first words old gruff, grumpy Hayden had delivered to the new recruits:

> ---Listen up, buttercups, ladies. You had better stand right. Then, hold the damn line. I never lie. I am a pain in the ass so that tomorrow you are better, tougher. I am the lead honcho grizzle gut that presently you are stuck with. You rookies probably think I am some sort of empty idiot, but I don't care if you like me or not. I am too old a bunny

> to be conned by wet diapers like you. I shouldn't have to remind you that I was not chosen for this job because of my pleasant personality or my strong skills at poker. Always think: DT for double time, since if you are slow, you'll probably get your lame flat ass handed back to you. My job is to make you better soldiers, sharp like the quills of a porcupine, leaner and sinewy and tougher, always more alert and in better condition, all to improve the chance that each one of you cry babies may one day get to go home to momma. So, now you whimpering sad sacks have to put up with me. I want no popping off or sassing back, is that crystal clear, greenie?

In remembering those words from Drill Sergeant Hayden, the soldier knew that he had been lucky to have such a grump as his DS, since he had made him tougher, smarter, quicker. Yes, I have been very lucky throughout the war. After that he said to himself, nearly out loud to the dark and quiet barracks:

> ---Ah, to heck with it. I might as well hit the hay, try to again grab some doss, plow the deep, go to the bottom of Davey Jones's Locker, but not to die, just to sleep.

And with that, he hoisted himself skyward as if he were himself a heavy duffel bag, so with a gigantic heave upwards, using his deltoids to the maximum and swinging his legs like steady metronomes arms, he flew up and then plopped himself downwards onto the middle of his brown Italian wool military blanket, the one with the six creme stripes, since there was no Hine Cognac about to sip upon and nor would there be any before morning; and too, as he found his small and dirty pillow smaller than a volleyball and nestled into the blanket, he told himself that I must say my prayers to God who knows more than I do about everything, and too, that I am ready to go to the land of poor Nod since I did not have to make the hard pee to the porcelain god or library which is a toilet or latrine, a Johnny Flusher to some. By the light of days which is only a couple of hours off, perhaps I then shall have and retain more clarity of thought, but only by God's kind Grace. Of that, I am sure. For some time now, my mind has been clouded, blocked, filled up with caking soot and greasy drivel, but after some decent ass rack time, that chapter will be finished, and the once-cogent lucidity of mine mind shall return. That clarity is something that now I miss, like an old friend from childhood. Where shall the battle be tomorrow? What new chaos will take place? How many of my soldier friends will croak or bite the big one or fall to dust? Pray tell me, Lord, when shall I join them?

And so, at the last, like nearly all soldiers do, especially ones that are flat-out tired, fatigued, worn out, he, the tired soldier, began to settle down to sleep, to stalk it cautiously and slowly before it would come gratefully to him, all as part of a new, fantastical dream of a beautiful and fragrant and naked woman coming to him with open arms, open and supplicatory arms, with she doubtless asking to be taken; with him thinking too that finally it was time for him to come to the water, to go to the water, the healing water, and there to accept, to ask to receive it, the water and the light, so that once again, ancona (and distinctly not the small city sulla costa Adriatica, Dilbert!), one may see. It is a simple thing for which to ask. All of this is simple, the

Cinque Sortite: Five Assaults Or Sallies Onto The Battlefield

soldier thought: So that one may see. He knew that many other soldiers including those sleeping nearby, stiff and frozen as molding logs scattered upon the damp forest's floor, are also weary, blind, and nervous from the endless battles, and too, he knew that they also would long to see. It is a simple thing, a simple request. The soldier thought how eventually everybody knows everything, and that nothing stays buried forever. However, he also knew that some in the regiment then sleeping like logs around him in the barracks were blind to all light and therefore did not wish to see, at least for that night and in the morning.

The soldier turned about some upon the bunk, stretching and squirming and re-positioning himself so that his right calf did not ache or throb as much, and also, he felt his back's lumbar, sore from the long trek, stiffen as if turning to hardening wood, and then the sweat from his long tramp, now dried, chilled on his washer board leaner bones and made him shiver some. He thought that it was time to no longer revere ourselves, like some puffed up generals or nincompoop colonels do, looking in the mirror to see the raised ribbons, the fancy chevrons, the braided eagles, the stars on the helmet. Those gents, a congress of louts and low-achievers, were resplendent and bedecked, but who cares for that? The tired and by now nearly asleep soldier had done his bit, at least for the nearly exhausted day; and too, he understood that it was well beyond tally time to ask Him for Grace so that he might better know what path to take, among all the dozens arrayed before him, what course might be best smartly followed to launch the next assault, the coming sally, the fresh foray, the proximate sortie. He will know and tell us precisely and exactly how best we might fight, which weapons to choose or disavow, what new battles may be eschewed or must be joined, and precisely where and when and how to commence them. He alone knows all the strategies that shall result in victory, a vanquishing of the enemy who lurks around every hillock, hides in every cave, lays prone upon every mountainside. The soldier was thirsty but understood also that there would be no beer in heaven, che non c'e birra in paradiso.

Therefore, he knew it was time to ask Him, and no false others, for help, to thus drink from the healing waters (yet, it must be said, not of lager, not of beer!) which He alone shall provide, and to once again, as if we were once again children and before all the adult besmirchments and entangling alliances had arrived, to once again embrace the friendly innocence of childhood, that once we did well know, and to accept a greater light into his hard soldier's heart, so that one might better see. Is such a thing too much to ask? The soldier knew that this job could not be accomplished alone, a solo, chancing by as a breath of fresh air or a light breeze, since this is the sort of operation where the true higher authority, and not some fouled up, jazz bow, bigshot major general with a lumpy belly and flattened ass from too much sitting, needs to be consulted.

Finally, now that the morning's faintest shards of light began to streak across the barracks, the soldier was on the verge or cusp of sleep, ready to drink copiously of that natural elixir which so far he had not found. Like many, as a last token and thinking again of the water, he remembered with the acuity of youth a favorite Foley song, whose beat and rhythm as he minutely edged towards sleep made a soft refrain inside his mind, a song which said:

> ---And let them who toil, let them come to the water. And let them who are weary, let them come to the Lord.

That trip would be a kind of re-baptism, or renewal, the tired soldier thought, something I sure as blazes could use, he mused. The song spoke clearly to him now so close to sleep. The soldier, whose back had now relaxed a tinge, whose right calf no longer ached or throbbed or pulsated, now warmed some under the heavy brown Italian wool blanket with the six crème stripes. Somehow as dawn approached and despite his exhaustion, the familiar song spoke to his heart, and unknit his fighting soldier's brow, telling him to toss quickly and carefully the duffel aside, so that it would neither impede him, nor be excessive in weight.

And so it was that finally the tired soldier, by praying some and playing in his mind Foley's song, said to himself that faith in this life was not something optional but necessary, something that any proper soldier required like food or his rifle, and one with plenty of ammo. It was like saying that any new recruit must be in tip-top shape if he is later to become a good soldier, someone fellow soldiers trusted and someone the higher-ups could depend upon. Like so many before him, the tired soldier thought to himself:

> ---Deo vindice. Only a God can still save us.

Thus, he pondered upon the need for faith, like all the legionnaires and crusaders and marines and seabees and paratroopers way back in time had done before him, joining with the many thousands of others who have fought these same nasty, treacherous battles.

Right away the tired soldier was rejuvenated by these thoughts and, thinking again like a soldier, he became instantly practical, saying to himself: Re-enforcements, more ammo, food! We must never run out of anything, that much is certain. What half-brain dingbat is in charge of ordering supplies? We must not run out of water, gasoline, diesel, food, Band-Aids, whiskey, all of it, do you hear me? Oh, to re-arm again and to get ready for the next battle which awaits! There is always another battle, another fight, so be armed and alert, gutter pup, rookie. The job is to get ready for war since it is coming out of the north like a big storm does in the fall, one which shall soon drench to sodden and pulp the once-dry countryside all around. The soldier knew that somehow or other the strong Hayden had given to him and to hundreds of others the gritty impetus to go on, and then to go on again, since such is war, any war, which is just an endless battle about gumption, as is life. He knew too that sometime soon he might be the last man standing in the field facing the enemy, the lone infantryman holding the only rifle with any ammo left, the one carrying the final, last bullet. Perhaps he would be last man, the last soldier in the fight. The wise and tired soldier dreams and is finally close to sleep, with no head fakes this time.

So, soon, the tired soldier is on the edge of a deep wood, one lost in a thick fog and the night, coo-cooing like an old, female owl might do, one upon the low bough who whispers into his ear: Stai attento, signore! Stay alert, sir! From his light, tossing sleep, he says to himself the names of his many comrades-in-arms already lost beyond Borgo Grappa and little Latina in the stinking Pontine Marshes.

Cinque Sortite: Five Assaults Or Sallies Onto The Battlefield

The death of his many friends must have happened beyond the fetid estuary and the swampy waters close to Fiume Liri. Whose lousy idea was this anyhow? Clark, Lucas, Churchill? Tonight, it does not matter one whit or iota which flat ass birdbrain made the bonehead call to go. So many men have been lost due to this combination of errors: In One Ear, Occlusion, Simple Tanglefoot. That about sums it up, that is, exactly how one gets taken to the cleaners. You don't mind a twiddle, do you? Sure, some of the dead stiffs were old and cranky doughboys from the Great War who could not stay away from any combat action since they just loved it so, more than a favorite dog, more than any luscious dame. Maybe it is time, the tired soldier dreams, to look for any trace of the large white bull or elephant on the edge of the dark forest now so deeply wrapped in thistly fog. My fellow soldiers: Zanin, Lallo, Pataca: Alas, they are all gone now. Please pay much better attention, mates! Yes, such a large white bull or elephant would then be a welcome sign of arriving health. For, a salvation and resurrection shall return, must return. Everybody knows these things, yet we act so slowly, like stiff stooges, or fuzzy rummies, as if we all are flummoxed or paralyzed or simply little-kid tentative and afraid to move. Frozen, we are stuck in this cloaking, enwrapping, impenetrable fog, la nebbia, yet that lousy, piss-poor condition is surely something of our own making. Nearby an old and lusty uncle who fully remembers everything is telling me tall and possibly randy tales one longs to hear, one craves to understand. He tells me long, windy jokes, one tafter the tother, and the telling makes me laugh and giggle as if I once again were a child, a tad. Too, he tells me that nothing we have belongs to us, that money cancels brotherhood, and that we shall and must in God's name meet all the bitter, corrosive arms that rise up against us only with the better weapons of faith, saying once again that that faith is something important, something required and necessary, something pivotal and vital, that last word relating to a better life. In other words, without it you are a sitting duck, and standing there upon the fractious, contentious veldt, you have your zipper down, and own neither rifle nor ammo. At this point, beyond dreaming and as if he had become transformed by this small, but key, epiphany, again the soldier is no longer tired, enervated, but rather, though now sleeping upon his bunk so close to the battlefield, he only gains in power and sinew. In his ascending dreams the soldier is fresh, feisty, and looks forward to the battles ahead. At the end of this long night in the middle of winter camped just below Monte Artemisio and Monte Peschia that both loom over the sleeping soldiers like sentries standing watch upon the rampart, the soldier thinks as precious sleep encamps within him: Who knows what five assaults that I may gain, what five sallies from Truscott that I shall inherit and that may not be postponed, what five attacks must be joined to win the battle that must be won, or else we shall be forever lost? Now that dawn was approaching, the thought made him smile once more like a youngster might have done, and he grinned at no one in particular in the bunkhouse, smiling broadly to the night since the now fresh, sleeping soldier once again looked forward to all the upcoming battles that would soon arrive, marching in repetition upon him, like so many waves from the sea that arrive one after the other upon the shore. Delighted, and as he closed and shuttered himself to solid sleep, he knew with confidence that there would much good work to do in the future.